Goodbye, Belvidere

A HUNDRED AND SIXTY ACRES

Joyce Wheeler

All scripture quote are from KJV

Maps

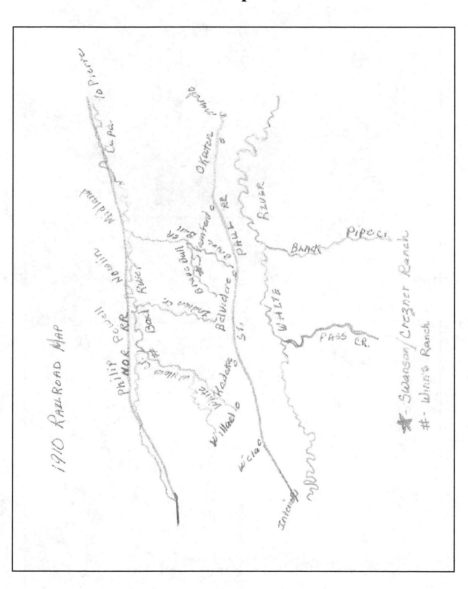

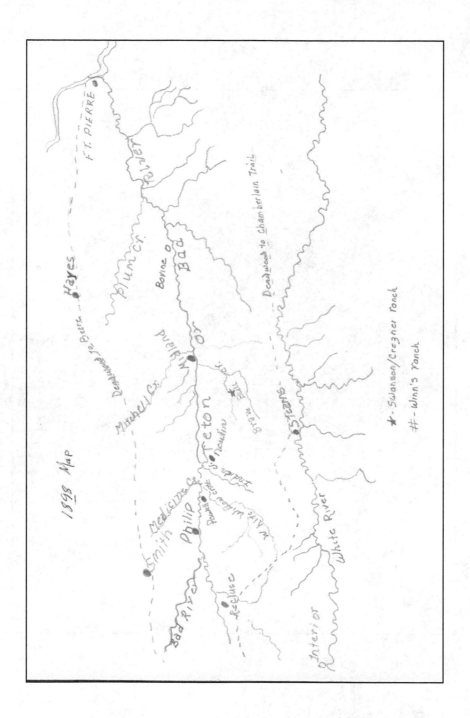

1898 Map

Hayes

FT. PIERRE

Cheyenne River

Plum Cr.

Bonne o

Deadwood to Pierre

Mitchell Cr.

Pumpkin

Bad or Teton

Chantier

Deadwood to Chamberlain Trail

Snowdin

Grave Bill

Willow

Smith

Medicine Cr.

Philip

Powder Cr. #

White

White River

Bad River

Recluse

Interior

* - Swanson/Cregner Ranch

- Winn's Ranch

Dedication

To the men and women who bravely settled the West River area of South Dakota. Your courage and stamina is an inspiration to all of us who live here in modern times, and still find it a challenge.

Introduction

November 1, 2012

Dear readers,

In the fall of 2010, I submitted *Laughter to the Wind* to the publisher and was mulling over thoughts of another novel. The idea came in bits and pieces: a homesteader story from the late 1800s, a series, a young man running from his family—and so Carl John (CJ) Crezner came into being.

A trek to my family's ranch started adding more pieces. Visiting the people in the area contributed more ideas. Family history became real and exciting. And the little town that started as Stearns and ended as Belvidere became the pivot point.

Goodbye, Belvidere was always the title in my mind. I could well imagine the emotions of people coming—and going from this spot on the prairie.

The list of people to thank is long. Much of the hours of research have been in the locally produced books of county history, both Jackson and Haakon counties. Many books that intrigued and explained came from my parents-in-law's library, which was extensive.

The Crezners, Swansons, Smiths and Tinners are fictional. But the people that come and go in the series have walked and ridden over these prairies and are a rich heritage in our area. Blended in is our own family history.

"A Hundred and Sixty Acres" finds us at the end of the century where the large cattle barons are facing an end to free grazing. The smaller rancher has come in, also utilizing the grasslands, but with an eye towards community, development, families living on the land. They're living next to creeks and rivers, which is an important factor in a land lacking in wood and water.

The climate is severe, forty below zero in the winter, well over a hundred in the summer. South Dakota unleashes hail, high winds, blizzards, floods, and drought in capricious moments, then turns around and charms with sunshine and gentle breezes, blue sky and horizons touching the earth.

The unwary homesteader, who locates on a quarter of land without protection from the elements, finds a cruel and vicious adversary in weather extremes. Many came with high hopes and left with broken dreams. Relinquishments on the same quarter were often listed eight or nine times and, in some places, as many as one hundred times.

Yet, they continued to come—1904 saw a huge increase of homesteaders in the area, 1905 brought May blizzards and July flooding, 1906 held the promise of railroads cutting through the endless prairie, 1907 begets towns springing up along the railroads and the beginning of communities.

Thanks to all my readers who have waited patiently for CJ Crezner's story. Your interest is so appreciated! And thanks to the people who have graciously given me permission to use their family's names in the story. It has truly given this book a great historical connection.

Sincerely,
Joyce Wheeler
Author of *My Lady* and *Laughter in the Wind, and the Goodbye, Belvidere trilogy*

One

July 15, 1898
Fort Robinson, Nebraska

Dear Mom and Dad,

We have finally arrived with the cattle at Fort Robinson. The Indian agency and some ranchers are buying most of the herd. I'm glad we have this part of the drive over with as it's been a long way from Missouri to here following slow moving cows and calves.

Giles has paid me, and he and the rest of the crew have left. I have a chance to go to South Dakota with a cattleman named Winn who is driving a small bunch from this herd to his ranch. From there, I will go to Pierre, South Dakota, and if you need to contact me, send a letter there.

My health has improved. Perhaps Doctor Regis was right when he said I had studied my brains out and needed some physical work.

Please tell Granddad for me that it will be later in the summer before I get back to Missouri and go into the ministry with him. Right now, I feel led to continue northward.

My love to both of you,
Your son, Carl John Crezner

The writer of the note muttered under his breath as he reread what he had written. "This doesn't sound right either," he grumbled and was of a mind to toss the letter onto the floor to join the other wadded up notes. The sound of booted steps outside his hotel room and a light tap on his door startled him, and he quickly laid the letter on the small writing table. Before he could get up to open the door it was thrust open. Dusty blue eyes in a freckled face peered into the early evening gloom of the small room.

"Hungry?" The one-word question was asked by his new trail boss, Winn. Carl John figured the man was probably several years older than himself. Winn seemed to have the confidence that men acquire when they've been their own boss for awhile.

Carl John nodded and slowly stood. He was taller than the average man of his day, slender built, with a suggestion of weakness in his frame. There were several who discovered it was a suggestion not connected to reality. After spending the greater part of his childhood running away from fights, Carl John learned even a preacher's kid should know the basics of self-defense.

"I guess I can finish this later." His hands made a sweeping gesture to include the papers on the floor.

"Trouble getting 'er right?"

Carl John gave a slight smile while he reached onto the bed to grab his hat. "Yes, sir, trouble getting 'er right." He followed his boss out the door, pausing to shut and lock it. The narrow hallway and the equally narrow stairway wouldn't allow them to walk side by side and he trailed behind Winn's stocky form as they made their way downstairs.

The unpretentious dining room was filled with off-duty army men, cowboys, and several traveling salesmen. Only a handful of women sat at the tables, and in deference to the ladies, the loud talk was mostly decent.

The house special turned out to be liver and onions fried to a crisp and tough as nails.

Winn's face was a picture of dismay as he cut into the well-done liver. "I hate bad food—even if it's served by a purty gal."

Carl John looked up in surprise. He had thought the young woman serving them was anything but pretty. "How long have you been nearsighted?" He gave a lopsided smile at Winn and hoped the older man wouldn't be offended.

Winn took a long time answering. He chewed slowly and methodically, and it took a lot of work to get the whole mouthful swallowed. "I know. She's homely as a mud fence, but"—he took a swig of coffee and pointed with his fork—"she has a purty cousin in the kitchen."

"How do you know that?"

"I'm a blooming fool for liking women who can cook."

"The pretty cousin cooked this mess?"

"Aw, no siree Bob! The purty cousin baked the pie that you remember I ordered right off the bat."

Carl John chuckled and tackled the equally tough beans that were a side dish.

"Now I ask you, how can you cook a bean to make it hard as a rock?" Winn proved his point by slapping the bean with his knife. They watched in amazement as it flew off the plate and bounced on the floor.

Carl John paused with his fork in the air for several seconds before he motioned to the waitress. She scowled to a stop beside their table.

"Ma'am, I, ah, neglected to order the same pie as this gentleman. Please bring two pieces for us when you come back." He didn't feel like smiling at her, so he didn't.

She nodded brusquely and left for the kitchen. Almost immediately, a young woman that Carl John decided must be the pretty cousin came out with a platter of plates that held berry pies. With one hand, she balanced the platter and, with the other hand, she carried a steaming pot of coffee.

She smiled at Winn as she approached their table, and he reciprocated by quickly taking two of the biggest pieces off the platter.

"Hope you enjoy this," she said as she refilled their coffee cups.

"Ain't no doubt in my mind that we'll enjoy every bite." Winn poured some cream from a small white pitcher onto the pie. He grinned at her. "Been thinking of this pie all afternoon!"

"How do you know it's good?" Carl John wondered aloud after the woman left.

"Had a sample."

Carl John pondered that while he forked the light and flaky crust into his mouth. It was mouth-watering good. The two men savored their bites in silence, and it was only when they scraped the empty plate several times with spoon and fork that he asked again. "How did you know she was baking a pie, and how did you get her to let you sample a piece?"

Winn grinned again and blinked his blue eyes. "There's some things that can't be explained." His eyebrows moved up and down in time with his blinking, a feat Carl John had never seen before.

Carl John shook his head. "Okay, I'm good with that." After a slight pause, he asked, "Are we still leaving in the morning?"

"Yup. First light. You already met Smokey, and there's a half breed that'll be coming along too. Don't know why they call him Joker— he's a serious feller."

"Well,"—Carl John pushed back his chair—"I better get that letter posted and my gear packed and my bill paid."

"Yup." Winn made no move to get up. "Yup. I might stay here a while and maybe have a little more coffee—and pie."

When Carl John paid his bill, he noted the piece of pie cost as much as the meal.

He wasn't sure when Winn and the other two men started calling him CJ. He decided the nickname must be a sign of acceptance, and after a week on the trail, they seemed to have reached an easy camaraderie.

The country was ever-changing as they headed northeast. Gradually, the overgrazed prairie around the fort gave way to taller grass. With the Black Hills on their left and the Indian reservation on their right, the four men kept the herd moving from early light to late afternoon. Joker always found a well-watered spot to rest the cattle and horses, and when the cook wagon stopped, the pace relaxed.

Winn was both trail boss and camp cook and his word was law. CJ discovered immediately that no one argued with him because he performed both duties very well. CJ made it his business to gather up firewood and haul water to the wagon. No one else wanted the job.

On the day thunderheads piled up in the western sky and the weather was crackling hot, Joker halted them earlier than usual beside a swift-moving creek. After the herd had started grazing, CJ made good use of the clear water to wash his extra shirt and overalls. After he draped them over some bushes to dry, he took off his boots and dived into the water, much to the amusement of the other men.

"Myself, I like my baths without clothes," Smokey scoffed.

"Well, take 'em off and try the water." CJ gasped; the chilly water after the hot summer days had surprised him. "Where is this water coming from?"

"From those beauteous mountains called the Black Hills. Don't drown."

CJ thought that was not a necessary admonition. The creek wasn't deep, but it was fast moving. He took the bar of soap and rubbed it all over the clothes he was still wearing and then lay on the rock bottom for the water to rinse the soap off. By this time, he was shivering in the late afternoon sun. When he finally waded out, he was thoroughly cooled down and ravenously hungry.

"Now, ain't you just the sweet little washerwoman man?" Smokey gave a slow grin and raised his eyebrows as CJ smoothed water out of his clothes.

"Sure. For money, I'll scrub your clothes."

"Nope. Got me my own sweet little washerwoman over on Brave Bull Creek."

"Ha!" Joker's voice was scornful.

Winn snorted. "It'll be a cold day when she takes on the likes of you."

"Now, Winn, that's an aggravating remark. And if she don't like the likes of me, I have other little sweet things scattered here 'n there."

CJ looked at Smokey's profile and thought that with his good looks and smooth talk he probably did indeed have sweet things scattered all over the country.

"Joker," Smokey said, "what's this 'ha' business? Do you know Joanna?"

"Grumpy squaw. Chase me out of her house with her broom. 'Out, out, out' she yip like a coyote. Made me stand outside until she got food."

"Well, darn it, that'll teach you not to come in without knocking and scare the little lady to death." Smokey chortled slightly. "I'll bet her food was good."

Joker walked over to the cook wagon disgustedly. "Out, out, out!" he said in a falsetto voice and made a sweeping motion with his hand.

"Come an' get it." Winn said, with a hint of laughter in his voice. "Us white folk get nervous, Joker, when we turn around and see you red folks right behind us. Gotta knock on the door, man."

"Don't know why you white folk need to knock. You walk like buffalo bull. Tromp, tromp, tromp. Wake the dead."

"Sometimes we're quiet." Smokey grinned.

CJ decided Smokey's words might hold double meaning.

The four men devoured the biscuits and rabbit gravy Winn had cooked. CJ finally warmed up after he finished his meal with a cup of steaming coffee. He was sleepy, and he looked longingly at his bedroll.

"We gonna have a blow tonight, Joker?" Winn puffed contentedly on his pipe.

"Maybe. There's lightning to the south."

"Lightning and wind. Hate it. Ruins my beauty sleep." Smokey stood up and walked over to the dishpan to wash his eating utensils. "That was good grub, Winn. Your mama taught you well."

"You betcha. Don't forget to wipe those before you put 'em away." It was common knowledge Winn liked to cook but hated doing dishes.

"It's rumbling off to the west. Makes me think we could get a storm all right. Maybe you better take the first watch, Joker, and CJ can take over at midnight." Winn blew a puff of smoke into the increasing breeze.

Joker heaved a sigh, spit, and slowly stood up while balancing plate, cup, and fork in one hand. "If there's a blow, I best ride the roan. He seems to think it's one big whoop chasing around in the dark." He glanced at CJ. "You best ride the bay if you're taking the midnight watch."

CJ nodded. He had noticed after the first couple of days on the trail that Joker spoke very seldom, but when he did, he was worth listening to. He was half-French, half-Sioux and had an uncanny sense of horsemanship. He also had a way of coming and going without making

14

a sound. It was eerie, and more than once CJ felt the hair on the back of his neck stand up as if there were a phantom in their midst.

By the time he bedded down, the wind had steadily picked up and the lightning was closer. It worried him to think of restless cattle with so few riders. All the cattle drives he had been on had big crews. There was comfort in numbers, he thought tiredly. Sleep caught up with him before he could fret anymore.

Midnight found CJ riding the bay towards Joker on his big roan. The lightning in the west danced across the sky, and the wind was gusting in fitful bursts of energy.

"Keep circling 'em. They're quiet; they just want your company."

Joker waved and headed slowly back to camp. Once again, CJ felt the aloneness that open range fostered upon him during the night hours. He started his slow circle around the bedded herd. The bay plodded a weaving course, its ears moving back and forth to catch any sound from the rider.

They made several uneventful circles but when CJ shifted in his saddle and vented a long deep sigh the bay stopped abruptly. CJ tapped his spurs lightly against the horse's side. With a disgusted snort, the bay resumed their course, and CJ began a one sided conversation.

"What am I doing out here in the middle of nowhere? I didn't study for the ministry to preach to cattle." There was no response from the bay even when the rider gave a self deprecating laugh. "On the other hand, why not cattle? They probably can get as much out of my sermons as people." There was a long pause before the rider burst out with raw emotion. "I don't preach good sermons, horse! I have no gift for it!"

As if for a response, the bay shied at some unseen thing in the dark. Moving clouds dimmed the light from the stars and moon, and if it wasn't for the lightning flashes, the night's darkness would have completely engulfed them.

"Well. Just great, horse. Dance around in the dark and dump me in a ditch." CJ muttered as they made another slow circle. Problems he had long pushed aside seemed to rise like ghostly shrouds in the darkness. He could almost see his granddad and his dad weave in

15

ghoulish frenzy and shake their heads in disgust at him. A Crezner not able to preach? Unheard of!

The entire next round was made in silence. Suddenly, the agitated rider gave another deep sigh and the sound of anguished words caused the bay to flatten his ears. "I can't go back. I can't be what they want me to be and I don't know how to tell them. How do I say that all I learned in seminary is the fact that the preacher's kid can't preach? It just won't work! It won't work. And I don't know how to tell them and I don't know what to do." The words caught rhythm with the hoof beats and were repeated over and over.

Suddenly, a more violent gust of wind rolled over the prairie and thunder rumbled. Cows mooed nervously, and several got to their feet with their heads held high as they faced the wind.

"Settle down, you old bats." The words didn't seem to comfort them.

Another flash of lightning was followed by a closer rumble, and several raindrops spattered CJ's hat. More cattle rose to their feet, and calves started bawling.

CJ wondered if the other men would get to the herd in time if the cattle became too restless. Once they started milling around, it would be hard for one man to hold them. He'd seen cattle when lightning lit the night sky and thunder cracked. They would start to bawl and fear would make them run. Racing after them to turn the lead cattle in a circle would be a heart-thumping experience. Even though horses had fair night vision, gullies and prairie dog holes could make any horse stumble and fall.

CJ decided he better try to get the cattle settled before that happened. Maybe he could lullaby them. He began a slow trot around the herd and started to softly hum a forlorn cowboy ballad. It seemed to have very little effect.

There were several more cracks and crashes in the heavens, an increase of raindrops. CJ decided he may as well use his lung power on a hymn suited for the event: "Rescue the Perishing." If he couldn't settle the cattle down with that old hymn, they might as well all perish and it would be a fitting epitaph.

CJ's strong tenor voice changed from humming into a quiet song:

Rescue the perishing Care for the dying,
Snatch them in pity from sin and the grave;
Weep o'er the erring one, Lift up the fallen,
Tell them of Jesus the mighty to save.

He hadn't sung in weeks. All the while he was on the trail drive, he let the other night guards sing. In fact, he hadn't sung the last months of college; he had studied long and hard and had felt no urge to praise God in hymns. Or even praise God in prayer. Or even, for that matter, to pray at all. His studying consumed him. Now he sang the ringing chorus several times.

Rescue the perishing, Care for the dying;
Jesus is merciful, Jesus will save.

The cattle were all on their feet. Calves were bawling in confusion. He trotted swiftly around them and started another verse. One thing about being a preacher's kid, he knew all the verses to all the songs— even, he mused to himself, the ones preachers eliminated if the sermons had been overlong.

Another bolt of lightning crashed around him. His horse whinnied in alarm, and both CJ and his mount braced themselves for the thunder that followed. It echoed over the vast prairie and the vibration and rumble continued for a seemingly endless time.

CJ kept his horse trotting around the nervous herd and continued with the chorus. When he had repeated it several times, he started on another verse.

Down in the human heart, Crushed by the tempter,
Feelings lie buried that grace can restore;
Touched by a loving heart, Wakened by kindness;
Chords that were broken will vibrate once more.

His vocal chords were vibrating right now, with more than a little anxiety. The cow that continually went the wrong way had her head up. She began running in the direction farthest from him. If she got away, he could imagine the whole herd erupting. He spurred his horse into a faster pace and hoped he could avoid ditches and holes.

It seemed longer than the few seconds it took to overtake her. "Get back where you belong you old rip!" He maneuvered past her and her calf. In the afterglow of another lightning bolt, he swiftly turned and chased her back into the herd. Hopefully, Jesus would be merciful and save him from any more races in the dark.

Tiny rivulets of water ran off his hat and dripped down his back. Once again, he trotted his horse in a circle around the herd. The wind was undecided on the direction it wanted to blow; it seemed like any direction CJ rode it whipped into his face and bent the brim of his hat into contorted angles

Why should I be discouraged, why should the shadows come?

CJ started singing a new song that had been circulating at seminary. As far as he knew, the composer hadn't even had it copyrighted yet. It was one of his favorites.

Why should my heart be lonely and long for heav'n and home
When Jesus is my portion My constant Friend is He
His eye is on the sparrow, and I know He watches me

The melody kept easy rhythm with his horse's gait. CJ certainly hoped someone in heaven was watching after him. So far, the herd was nervous, but not bolting. He sat straighter in the saddle and sang a little louder.

His eye is on the sparrow, and I know He watches me.
I sing because I'm happy, I sing because I'm free;
For His eye is on the sparrow, and I know He watches me.

He was neither happy nor free, but at least the cows were contained. He reasoned if a cow could think, she might decide she liked being serenaded rather than chased and cursed if she stampeded.

'Let not your heart be troubled,' His tender words I hear,
And resting on His goodness, I lose my doubt and fear

The rain suddenly became a downpour, lasting only a few minutes before it tapered off into a light shower. He was drenched, but the cows still stood in their spot, mooing plaintively as he rode past them.

He had sung to congregations since he was a little boy. His voice had changed from a piping soprano to a deeper tone, but the quality and timbre remained with him. He sang because it came as naturally as breathing to him; he couldn't remember ever being nervous in front of a crowd when he sang. Preaching, however, was another matter entirely.

By the time CJ finished the rest of the song and sang another hymn for good measure, the storm had split, with part of its vengeance heading north and a smaller part moving to the south.

The cattle grazed and some of them folded back down and started chewing their cud. In the distant eastern sky, a slight sliver of light could be seen. When it seemed as if all was quiet and the wind was ebbing, he stopped the bay on a small ridge.

The slight sliver of light was widening, and a sleepy birdsong was beginning. The air after the rain had a chill that sent a shiver down his back and made him long for a cup of hot coffee.

The bay gave a slight snort and turned his ears towards camp. Out of the gloom, CJ could see an outline moving towards them; he recognized Winn's solid form.

"Thought after that concert you might need something to whet the whistle," Winn said and held out a wrapped pint jar.

CJ took off the lid and steaming coffee aroma wafted upward. With delight, he took a swig. "That hits the spot."

"Yup. Well, looks like it all blew over. Had me worried for a while when I heard some bellowing."

"You mean the cows or me?"

Winn chuckled. "You sang so good old Smokey is back at camp sitting on a log and thinking of repenting."

CJ laughed and took another swig. "That'll be the day."

"Yup. Well, it does a body good to hear those hymns. Not too many fellers can sing the cows quiet. They must have enjoyed hearing you."

"Good thing the clouds split and went around us. I thought for a while it was going to get nasty."

"I was thinking the same. Me 'n Joker was getting ready to saddle up when we heard you singing."

"I'm out of practice. Haven't sang for a long time."

"Better keep in practice CJ. You wouldn't want to lose that gift." Winn turned his horse around. "I'll send Smokey out to relieve you shortly. He's had all the beauty sleep the rest of us can stand."

CJ and the bay stood on the knoll and watched the dawn slowly shed its light over the land. The bird chorus had gradually increased and cows were up and grazing again. Calves remembered it was breakfast time and, with tails cranking, they quickly found their mamas. It was a peaceful scene, and after the wind from the night, it was appreciated.

"Well, horse, maybe Winn has something there. Singing is a whole lot easier than preaching. I guess I could at least do that in church." That thought didn't give him half as much pleasure as watching the sunrise.

Two

August 10, 1898
Recluse Post Office, South Dakota

Dear Mom and Dad,

I've never seen grass country like this. In fact, I've never seen so much sky and prairie and been in as much wind as I have these past several days.

We have the cattle at Smokey's place and branded his part of the herd. Tomorrow we'll head out with the rest of the cattle and should be at Winn's place in a couple of days.

I think the cook/boss has managed to add some pounds to this skinny carcass. We have feasted all the way from Fort Robinson.

It is a wild and raw country, and I don't know why, but I like it. Smokey has a nice ranch along the Bad River. There's a rock tower on a high ridge they call Stoneman. The Indians used it as a guide to find water. I guess it's where another creek falls into the Bad River.

Hope this finds you all well. Perhaps, for this fall, it would be best if Granddad found someone else to help with his pastor duties. I plan to be home for the winter, but this is bigger country than I realized, and it will take me a while to get to Pierre.

Love,
Your son, Carl John

Carl John had swiftly written his letter with little thought other than to let his family know where he was and when he might be back in Missouri. He quickly sealed the note inside the envelope and handed it to the postmistress of the newly named Recluse Post Office. Just a few pigeon holes on the wall of the partial dugout and log home gave evidence this was where the US mail was received and distributed.

He was surprised to see a piano resting unevenly on the dirt floor. The postmistress followed his glance. "I play the piano, and my husband, Charles, plays the fiddle." She took his letter and placed it in a leather bag. "The stage should be through here tomorrow."

"Thank you, ma'am," CJ said and remembered to take off his hat while talking to a lady.

"Where are you from?"

"I'm from Springfield, Missouri, ma'am. I'm just up here helping Winn and Smokey trail their cattle, and then I'll be heading back."

"Going back to family?" She seemed to ask the question a little wistfully.

He nodded. "How long have you been here?"

"Here, meaning here on the south fork of Bad River?"

He nodded again.

"Well, let's see. I suppose in this spot about two years. Before that, we were on down the Bad River, where the two forks come together."

"There's not a lot of people in this country, is there?"

"No." She paused before continuing, "But Charles likes it that way. He wouldn't care if he never saw another town again." She smiled at CJ and shrugged. "I guess we just like the openness of the prairie. 'Course, looks like the Thompsons are adding to the population. Those are all our children outside listening to Winn."

He realized suddenly that she probably had more to do than visit with him. He politely told her goodbye before he put his hat back on and headed out the door.

"Done already?" Winn was in the middle of a story, which was enthralling his young audience. Clearly, they wanted him to continue. CJ nodded and joined Smokey on a rough bench placed against the outside walls of the log home.

"See that feller riding in?" Smokey pointed to a lone horseman coming across the prairie from the south leading a packhorse. A group of hunting dogs followed him; some running and some walking slowly with their tongues hanging out. "That there is Wolfer Thompson. Don't sass him. Ain't no better wolfer in the country, but if he don't like you, it ain't good."

"I'll try to keep my witty remarks under control," CJ said with a slight smile. As far as he knew, he was the most humorless person in the world.

"Sure, well, just warning you. Old Wolfer and his wife run this post office, and those young uns Winn is lying to are their kids— Winn!" Smokey's abrupt call almost made CJ jump. "Better wind up your yarn. The boss is coming home."

Winn nodded, and within minutes the tale was done, and several bright pennies were distributed to his listeners. The children seemed to vanish as quickly as mice seeing a tomcat, CJ mused to himself. By the time the rider and his packhorse and his dogs were by the house, only one child stood beside Winn.

The horse gave a slight grunt as the big man dismounted. Wolfer Thompson stood well over six feet, and all of him was solid muscle. He wore his pistols with the easy grace of one long accustomed to firearms.

In a short length of time, some of his children led his horse and packhorse towards the barn, others were feeding the dogs, and his wife had brought him something to drink. He gave her an absent smile and stood silently while he surveyed the three men. CJ thought Smokey seemed unusually tense

"How you doing, Wolfer?" Winn asked.

"Other than being hot, I can't complain. Got the wolves that were killing the *15* Irons horses, but not before they hamstrung some and ate 'em alive. Always makes a man sick to see it."

CJ looked down and shook his head. He'd heard a lot of stories about the habits of grey wolves. He wondered what he would do if he ever saw a wolf eating the nose and ears off a horse while the horse was still alive and screaming in pain.

"Did you trap 'em or shoot 'em?"

"Used Newhouse traps and my Remington." Wolfer suddenly grinned. "And of course, my dogs."

"Ah, how's your dogs?" Smokey's voice sounded strained.

"Good. How's your cattle?"

The abrupt answer seemed to rattle Smokey, and he sprang from the bench as if an invisible force had jerked him. "I bet you don't know this feller—CJ Crezner. He came up with me 'n Winn from Fort Robinson."

CJ rose slowly. "Nice to meet you, sir." He waited to see if Wolfer wanted to shake hands with him. The big man merely nodded.

Smokey cleared his throat and mumbled, "Well, Joker might be getting tired of watching those cattle by himself, so maybe I better get going." He hastened to untie his horse from the hitching rail. CJ watched with perplexity as Smokey quickly mounted and, with a farewell wave, rode away by himself.

Wolfer Thompson watched him leave. He turned to his wife and gave her a wry smile. "First sheep, then Smokey. I don't know which is worse to have in the neighborhood."

She watched the departing subject ride away at a clipped trot. "At least the sheep people had their wives. Smokey just seems to have a lot of—" She stopped abruptly and looked at CJ and Winn. With an embarrassed laugh, she turned towards the house. "I have work to do."

"Well, sir, I can tell you what's worse," Winn spoke up after she left. "The dang railroads are gonna be coming in. Lots of talk about 'em bringing in homesteaders, and when they do, we'll see people on every blasted hundred and sixty acres. Ain't no way they can make a living from this land on a quarter. And it won't be purty."

"You'll see it, Winn, not me. The missus 'n me will be gone. We ain't gonna stick around to see the soddies come in. I've seen it before. First the shacks, then a town. I hate it."

CJ walked over to the hitching rail and untied his horse. Homesteaders, soddies, honyonkers—he'd heard all the talk before from cowboys. They wanted this last piece of open country to stay as it was with its miles of grasslands. He didn't plan to make it any of his business. Yet in a way, he could understand what they meant. There was something about the sound of wind in the grass under endless blue sky that triggered a sense of freedom. He decided the two men might want a private conversation. They seemed to know and understand each other. He noticed Winn seemed in no hurry to leave.

He tightened his cinch before he slowly mounted. "I better be going too. Gentlemen,"—he raised his hand in a quick salute—"have a good day."

Wolfer Thompson nodded in his direction. "Next time you come, better let the missus play a song on her piano for you to sing."

CJ looked at the man in puzzlement while Winn burst out laughing. "Talk travels fast here, CJ. Prairie grapevine. New feller in the area that can actually carry a tune is gonna be talked about."

"Especially when the new feller isn't much good at anything else," CJ answered with an embarrassed grin. "I'm most likely heading back to the east, sir, but if we ever cross paths again I could sure do that."

He heard both men chuckle as he turned his horse and headed down Bad River to Smokey's ranch. After he crossed the shallow crossing onto the north side, he started up a long ridge. His horse moved slowly, which was fine with CJ. He wanted to take the opportunity of being alone to savor the countryside. Along the rivers and creeks that they had passed getting to this spot, he noted a few rough log homes, small barns, the beginnings of communities.

Funny thing about this land. It gets to a person after awhile. The bigness, the openness, the challenge of it. I suppose you either love it or hate it.

His horse came to a stop on the top of the ridge, and Bad River valley stretched out before him. The river snaked towards the east and then, as if it quickly changed its mind, it veered towards the north. In the distance, below the Stoneman, it made a turn to the west. It was a dirty, yellowed water, Smokey informed him, until it chose to clear up, and it then became a nice little stream rushing over shallows, or plunging into deep holes.

He glanced towards the south and took note of a weaving creek that meandered toward the Bad River. Little Buffalo Creek, Smokey called it. CJ wondered what it must have looked like years ago when the buffalo grazed on the land, dotting the whole area with herds of massive proportions.

Guess it all comes and goes. Buffalo, Indians, cattle barons. Only God remains unchanged, today, tomorrow, forever.

His horse blew and stomped flies away. CJ remained motionless.

This is humiliating, Lord. The preacher-in-training can't seem to get it right. I wonder what the family will say when they get my letter and read 'Grandfather should get someone else?' It ain't gonna be purty.

CJ suddenly grinned. Winn's colloquialism had unintentionally invaded his muttered prayer and, probably in few words, accurately described the situation. From the time he could remember, he had been told that he would make the fourth generation of preachers in the Crezner family. He had believed it, studied for it, and had no other objective in mind but to follow their footsteps. He had never once considered that his sermons would be anything else but powerful. Powerful was how his father, grandfather, and great-grandfather had preached, and it was expected of him.

What happened, God? Somewhere along the line, while I studied for the ministry, memorized enough scripture to float a boat, learned how to behave myself properly, poured over theological and religious doctrines---somewhere in all of that, I lost sight of You.

He gave himself a mental shake and shifted uncomfortably in the saddle. "Come on horse, let's get going." He tapped the horse's side lightly with his spurs. His horse responded with a bone jarring slow walk.

This isn't good. Could it be I was so intent on being a great preacher that I never considered—but of course, that's absurd. Absolutely absurd.

A frown worked its way from his squinted eyes to his mouth and seemed to wash over his entire body. The thought he almost thought was preposterous. Of course, it was.

This country is making me ask too many questions that I can't answer. I can't have gone all these years without considering it's possible I'm not a true believer. That can't be the case at all. Look at all the good things I've done. Look at all the bad things I've not done. Look at the time I've spent learning the Word of God. What's the matter with me, anyway?

With that thought he spurred the plodding horse into a trot, and was relieved to see Smokey's log house come into view.

"You see those pens over there?" Smokey pointed to the set of corrals they used to hold the cattle and brand Smokey's part of the herd. The pens were well built and sat on the same river bench the house was on. "Those were put up by a sheepman," he continued without waiting for CJ's response. "See that dugout up by the riverbank over there?" He pointed in the opposite direction, and again without waiting to hear from CJ, he said, "A guy by the name of Lewis was here with his family and sheep. He got caught out in a blizzard, came back, and found that a bunch of cattle walked over the dugout. The roof fell in, killed the wife and kids."

Smokey was reflective. "Sometimes, I don't much like this country. It's rough. Takes a terrible toll on women and kids. People think free range, free grass. They think it's easy. It ain't easy. This place here—ain't easy. Sure, it's purty now, but wait 'till the Bad gets on the rampage. Wait till snow covers everything and the cattle can't graze. Forty below zero and miles from anywhere. I guess I don't much like it."

"Why are you here then?" CJ asked and stretched his legs straight out from the hardback chair he sat on.

"My dad runs a post office and store down on the Chamberlain to Deadwood trail, near the White River. He sees all sorts of people. Heard the sheep folks wanted to move, so took up the relinquishment from 'em. Maybe he thought I'd settle down some if I had some land."

CJ grunted in acknowledgement. He knew what it was like to be in a place where other folks thought you should be.

The two men sat on the porch of Smokey's comfortable log house. Smokey had a cigarette he'd rolled from a pouch of Bull Durham, and CJ had a glass of water.

"I was wondering if Joker might need some help," CJ broke the silence. "Maybe I should pack some grub and ride out to where he is."

"Sure. Help yourself to whatever's in the house." Apparently Smokey had lost all his earlier stated inclination to help Joker with the cattle.

Smokey's pantry was well stocked, and within a half hour, CJ hit the trail with a fresh horse. He crossed the Bad River where they trailed Winn's cattle earlier, and followed the obvious marks of the moving herd. Winn's place was about fifteen miles northeast and Joker had volunteered to haze them in that general direction while the rest of them went to Recluse.

It was well over an hour later when he finally caught up with Joker and the herd. Together the two men kept a methodical push to keep the cattle moving. Finally, in the late afternoon, the thirsty cows caught the scent of water and began a hurried trek towards it.

"What's this creek called?" CJ asked his silent partner.

"Bad River."

"Bad River? How can that be? I thought we left that behind us."

Joker spit and dismounted from his horse. "It turns and comes east, and it keeps going east until it falls into the Missouri at Fort Pierre."

"Oh. So, I need to follow this to get to Pierre?"

Joker nodded. "Don't camp by it. When it rains, many waters come fast."

The heat of the day had begun to give way to cooler evening air by the time they had their own campfire built. Joker followed his own advice and found a spot above the river. Smokey's tinned beef and sack of crackers filled the hollow spot in their bellies. CJ was thinking a cup of Winn's hot coffee would taste good when he heard the rattle of the cook wagon coming towards them.

It didn't take long to realize their usually congenial trail boss and cook was completely out of sorts. Joker and CJ looked at each other as Winn grumbled about the wind, yelled at his team as he was unhitching them, and stomped around their camp without a civil word to either of them.

Finally, he caught one of the horses and threw his saddle on it. "I'll take first watch," he said and rode off into the darkness with dire threats to the horse if it stumbled with him.

"White men," Joker said in disgust as he watched him leave.

CJ stood with his arms folded across his chest and shook his head in puzzlement. "I figured Smokey would be coming with him."

Joker spit a perfect arc into the campfire. "Nope."

CJ looked at him sharply. "I must have missed something here."

"Most likely." Joker laid his lariat rope in a circle around his bedroll, a precaution he informed CJ earlier on the drive, to keep snakes away from his sleeping form. He slid under a thin army-issued blanket. "Taking midnight watch, CJ?"

"Sure." The answer came out clipped and cold. CJ was beginning to be irritated at the unspoken law of the range—whatever that meant. These men had all sorts of meanings in their silence. A slight nod spoke volumes. A well-directed spit meant something else.

He walked over to Winn's wagon and rummaged for the coffee pot. Soon the pot was filled with water, a handful of coffee grounds were thrown in, and the whole shebang was set on the fire's hot coals. It was all accomplished with a great deal of muttering and grumbling on his part.

By the time he filled a tin cup with his creation and wandered farther up the hill in the deepening twilight, Carl John Crezner was in no mood to meditate on the beauty of the prairie. He found a small bank that made sitting down with a hot coffee cup a little easier than sitting flat on the ground, and after checking for cactus, rattlesnakes, or who-would-know-what-else, he sat down gingerly. He noted a bit surly that the sunset had lost its grandeur and had diminished into bits of pink fluff on the western clouds. He could see the dark forms of Winn's cattle a slight distance east of him and pointedly turned away as if Winn could actually see that unfriendly gesture in the gloom.

He took a sip of coffee and noted it was a halfway good brew. He let his mind wander and slumped slightly as a mental weariness draped over him.

I've been on summer cattle drives since I was twelve years old. Dad always said I needed to see the other side of life. He trusted Giles to keep me out of serious trouble, and Giles always came through. I can't say, though, that I understand cattle, or cattlemen, for that matter.

He took another swig of coffee and heard the nearby whoosh of a night hawk.

I should thank Dr. Regis for sending me on this drive. I finally quit having headaches and gut aches, and all the other things that come from sitting inside and pouring over books.

It wasn't that he minded being the son of a minister, or even studying for the ministry, he mused, while the glow in the west steadily diminished. That didn't take away the fact that he was dawdling here in the North Country rather than heading back to Missouri. He realized suddenly he would rather put up with the vagrancies of cowboys than face a congregation back home.

At least, there is action here. Sometimes, it seems Dad spends a lot of time ironing out misunderstandings among the flock. He tries so hard to be the peacemaker. I wouldn't be as patient as he is.

When he was away from church and parental influences, he saw life differently. Maybe he understood for the first time that a life without God can be a troubling journey of uncertainty.

The evening prairie sounds washed over him. The crickets, the breeze rattling the tall grass, the gentle calling of cows to calves, the ending of the day sounds. He looked down at camp and could barely make out Joker's sleeping form. The banked up campfire had only a few coals glowing in the dark.

A lone coyote found a high hill and sent out his mournful cry. The sound echoed throughout the Bad River breaks and caused CJ to wonder if the mangy critter had his own sorrows about life.

A long sigh escaped him, and he shook his head grimly. *I don't know what I am good for, probably not this life, even though I enjoy it somewhat, probably not the ministry, since I can't preach a good sermon. What then, Lord? What do you want me to do? I just don't know anymore. I can't seem to come to any decision.*

It was a small concession on his part to admit he needed guidance. He hardly realized at the moment that it was the beginning of an improved relationship with the God he knew, but had chosen to keep at a distance. He gulped down the rest of the coffee and rose stiffly from the makeshift chair. Tomorrow would bring its own worries, but hopefully this evening would just bring sleep.

Three

August 17, 1898
Philip, South Dakota

Dear folks,

Wanted to tell you that I will probably be in this area for awhile, as Winn has decided I need "some learning" about this part of the world.

There's a lot that goes on here. If I had mailed this letter in May, I would have addressed it from Powell, but now a fellow by the name of Morrison has the Powell post office and the name was changed to Philip. It's along the Bad River. Winn tells me the name goes back to 1890 when they named the post office after a guy named Scotty Philip who ranches east of here. Winn used to be his cook.

Winn's home is along a nice creek called White Willow Creek, and he has a good spring behind his house. He's been in the area for quite awhile, seems to know a lot of people and also knows a lot about cattle.

Of all things, I see sheep around here. Some pretty big herds. And there is a man from Tennessee named Waldron who has a horse ranch on east along the Bad River.

I could go on forever, but will close for now. I hope to catch up to your letters when I get to Pierre. It might be a while. Hope all is well at home.

Love,
Your son, CJ

"Man, you wrote that in a flash," Winn commented as CJ walked out of the log home that doubled as a post office.

"I'm thinking the ride back to your place could be hot. No use wasting time trying to figure out the right words."

Winn gathered the few pieces of mail he had been looking at and slowly stood up. "These young bucks are always in a hurry," he grumbled to the postmaster. Even though it was only eight in the morning, the day held early promise of being scorching hot. It seemed odd that even the birds were silent, a fact CJ commented on as they crossed the river and headed southeast.

They leisurely walked their horses up and out of the breaks and came to flatland prairie. After a while, they were once again descending into rugged hills and forded White Willow Creek. From there to Winn's house was only a short distance, and even though they covered the miles slowly, their horses were still wet with sweat from the hot, still air.

"Ow!" CJ gave a sudden jerk in his saddle and swatted a spot on his neck. He quickly squashed a deerfly between his fingers and gingerly rubbed the rapidly swelling bite. "I think I've been bit more times here by deerflies than anywhere else! Blasted things anyway. How come they never bite you?" He gave Winn a reproachful look.

"They don't like me. Neither do mosquitoes. Has something to do with all the garlic I eat," Winn replied with good humor. "'Course, the down side of that is the gals don't much like me either."

Winn had built a two-roomed house with an east porch on the banks of White Willow Creek and a small barn in the shelter of some tall cottonwood trees that ringed a horseshoe bend. After they unsaddled their horses and turned them into a small fenced pasture to graze, the two men slowly sauntered towards the house.

The cattle they had branded several days ago with Winn's brand grazed along the hills towards the south. Winn had decided CJ could help him put up some prairie grass in the creek bottoms, and after it cooled down in the evening, the men planned to stack it.

"If these old girls can just have an open winter to graze, I might make a little profit on 'em," Winn said, looking at his newly acquired herd. "Keeping 'em fed in the winter gets to be the big problem, you see." He looked at CJ and seemed to think CJ didn't see anything at all about cattle and South Dakota winters. "The old timers here tried to have thousands of cattle and winter 'em like the buffalo. You know, a buffalo can survive a blizzard 'cause they bunch up in a circle and the old bulls face the storm and protects the cows. Ain't no cattle bull gonna do that trick. The whole bunch usually just drifts with the storm, until they freeze to death. And that ain't purty."

"So how are you going to stop yours from drifting?"

"I'm gonna feed 'em in the winter. I'm gonna feed 'em here in this protected spot, and hope the dumb bells will think to come here to fill their bellies and get in that heavy timber and weather it out."

"Winn, how can anybody be an old-timer out here? I thought the Indians were the only ones allowed to live on a reservation."

"Well, you see, if you marry an Indian, you could live here. That's what some of 'em done. My boss, Scotty, he and his wife live on down Bad River. They were here in the early eighties. But they moved to Fort Pierre to get their kids educated. And there's John Utterbach. He married a sister to Philip's wife and lives along the White River. The government opened up this part of the reservation to whites in about 1890."

"So, anybody can live here now?"

"Yup, even an educated pup like you could live here if you wanted to. Course, you'd have to figure out how to survive, and build a claim shack, and plow up some acres, and dig a well; you know--follow all the government's rules, and that ain't easy."

A hot breeze moved the limp leaves on the cottonwoods along the creek and then, as if nature was displeased with heat and bugs, a whirlwind whipped over the ridge of the hills.

"What do you think of homesteaders?" CJ asked while he watched the grass from the whirlwind move in agitated circles.

"They're usually miserably uninformed." Winn gave a disgusted snort. "All the newspapers in the East say cattlemen are greedy and don't want anyone else out here. That ain't the case. The cattleman knows you need a lot of acres here. It ain't like other places and that's just a cold hard fact."

CJ gingerly traced the welt on his neck from the deerfly's bite. "Maybe another cold hard fact is that the people who want to settle here just want a piece of land, even when they know it could be cactus and nothing but hard work. Maybe though, like Smokey says, it's hardest on the women and kids."

"Smokey said that?" Winn scowled. "Maybe for once he said something smart."

"Winn," CJ began, as they mounted the porch steps, "I never quite figured out what happened to Smokey. It's not my business to know, and you don't have to tell me. I just haven't figured out why he never came along."

Winn held open the screen door and CJ walked into the kitchen. After Winn came in and dipped each of them a glass of water from an enameled pail, he motioned for CJ to pull up a chair and sit by the table.

"I guess I can tell you. Smokey is a hard fellow to figure out sometime. He was suppose to pay me for his part of the herd, but when I got back to his place from Recluse, he waved that off and said to go to Stearns, where his dad runs a store and post office. He told me to get the money there." Winn scowled at his glass. "I wasn't happy at all about that. Had other plans. Then I got to thinking how maybe you might like to take a little side trip with me. What do you say? Are you up to seeing more of God's country?"

"Sure, why not? Where is this place, anyway?"

"It's south of here, along the White River. And while we're heading that direction, I'm going take a couple of shirts along and have that purty washerwoman Smokey claims is his clean 'em up for me."

<hr>

It was a couple of days later when the two men finished haying. They saddled their horses at dawn and headed southeast. After they left Winn's home range and the yucca-covered hills, they crossed several creeks that Winn called by name. The steeper hills had given way to rolling prairie, and the grass, even in August, waved in the gentle breeze and was almost as tall as their horses' belly.

They were in no hurry, and the miles passed in pleasant conversation. When the sun hadn't quite reached the ten o'clock hour, they crossed a dry creek bed and rode up to a house and barn tucked into a horseshoe bend.

"Hello! Hello!" Winn called as they approached the house. CJ noticed that a short distance from the house was another smaller building. He saw movement in its clean glass window, and suddenly, a small barefooted boy darted out and stood outside the door, a slight smile on his face.

"Are you the master of the house?" Winn grinned at him and winked.

"I'm Isaac," the boy answered uncertainly.

"Well, Isaac,"—Winn dismounted and handed CJ his horse's reins—"we were wondering if the lady of the house still took in laundry."

"Oh yes, sir!" Isaac brightened perceptively. "I'll fetch 'er!" In a flash, he darted away and CJ watched his small form zip between some chokecherry bushes and momentarily disappear from view.

"Hello, there!" Winn called out suddenly to someone approaching from the barn. CJ turned in his saddle and saw a tall thin man walking hurriedly towards them. He wore the bib overalls of a farmer, and his smile stretched from ear to ear.

"Well, by jingles, hello there, yourself! Didn't hear you ride up! Better come in the house and have a cup of coffee."

It was the hospitality of the west, CJ thought to himself as he slowly dismounted. When you came to someone's place, the offer was immediate. Come in. Have coffee. And if there was something to go with the coffee, take all you want.

He led both horses to the hitching rail and tied the reins while Winn was introducing himself. He overheard the man say his name was Simon, his boy was Isaac, and Joanna would be up shortly. She was in the garden, he offered, and when both men started towards the house, CJ followed and took note of the small frame home with irises growing by the front door step.

Simon wiped his feet on an old rug before he opened the house door and looked pointedly at Winn. CJ wondered if Winn would get the unspoken message that he was to do the same, and sure enough, Winn industriously followed suit, as did CJ.

"This here fellow is CJ Crezner," Winn told Simon as the three men entered the house.

CJ nodded a hello and offered his hand. Simon gave him a bone-breaking handshake and a pat on the shoulder that nearly knocked CJ over. CJ noticed Winn looked very amused.

"I'll get us some coffee while we wait for Joanna. She usually has something good around here to eat." In no time, three cups were produced, and the coffee that had been warming on the back of the cook stove was poured.

While Simon was busy with that, Winn was telling him how he and CJ had some shirts that needed a woman's touch and Smokey Stearns told them all about the good job Joanna done.

And while Winn told Simon about his laundry woes, CJ made a careful study of the room they were in. It was a bright and homey-looking kitchen, dining room, and living room all in one. Some comfortable chairs were grouped on one side, and proudly standing by them was a full and almost overflowing bookcase. A rag rug added color. The table they were seated around was in the middle of the room, and a counter with cupboards finished the other side of the room. A door led into the lean-to at the back of the house, and CJ supposed a bedroom was in that part.

He was struck by two things. One was the absolute spotlessness of everything, and the other thing was he had been in male company and their homes for a long time. Leave it to a woman, he silently mused, to make a house a home. The rugs, the prairie flowers in a vase on the table, the sparkling clean windows with their equally clean curtains all showed a woman's touch.

He was curious about the kind of woman who would venture into prairie country with its weather extremes, Indians, isolation, and hardships. He didn't know what he expected, but the no-nonsense young woman who strode through the door startled him.

Joanna's attitude indicated she was a busy woman and interruptions in her schedule irritated her. Her dark eyes seemed to miss nothing, and her slender form was dressed in immaculate attire. CJ wondered if even dirt and dust was intimidated by this woman.

He politely rose and nodded his head when Simon made the introductions and was relieved when she merely nodded back at him.

Winn, however, seemed to think she was worthy of his flattery. He grandly came around the table and reached for the metal dishpan she carried in.

"You raised all that in your garden?" He looked with longing at the vegetables that filled the pan.

CJ didn't think he liked the quick look of irritation that flashed over her face. However, when she answered, her voice was mild.

"Isaac and Simon help me. You can set it on the counter." She relinquished the filled pan to Winn's grasp. "And Isaac tells me you were asking about washing something for you?"

"Oh yes, ma'am," Winn said, setting the pan carefully on the counter and turning around to face her. "Me 'n CJ both have some shirts that ain't purty no more."

"Well, let's look at them."

"They're in our saddle bags. You want I should bring 'em in here?" Winn asked.

Again, CJ noticed a flash of irritation cross her features. He spoke before he thought. "Of course, she doesn't want our dirty shirts in here, Winn. I'll go get them and she can look at them outside."

She snapped a look of surprise in his direction and followed him outside without saying a word. In fact, she never said anything until he pulled the clothing out of the canvas bag he had slung onto the back of his saddle.

"Whoa! Does he take a bath in garlic?" She shuddered as Winn's aromatic clothes were carelessly tossed onto the saddle. CJ noticed the horse's ears flattened. The smell must be pretty bad if it bothered a horse.

"He just likes garlic, ma'am, and wild horse radish and lots of onions."

"Thank you for keeping them out here," she said flatly and reached for one of CJ's shirts that had a three-cornered tear on the pocket. "Do you want me to mend this?"

"Yes, and there's some buttons in the other pocket that could be sewn on, if you do that." He knew he spoke rather coldly to her. For some reason, she aggravated him.

"Twenty-five cents a shirt for laundry, overalls are fifty cents, small tears and buttons cost five cents apiece."

"I suppose you have a corner on the market out here." CJ snorted at the outrageous price.

"Yes, I do. Take it or leave it."

He looked at her slender frame standing motionless before him and then glanced at her hands. They were not what he would have expected for a washerwoman. Maybe she priced herself out of business. Her slim hands were tanned and strong-looking, but not raw or callused like he thought they should be.

He pushed all the clothes back into the canvas bag. "Where do you want 'em?" he growled, uncharacteristically surly.

She gathered her skirt in one hand and pointed to the small building he had first noticed with her other hand. Without another word, she started towards the house.

"Little snip," he growled to himself and strode towards the little building. He had scarcely reached the door when Isaac hurried towards him, half-running, and half-hopping.

"Joanna says to put 'em on the outside step," he informed CJ breathlessly and pointed to a big rock step that led into the building.

"Isaac, how old are you?" CJ set the canvas bag on the step as instructed.

"I sorta think I'm pushin' six."

CJ swatted at a fly that buzzed through the air and landed on his arm. "How long have you and your family lived here?"

"I sorta think…like maybe over a year." He scratched some old mosquito bites absently while he thought about his answer. "Yup." He nodded his head. "Yup, 'cause I was four when Ma died, and we all moved here that springtime after that bad wintertime when Ma died." He bobbed his head again and squinted up at CJ. "Yup, 'cause Joanna baked me a real good cake that had five candles on it, and that was last year when it become like falltime."

"Was that the last time she baked a cake?" CJ asked sourly.

"I sorta think it was the last time she baked something that had candles on it. Pa said he didn't want candles on his birthday cake, and Joanna said that was good 'cause it might start the house afire." A worried look crossed his face. "Do you think six candles could set a house afire?"

"No, sir. Six candles wouldn't, but twenty-six might. Do you know your numbers?"

Isaac threw him another squinted look. "Is that like rel'tives? 'Cause I can't remember the rel'tives."

CJ grinned and tousled the boy's hair. "Numbers are—sorta like ciphering."

"Oh, yup. I know ciphering. Joanna has me do that when she's sewing on buttons and mending. She sez, 'Isaac, get your pencil and cipher for me.' Then she tells me how many she's sewed on that day, and I cipher 'em for her." He gave a big sigh. "Sometimes, it takes a lot of ciphering."

CJ looked at him sharply. "Is she busy most of the time?"

"Yup." Isaac started towards the house and motioned with his small hand for CJ to follow. "She's getting some cookies for us. We best not keep 'er waiting."

Lord, help the man who keeps Joanna waiting, CJ groused to himself as he followed Isaac's quick steps back into the house.

Four

August 27, 1898
Stearns, South Dakota

Dear Mom and Dad,

I've seen some beautiful grass country and met some fine people. Believe it or not, tonight I'm going to a dance here at Stearns. I can't imagine what kind of music or what the musicians will play, but this little burg is bustling with activity. The folks who live downriver, by the name of Thode, are doing what they call a pit barbecue. They've invited all the surrounding folks to come and enjoy the roasted meat and then stay for the dance. Since they also have a store in Stearns, they probably hope the folks will do some buying as well.

Mr. Stearns, who runs the post office and a store, is Smokey's widowed father. I don't know if he was glad to see Winn and me or not. Winn wanted his money for the cattle and wasn't exactly patient about getting it from him. Mr. Stearns didn't seem to know his son had bought cattle and he done some hemming and hawing, but finally gave Winn cash for them. After tempers cooled down, Smokey walked in. His father didn't act pleased to see him either, but Smokey has a way of congenial bantering that soothes everyone. Plus, he bought drinks for all of us.

The White River is not "purty" as Winn would say. It runs thick white water when it's riled up, and even when it settles down, the water is not clear. However, it does keep the trees and vegetation watered around here, plus providing good rough cattle country. The Pine Ridge Indian Reservation is on the south side of it.

Running out of paper. Will see you later.

Love,
CJ

"I say, CJ, if you get any faster at writing these notes to your folks, I won't even have a chance to sit down." Winn shook his head at the rest of the group in the crowded store that doubled as a post office. "I think it's this guy's goal to mail a letter from every post office in the country."

"Who knows?" Smokey retorted. "A hundred years from now people will see those letters and wonder where in the world Stearns, South Dakota, was. Same way with Recluse. Better tell the family to save all the letters, CJ. Your grandkids might be able to sell 'em for a few cents." The words were barely out of his mouth before he jumped down from his perch on a keg of nails and hurried to the door. With a grand swoop, he opened it to admit Joanna.

Everything about Joanna looked perfectly in place—from her starched white collar to the barely discernible bottom of her white, lace petticoat.

"Aren't you the perfect gentleman?" she said briskly, nodding at Smokey. The feathers in her hat waved gracefully. She entered the male-dominated store and post office with scarcely an acknowledgement to the motley crew, carefully stepping around the obstacles that were scattered in front of the pigeon holes which represented the US mail.

"Any mail for us, Mr. Stearns?" She didn't wait for his reply but searched for herself among the tied up bundles that were thrust into the slots. "Oh, good!" She pulled out a stack of letters and turned around to look at the strangely silent group. "Anyone who left laundry with me can pick it up at my buggy. Isaac is waiting there to do business."

She placed her mail into a seemingly bottomless reticule and picked up her skirt with one hand. She gave a smart little salute with the other as she left the silent men and walked out. Smokey followed her, shutting the door firmly behind him.

"Oh, that is a purty woman," Winn said softly. "And can she ever cook. Me 'n CJ had dinner with them a few days ago. Mmm, good!"

CJ decided to hunt down his laundry. He had heard Winn's raving about Joanna's cooking all the way into Stearns the day before. Her cooking was good, but, he decided, her attitude was terrible.

The little outpost of Stearns baked in the afternoon heat. Closer to the White River, the huge cottonwood trees gave welcome shade to the gradually swelling population. Word of mouth had spread quickly that food, friends, and visiting was in the works. Cowboys, Indians, cattlemen and their wives, and sojourning strangers had gathered to share a break in the routine.

CJ noted that tables had appeared out of nowhere, and it looked like everyone had brought something to add to the feast. A place to dance had been roped off, and even now a small group of musicians who brought instruments were tuning up. Discordant notes and laughter were heard as they struggled with some songs.

He saw Isaac standing in a black buggy parked in the shade of another store and watched with amusement as the little lad conducted his business with all seriousness. Joanna and Smokey were standing a short distance from him. CJ doubted she would let a penny go unwatched.

"Hi, CJ!" Isaac's greeting was full of smiles.

"Guess you're learning more ciphering today, right?"

"Yessir! And here's your package and you owe—" Isaac puckered up his forehead as he read the amount on the paper. "Twenty-five cents."

CJ frowned and looked at Joanna. He knew he owed for one pair of overalls, two shirts, and probably a host of buttons and torn places. It should be more like one dollar plus.

Isaac was patiently waiting for the money. CJ paid him and then ambled over to where Joanna and Smokey stood. Their conversation faded into silence as he came closer and Joanna's smile disappeared.

"You don't look happy, Mr. Crezner."

"Ah, well, Miss Swanson, perhaps happy is not the right word. I'm perplexed. I thought I left two shirts and one pair of overalls, and from the looks and feel of this package, there is one pair of overalls and no shirts."

"Oh, oh, oh, Joanna." Smokey whistled and winked at CJ. "A dissatisfied customer. I better leave the two of you alone to discuss business." He gave Joanna a rakish grin. "Remember, you promised to dance a whole lot of dances with me." He patted her cheek and sauntered off.

"Yes, well." There were small red spots on Joanna's cheeks as she turned her attention back to CJ. "I washed and mended them, but even I could not fix all the splits in the seams. Mr. Crezner, those shirts are way too small for you. Like the one you're wearing now."

CJ stood a little taller and felt the usual tightness under his arm pits. "What?" he yelped, a little louder than he intended.

"You apparently aren't the skinny little weasel you used to be," she answered firmly. "I only charged half price for the overalls." She lifted her chin a bit defiantly. "Of course, if you want shirts that don't fit you anymore, I could charge the whole amount, which would be one dollar and twenty cents."

He took a deep breath and counted to ten. In the process, he realized the buttons over his chest were about ready to pop.

"Just great," he finally muttered. "I wasn't planning on buying new shirts."

"You must still be a growing boy."

"Young lady," he said quietly, "I'm neither a weasel nor a boy. Most likely, I'm older than you are." He walked away before he could say more than he should. She was a most infuriating woman.

⚬∞⚬

The afternoon shadows were long, and the cottonwood trees graciously lent their shade to the perspiring dancers. The musicians had worked up a variety of songs together, and their efforts were appreciated. In fact, CJ mused, they sounded good. He had watched the gathering with a great deal of enjoyment, even if his new loose-fitting shirt was hotter than his old, thin tight one.

The prettiest woman there was a smiling young lady who seemed to think it was her duty to dance with every gentleman present. She was coming his way and had a determined look. He had managed to disappear into the crowd before. It would be rude, he knew, to not share a waltz with her.

"You all must be the most bashful fellow here," she drawled, and her accent was beautifully southern. CJ decided she was even prettier close up.

"They are playing the Missouri Waltz, and I hear you are from that great state, as I am—I believe it must be our dance!" She tilted her head to one side, and a blond tendril moved along her cheek in the light breeze.

"I believe it most certainly must be our dance," CJ said and took her offered hand to lead her towards the swaying couples.

When she smiled delightedly at him, he noticed the dimples in her cheeks. "Isn't this just a marvelous, marvelous gathering?" she asked as they started dancing. "I'm visiting friends and am so excited to meet everyone. I live in Pierre, and my daddy told me to get out into the country and invite people to our tent meeting next week. I'm combining business with pleasure, and so, sir, I'd like to invite you also. Now, please say you'll come and bring all your friends!" She gave the whole speech with drawls and smiles and never missed a step of the waltz.

"What kind of tent meeting?" CJ wondered if her daddy might be a con medicine man who sent his beautiful daughter out to gather in the local yokels.

"We are having a revival to spread the message of Jesus Christ!" She acted as if she didn't notice that CJ stumble a couple of steps and went on talking merrily. "Our church in Missouri sent us here to South Dakota to meet the spiritual needs of the west, and Daddy and Momma thought what better way for people to see and hear Daddy preach than to have a wonderful big tent meeting!

"And, Mr. CJ Crezner, I also have something more I'd like to talk to you about. Oh yes! I know your name." She laughed at his surprised look. "Mr. Smokey told me, and he also told me you have a wonderful voice, and since I was asked to sing a few songs, I'm just begging you to sing with me! Smokey says you know all sorts of hymns, and I know it would lift up people's hearts to hear praises to the Lord!" Her dimples flashed and she seemed to float in his arms as they dipped and swayed to the music.

He smiled down at her, and wondered if anyone ever refused this delightful creature anything.

"Ah, Miss—"

"Oh, just call me Deborah Lynn. My daddy is the Reverend Joseph Smith, from the First Baptist Church in Pierre, and even if we don't have a church building yet, we will in the very near future. If it's the Lord's will, of course."

"Of course." CJ made a few steps without saying anything, and then asked, "What songs do you have in mind?"

He figured correctly that Deborah Lynn knew exactly what they were going to sing and when they would be singing. She launched into another speech and her blue eyes twinkled all the while she informed him of his role and what songs they would sing, and what key they would sing them in. He was smiling broadly by this time and was surprised when he looked up to see Joanna and Smokey dancing close beside them. He was even more surprised when Joanna rolled her eyes and shook her head at him. He lost his smile immediately and glared at her. Smokey chose that moment to whirl his partner in a different direction and CJ found himself glaring at Joanna's back.

"Well, now, that is a dark look. I certainly hope I'm not the cause of such irritation." Deborah Lynn's voice carried a tiny bit of reproach.

CJ hastily assured her that she was not the cause of any such thing, and before more could be said, the music stopped. It was the last song of a set, and CJ supposed the correct thing to do was to escort his partner back to her friends.

She made sure that he would indeed sing with her, and he agreed. He didn't loiter with her and her friends, but instead took a quick tour around the crowd while he looked for Smokey. He had a few things to say to Mr. Stearns.

Instead of Smokey, he found Joanna fanning herself beside the lemonade table. Come to think about it, he also had a few things he wanted to say to her.

She raised one defined dark eyebrow at him as he approached her. "If you've come to ask me to dance, you'll have to wait a minute. I'm cooking."

He opened his mouth to say that was probably the last thing on his mind, but decided such a remark would be rude. "Well, while you're cooling down, maybe you'll tell me what the rolled eyes and so on meant." He knew his words were short and clipped.

She looked at his shirt. "You have a nice new shirt. The right size. But good grief, the collar makes you look like a preacher." She shook her head in obvious frustration at his inability to dress correctly.

The music started again, this time a slow two step. Without thinking, he steered her rather unceremoniously onto the makeshift dance floor and tersely gathered her into his arms to dance. For a brief moment he thought she was going to break away from him and return to the lemonade stand. He held her tighter and she looked at him questioningly.

"Miss Swanson." He couldn't keep the edge from his voice. "Do you know why it makes me look like a preacher?" He answered his own question with brusqueness. "I am a preacher, and, ma'am, I would be pleased if you keep that information to yourself." He took momentary pleasure in seeing her eyes widen in shock.

For several moments they danced in silence. He felt her take a deep breath and then she looked up at him with her eyes narrowed and speculating.

"The J in CJ must stand for Jonah."

"What?"

"The J in CJ must stand for Jonah. He ran away when the Lord wanted him to preach too. I wondered why an educated man like yourself was wandering around with the locals."

"What? What?" Each *what* became louder until the dancers next to them gave him a startled look. He managed a forced smile and quickly whirled Miss Swanson a little farther away from the rest of the crowd.

He muttered close to her ear. "You always make the most irritating remarks!"

"I know. It's a bad habit of mine." For a second, she looked apologetic. "But," she added with exasperation, "When people aren't quite what they seem to be, I think they're trying to run from something."

"Not what they seem to be?" He scowled at her. "Now just what does that mean?"

"Hat, chaps, and boots don't make a cowboy."

"What?"

"Oh, pipe down." She looked at him with evident disgust. "I can't explain it, but I knew right away you weren't exactly the run of the mill cowboy."

They danced without smiling.

She continued, "So, why aren't you preaching out here? We have all sorts coming through, but not many preachers."

He didn't answer for a while. He wished with all his being that he wouldn't have told her. Not that he thought she'd say anything, but he wasn't quite ready to be a man of God. Being a wandering cowboy was much easier. He sighed. Maybe he was making the whole matter a lot more difficult than it really was.

"I needed—I wanted—time. Time to—I don't really know. Just time to pull it all together, time to get ready for what my family wants me to do."

She looked over his shoulder without saying anything for a while. "What does your family want you to do?"

"Join in with my grandfather at his church. Preach. Become the next pastor and follow in his footsteps."

"What's the problem with that?"

"I'm a lousy preacher." She was the first person he had admitted that to. He vaguely wondered why he was so honest with her. Probably because he would never see her again, and he doubted she would concern herself for any length of time over his troubles.

"Well, that's pathetic! Why don't you improve yourself? Get more fired up. You seem so…so…"

"Bland." He supplied her missing word.

She studied him with a thoughtful expression. "No. That's not the right word. I can't think of it right now." They finished the last steps of the song, and after the music ended, she put her hand on his arm. "Mr. Crezner, running away doesn't solve anything. I know that first hand."

"I wouldn't call it running away. I'm just not quite sure." He couldn't seem to finish his thought and was irritated at her for no other reason than the fact she said squarely what his mind refused to admit.

Five

September 12, 1898
Pierre, South Dakota

Dear Mom and Dad,

I hope my telegram didn't alarm you. I wanted to let you know I arrived in Pierre, and I would be staying here for a while. I was so busy that it seemed best to send a quick note.

I've been helping Reverend Smith and his family with tent revival meetings, and it was a full two weeks of being the song leader with numerous other duties. Reverend Smith has been able to garner immense enthusiasm towards the building of a church and has asked me to continue working with him. It seemed like a good idea, especially after I read Granddad's letter which indicated cousin Kentworth and his family were planning to work with him. That has relieved my mind considerably. I was worried I had seemed ungrateful for the position my granddad offered me.

However, this past week, the Smith family received word that Mrs. Smith's mother in Missouri has become very ill. The family has asked me to escort Mrs. Smith and her daughter, Deborah Lynn, back to Missouri for an extended visit and I have agreed to go with them. Reverend Smith will stay in Pierre to continue with the building plans. After I have delivered the Smith ladies, I will be able to travel to Springfield to be with you for a couple of weeks.

We are leaving in two days, so I will probably be home before this letter reaches you, although I understand train connections are a little dubious going north and south.

Thanks for all the letters from home that were waiting for me at the Pierre post office. It was good to read the news. I am looking forward to seeing the family.

Love,
Carl John

CJ slowly reread his letter. It had been difficult to condense the past weeks into a couple of paragraphs. Life with the Smiths had thrust him into the middle of church life once again. He found he remembered exactly how to speak and act so he wouldn't be contentious. He remembered to murmur "Praise the Lord" at all the appropriate times. He knew church life. He wasn't sure if he knew what God wanted from him as well as he knew what the church expected of him.

He carefully folded the letter and placed it into the envelope and, just as carefully, sealed it shut. For several minutes, he sat looking out the window of his small room in the boarding house. The street below was quiet in contrast to the bustle of the town.

Pierre, South Dakota, was excited to be the new capitol of the state. It was growing, and it was building. Situated along the banks of the Missouri River gave it an ambience of a watered oasis from the brown of the prairie.

After the Stearns dance and feed, Winn had decided to accompany CJ to the stage stop at Midland where CJ would board the stage for the ride to Pierre. The two men had ambled down Brave Bull Creek with Winn making stops at every place to visit. He loved to tell whoever would listen how CJ and that purty blonde gal sang so good together that right on the spot she asked him to come with her to Pierre to help with her daddy's revival. Winn gave a great account of how CJ stuttered and stammered and finally said yes.

CJ would shake his head at Winn and knew from the looks of Winn's audience it made a good story and would be repeated.

CJ pushed back his chair and decided a walk to the post office would be a refreshing change from sitting in his room and thinking too much. He reached over to the peg where his hat rested rather forlornly. When he arrived in Pierre, Deborah Lynn had teased him and said his hat looked passable only when he was chasing cows. Since he was with the Smiths every day, and both parents looked the same way at the dusty and battered head gear, he parked it on the peg.

For a moment, his hand hovered indecisively over his Stetson, but defiance in this tiny matter took over, and he placed it firmly on his head, grabbed his letter, and walked out the door.

"Mr. Crezner!" His landlady stood at the foot of the stairs with her hands on her hips. "Mr. Crezner, the Smith ladies are here and are a-wantin' me to fetch you."

"Oh. Well. Tell them I'll be right down." With those words, CJ slowly reopened his door and placed his tan Stetson back on its peg.

He often wondered when he saw Deborah Lynn Smith if a more vivacious or lovely lady existed. She could charm a rattlesnake if she chose to, he thought, and he had never encountered her when she wasn't charming.

Today was no exception. As soon as he entered the parlor, both ladies bounded out of their chairs and began talking at once. Deborah Lynn laughed and gave her slightly shorter mother a hug.

"You all go ahead, Momma. I'll let you tell him the news!"

The elder Smith lady began immediately. "CJ, we have a small monetary gift for you which the Reverend said you well deserved." She handed him an envelope. "But this is what we are so excited about! When we were walking past the general store, what did we see in the window but the perfect hat for you?" She took a deep breath and added with an adrenal rush, "And it's on sale!"

"Well." CJ tried again with more enthusiasm. "Well!"

"Now, we can't take any more time to go back with you, but we did tell the proprietor that you might be coming down. So—"

"Oh, I get to tell him this part, Momma! So the store is holding it for you until you get down there. We all just rushed up here right away to tell you! We felt so bad that you've gone bareheaded all these days. Daddy says a man should have a hat!"

"I was just going to the post office to mail a letter, so I'll—I'll check it out on my way back." CJ put the envelope in his shirt pocket.

He had unhappy visions of what kind of hat the two ladies might think was perfect for him. Probably a derby or some other kind of sissy-type hat. He shuddered.

"Now, CJ." Deborah Lynn put her arm through his. "We'll just walk down to the post office with you. It's on our way home." He was ushered out the door and onto the street before he realized it.

The two women talked about the trip back to Missouri and how they had been praying for Mrs. Smith's mother. They talked about the building plans and the excitement of starting a new church. When they arrived at the post office, they reminded him they were expecting him for supper that evening, and Mrs. Smith she hoped he'd be wearing his new hat.

He waved a rather weak goodbye to them and gave an inward sigh. After he posted the letter, he decided he may as well get this nightmare over with and slowly walked to the general store.

The owner seemed to be waiting for him. "Mr. Crezner? Say, I want to tell you I sure enjoyed hearing you sing. You've got quite a voice there, young man."

CJ thanked him. "Ah, I'm told there is a hat here?"

"Oh yes, sir. The Smith ladies picked this out for you. I think you'll like it!"

CJ wondered if there was a little smirk on the guy's face and braced himself for whatever was going to be presented. With a grand flourish, a hat box was brought out and set on the counter.

"Are you ready for this?" The owner snapped off the lid and proudly pulled out the hat with great pomp and ceremony.

CJ's jaw dropped. He stared uncomprehendingly and was totally speechless.

"Yup. Thought you'd like it," the storekeeper said with obvious satisfaction. "The two ladies looked it all over, pointed out a few flaws they noticed, and told me to hold it back for you. I can take cash, or if you can't pay all of it right now, I can do a little bit of credit."

"Well. Ah, what are you needing for it?" CJ finally found his voice.

The storekeeper puffed up his chest. "A Stetson of this caliber usually sells for four dollars and fifty cents. But, as the ladies pointed out, there are some spots on the crown, plus a tiny slit in the silk lining. I don't know how that happened. But anyway, I took off one whole dollar. And because I sure like your singing, I told the ladies I would sell it to you for three dollars, but that's just for you and just for today."

It was quite a speech. When he was finished, he looked at CJ speculatively. "You ain't gonna find another bargain like this. 'Boss of the Plains' is the best Stetson they sell. Made of nutria fur—best there is—and the brown color, perfect for you, sir."

CJ quickly took the envelope Mrs. Smith had given him from his shirt pocket. When he opened it, he counted out the money and laid it on the counter. Then he dug into his pockets. He found enough coins to total three dollars, with two pennies left over.

"I—well, I sure never thought I could afford something like this!" CJ shook the beaming man's hand. "Boss of the Plains! A lot of guys I rode with talked about this Stetson!"

The storekeeper carefully put the money in the register and wrote up the bill. He scrawled Paid in Full on it and handed it to CJ. "You want me to shape it a little for you?"

CJ had already put it on his head. It fit a little loose, but some paper in the band would take care of that. He found a dusty mirror in the store and a quick glance told him it was just fine the way it was.

"I believe this will work."

"Yup. Looks mighty fine. The ladies said you were escorting 'em back to Missouri. Too bad about Mrs. Smith's mama. Oh, you want the box it came in?"

On his way back to his room, with a fine Stetson on his head and the empty hat box in his hands, he thought about the Smith ladies. How did they ever convince the store owner to mark this hat down and then come up with almost enough money to buy it? And the wonder of it all—to pick out a hat that he really wanted? Amazing. They were amazing women. Visions of blue eyes and dimpled cheeks sifted through his mind. Tactful. Talented. Terrific. Beautiful. And he was the lucky man who would be escorting Deborah Lynn (and her momma) back to Missouri. Wonderful!

Six

October 18, 1898
Springfield, Missouri

Dear Isaac,

I'm sending you this crate of surplus books from our church library in Springfield, Missouri. I thought you might like them. I also included some books for your father and your aunt.

I'll be heading back to Pierre in a couple of weeks. The Reverend Smith had asked me to escort Mrs. Smith and their daughter, Deborah Lynn (you remember she's the one who sang at Stearns) back to Missouri earlier because of illness in their family. Sadly, Mrs. Smith's mother passed away shortly after we arrived in Missouri.

The fall colors are beautiful and the trees look like a painter has been splashing colors all about. I will be anxious to see what South Dakota looks like in the fall.

I hope you enjoy the books.

Sincerely,
Carl John Crezner

The wooden crate was full and heavy and it would cost a pretty penny to mail. His mother had carefully packed all the books in solidly and even found nooks and crannies to add some hard candy.

"If you're finished, Carl John, we'll get the lid nailed on." His father was waiting with the hammer.

"Finished." CJ quickly stuffed the letter into the envelope and laid it on the top of the books.

Within minutes, the lid was nailed on, the address to Mr. Isaac Swanson, Stearns, South Dakota, was written in bold letters, and the return address of CJ Crezner, Pierre, South Dakota, was also added.

It was a lazy afternoon in the Missouri autumn. The curtains in the parsonage dining room fluttered silently from the slight breeze of the open window. It was, CJ reflected, the only time since he arrived that the pace of the household slowed down.

There had been several unexpected deaths in his father's congregation. With consoling the grieving families and preparing for the funeral services, his father had given CJ list after list of details to attend to and time seemed to evaporate. And while his parents had both expressed pleasure at his physical improvement, there had been an undercurrent of concern about his spiritual state of mind.

"Doc Regis was pretty proud his diagnosis of you was correct." CJ's father pulled back a dining table chair. He motioned for CJ to sit down and join him.

CJ smiled as he sat down. "Doc Regis is a crusty guy with a heart of gold. Did I ever tell you that he taught me how to fight when I was being bullied in the third grade?"

"Oh yes. I knew all about it." Humor glinted from his father's eyes. "A preacher doesn't teach his son to fight, but if the family doctor takes the boy to the barn and shows him some protective moves, praise the Lord."

CJ looked at his father with dawning comprehension. "And if the same family doctor has a brother Giles who is a trail boss, praise the Lord again."

"Exactly. You needed experience that I couldn't give you. I sometimes wish my own father had sent me away for a while. But your temperament and mine are different. I—never had the questions about my faith that you seem to have." His father gave a sigh and shook his head. "I'm glad you came home for a visit, son. Your mother and I were beginning to think you might end up in Canada."

"Well, the prairies of Dakota might seem like the end of the world for some people. I guess I like the open space. I miss it more than I ever thought I would." CJ fidgeted slightly in his chair. "It's not that I question God, or that I doubt Christ. It's more—it's more like I don't have any enthusiasm." He found the words hard to say and looked down at the table. "I don't have any enthusiasm to preach." He looked at his father pleadingly. "I'm sorry, Dad. I know I've disappointed you and Granddad. I'm—I'm very sorry."

He abruptly pushed back his chair and stood up. "I listen to you and Granddad preach, and Reverend Smith, and there's passion in your message." He shook his head and began to pace back and forth in front of the window. "I don't have that zeal. I don't have a voice that has any conviction. I can't muster up anything but dread for the pulpit. If I were to take Granddad's church, the whole congregation would stop coming. I would feel like a hypocrite every time I preached. It's not in me!" He slumped back into his chair. "It's just not in me," he repeated slowly.

His father looked at him steadily. "I have begun to realize we always took it for granted that you would be another generation of Crezner preachers. We made the mistake of not asking the Lord if this was His will."

"I have absolutely no idea *what* His will for me is," CJ said, a little bitterly.

"Not everyone is called to be a preacher, Carl John. There are many who serve the Lord quietly and touch people's lives. You'll find your calling. And while you're waiting, study the Word and pray."

"Was—Granddad totally disgusted with me?" He still hadn't made the twenty mile trip to his granddad's church.

"Surprisingly, no. Your cousin Kentworth unexpectedly married a woman with three children, and they wanted to raise them in a small town. He contacted your grandfather late this summer about moving from Kansas City and coming to help at Dad's church. Actually, it has worked out very well. The Lord moves in mysterious ways, Carl John. Maybe it was His nudging that prompted you to head north."

CJ frowned and looked down at his hands. Maybe it was. Maybe it wasn't. He was never sure where the nudges came from.

He heard his mother's voice through the open window and then two other very southern voices that he knew quite well. His quick look out the window confirmed that, indeed, his mother and the Smith ladies were almost at the door.

"Did you know we were having company?"

His question was answered by the puzzled look on his father's face. "No. Do you recognize the voices?"

"The Smith ladies." He barely had the words out of his mouth when three happy and chattering ladies entered the dining room.

"Look who I met at the luncheon!" His mother's voice was full of enthusiasm. "Imagine my surprise when I found out that Miss Rovey's niece, who was our singing entertainment today, was none other than Debora Lynn Smith! And her mother is here also!"

"Oh, I love surprises!" Debora Lynn had reached the now standing CJ and she patted his arm with obvious pleasure. "When Auntie Coramae asked me to sing, I just knew we could surprise you and your family by coming to Springfield! And to think—you and Auntie are neighbors!"

To think, CJ mused to himself, the gregarious maiden auntie who fussed over every little detail in life was this lovely creature's relative took more than a little imagination.

"And you must be Reverend Crezner!" Mrs. Smith greeted CJ's father with outstretched hand and her usual winning smile. "We are just delighted to meet CJ's family. He is a very fine young man, you know, and has just taken absolutely wonderful care of Deborah Lynn and myself on this long and tiring trip. I simply don't know what we would have done without him." She paused for breath before continuing. "And, when you hear him and Deborah Lynn sing, it will warm your heart, just simply warm your heart. And, we have some huge plans for him to sing with Deborah Lynn tomorrow at the gospel meeting at your church. It was Coramae's idea that these two young people could sing several songs before the meeting and several more afterwards. Oh, I just know everyone will love hearing them. Of course, that is if CJ is willing and all that."

She paused once again and Deborah Lynn looked at CJ with pleading blue eyes. "Please, please say you will, CJ. Momma and I have some songs that we think will sound so perfect for the meeting. And Auntie approved of all of them last night. Please?"

CJ looked at his father blankly. "Gospel meeting?"

"My goodness, yes. In all the hustle these past days, I never mentioned to you we have planned a special meeting to preach the gospel. Several ministers are coming. Even your grandfather."

"Well." He managed a smile for Deborah Lynn and sighed inwardly. South Dakota was sounding better all the time. "Well," he repeated, "this is short notice. What songs did you have in mind?"

Within moments, he was herded to the piano in the parlor, and excited chatter from everyone was swirling around him. He had a sinking feeling clear to the end of his booted toes. Gospel meetings. Blood and thunder preaching. Halleluiahs and Praise the Lord. *Oh God, why did You send me home to take part in this? What would have been wrong with just a quiet visit with my parents?*

Everyone said they had never heard him sing better or with more feeling than when he and Miss Deborah Lynn sang the closing hymn, "Rescue the Perishing." It seemed to hit a tender note with the crowd and certainly added a grand finale to the meeting.

Afterwards, a bountiful lunch was spread on the tables outside in the late afternoon sunshine. Platefuls of sandwiches and dainty cakes were urged upon the enthusiastic gathering. Deborah Lynn walked with him with her arm tucked sweetly around his, and graciously said "Praise the Lord" when people would stop and congratulate them on a job well done.

"I declare, CJ, I could drink a whole pitcher of lemonade, my throat is that dry," she told him as they passed through several groups of people.

Upon hearing her remark, a tiny lady turned towards them. "CJ? Now, Miss Smith, when did the Reverend Crezner become merely CJ?"

"Hello, Mrs. Kraft, it's good to see you!" CJ took her tiny hand and gently brushed his lips across the gloved fingers. "Deborah Lynn, let me introduce you to my favorite teacher!"

"I taught him high school English and elementary Christianity." Mrs. Kraft beamed.

Deborah Lynn looked puzzled. "Reverend?" She gave her liquid laugh that always seemed to float into a musical arrangement. "Reverend?" she repeated and looked at CJ for an explanation.

Mrs. Kraft didn't wait for CJ to explain anything. "Yes, my dear. Reverend Crezner, the next generation of Crezner pastors. I, myself, attended his orientation, and even if I do say so myself, I take great pride in having taught him Sunday school for many years. Yes. Yes. He will preach as good as he sings."

He gently hugged the tiny form. "Mrs. Kraft is, of course, prejudice, but that still doesn't keep her from being my favorite teacher."

"And you, young man, were my favorite student. But I must scold you for not writing to me while you were gone. Of course," she added thoughtfully, "when I last saw you this spring, you didn't look healthy enough to even make it to fall." She tapped him on the arm with her fan. "Sunshine and cattle drives must be good for you. You look the picture of a strong young man now! When are you going to take your grandfather's church?"

Deborah Lynn looked even more puzzled and seemed to be at a loss for words. A very rare thing, CJ mused to himself.

"I'm going back to South Dakota with the Smiths, Mrs. Kraft. Grandfather is very blessed to have my cousin Kentworth at his church."

Mrs. Kraft clucked and shook her head. CJ knew she had more to say, but at that moment, Mrs. Smith swept towards them with glasses of lemonade in her hands.

"My dear children, you must be famished for something to drink!" She handed them each a glass and, with her usual gentleness, began a conversation with Mrs. Kraft.

CJ felt a gentle tug on his arm. It was clear that Deborah Lynn wanted a word with him in private.

"*Reverend* Crezner?" she asked when they were beyond the hearing of others. "Reverend? CJ, why didn't you tell us you were an ordained minister?" Her blue eyes looked slightly stormy.

"Well." He wanted to choose his words carefully. "It really didn't seem important. You didn't need a minister; you needed someone to sing with you. Do the little jobs. I was glad to help you and your folks in that manner." He smiled gently at her, hoping that would take away the storm which seemed to be brewing a little stronger every minute.

"But it was deceiving of you!" She took a long draught of lemonade, and then a deep breath. He waited for the storm to break. "I can't understand why you aren't proud to be an ordained minister for the work of Jesus Christ. It—frankly, CJ, it puts you in a different light, at least, for me, it does."

He immediately took offense at her words. "There was no deceiving on my part. Pure and simple, I was ordained in the spring, I don't have a church, and I'd just come off a cattle drive." He looked into her troubled eyes with an edge of annoyance sparking from his own hazel ones. "You took it for granted I was a cowboy. I never said I was or I wasn't."

She said nothing for several seconds. Neither did he. Finally, she looked down and said softly, "CJ, we'll have to continue this discussion another time. Momma will be wanting me to mingle with the people." She swiftly walked away, her long skirt brushing through the grass with a swishing sound.

He gulped down his own glass of lemonade and set it on a nearby table. He turned towards the church and walked the brick pathway towards the steps that led into the sanctuary. Only as he reached the top step did he realize his grandfather was standing just inside the double doors, watching him.

"Carl John," his grandfather said in his sonorous voice. "Come inside. I have been wanting to talk to you."

Seven

November 7, 1898
Pierre, South Dakota

Dear Grandfather,

I have taken your suggestions and advice, and I so appreciate your time and wise counsel. I especially am grateful for the truths you revealed to me as we visited the graves of my older brother and younger sister. You enlightened me on many issues I never felt comfortable asking my parents concerning my siblings' deaths from diphtheria. I was five years old when that sadness crept into our family. You pinpointed the weight of responsibility I have felt since then to make my parents happy. I suppose, as you suggested, I have always tried to be extremely obedient so as not to cause them any more grief.

On your advice, I immediately had a private conversation with Reverend Smith after we arrived back in Pierre. He was understanding about the reasons I had not divulged what I considered unimportant pieces of information to his family. I have continued working with him on their building project, but I have also taken another piece of your advice and now am employed at the lumberyard, doing their book work and filling in as needed in other places.

I believe we have parallel opinions concerning the lovely half of the singing duo. Greet Grandmother and give her a hug from me. Thanks once again for your insight and concern—you have relieved my mind considerably!

Love,
Carl John

A cold blast of wind rattled the windows of the boarding house. After spending the day working mostly outside at the lumberyard in the wind and spitting snow, Mrs. Ordin's hot meal and warm house had been a welcomed relief.

He slowly folded up his letter and sealed it while Mrs. Ordin brought her guests the last round of coffee for the evening.

"Mr. Southerner," she said, addressing CJ with her bantering grin, "the way I see it, a Missouri kid like yourself is a-gonna' freeze his tail off here in the North Country."

Mrs. Ordin was a middle-aged spitfire who claimed her third husband was the best of the lot, and even if he wasn't blessed with as much get-up-and-go as she had, she was going to keep him.

CJ agreed with her. "Any advice?" He put his letter in his shirt pocket and took the offered cup of coffee.

Her husband snorted from his corner chair. "You got a couple of hours? Hily always has advice." He ducked with good humor as she gave him a light-handed cuff.

"Layer up and keep your feet dry and warm. Now the way I see it, more folk get sick 'cause they ain't got dry socks. And they ain't got dry socks 'cause they ain't got good rubber boots and just a-walkin' around in those leather-soled fancy boots. You can't look fancy and keep warm at the same time." She paused for breath and the dangle earrings she always wore swayed in excited little swirls.

"And I sez to the young, good-looking fella that came to see about a room this afternoon, and him all looking like he was froze, I sez, 'Better get some warm duds, brother,' 'cause he has a collar like a preacher, and he sez, 'I'm on fire for the Lord!' and I sez, 'Good. Get some warm duds or you all will have fire for a temperature when you catch pneumonie.' That's what I told him, and he just laughed, took a room, and went to see the Smiths."

CJ became interested. "I heard another minister was coming to visit them. Will he be coming back this evening?"

"Nope. Said he was a-stayin' at the Smith's tonight, but planned to be here for a couple of weeks and didn't wanna bother 'em that long." Mrs. Ordin took her own cup and sat down in the rocking chair reserved for her beside the stove.

She took a drink of her coffee. "How long are you all planning on staying, CJ?"

"Well. That's a good question. Right now, with helping the Smiths and working at the lumberyard, I have a little income. I guess I'm planning on staying the winter anyway."

Mr. Ordin snuffled a bit and blew his nose. "I always say a person who wants to live in this country should spend a winter here before they make up their mind. If they can tolerate winter, then they should stay a hot summer. If they can handle both them weather extremes, they might make a South Dakotan."

One of the other boarders asked what the coldest temperature the Ordins remembered was.

"Oh, mercy!" Mrs. Ordin said. "Did you ever notice that funny looking pine tree out front? One night, when it was way below zero, one of our boarders rammed into it, and it was so cold a branch just popped off near the top. 'Course it was a little feller than. Now it's a growing funny, so I call it the cold tree."

"It was forty below zero that night," Mr. Ordin stated with authority.

"What's the hottest you've ever seen it?" CJ asked.

"Hundred and fifteen. And that was in the shade." Mr. Ordin replied.

"Well." CJ stood and put his empty cup on the tray. "Guess I'll turn in, folks. Good evening, everyone." The other boarders looked reluctant to leave the warmth of the fire for the cold upstairs rooms. There was a chorus of goodnights for him as CJ left. The conversation was back to the weather as he started up the stairs.

He was going to take Mrs. Ordin's advice and use the new warm wool socks he had just bought. He was going to dig out his new rubber boots too. She was right. Better to be warm than have cold feet. He had hesitated to wear them because he thought he'd be the laughing stock of the lumberyard. He decided they could laugh all they wanted—he had felt chilled to the bone when he finished work this evening. A southern softie like himself had better take all the precautions.

Mrs. Ordin had given him a room on the southeast side of the house, and the chimney was also in the corner. She had pegged him as a southerner after she heard him talk. "A good old Missouri boy," she said and admitted she was "a good old Missouri gal." He was doubly grateful to her when the wind howled in from the northwest.

For all the weather extremes, CJ was comfortable in his new surroundings. The Smiths invited him often to their home, but there was an unmistakable coolness between him and Deborah Lynn.

It was probably more his fault than it was hers, he reflected as he got ready for bed. She had made sure they never had a moment alone coming back from Missouri. It had irritated him she so pointedly preferred everyone else's company to his.

After his visit to Reverend Smith, she had thawed considerably, but CJ remained aloof. If the new preacher was "on fire for the Lord," he would definitely be a match for Deborah Lynn. CJ couldn't begin to count the times she had made the same impassioned remark to him. She would look at him searchingly, as if waiting for verification that he felt equally passionate for the Lord, and would turn away in disappointment when he said nothing.

"I'm sorry, Lord," he muttered as he unbuttoned his shirt. "I wonder if I will ever reach a point in my life when I say I'm on fire for the Lord. All I'm able to muster up right now is to be a good and faithful servant. No fire." He shivered.

He felt the envelope in his pocket as he hung his shirt on the back of the chair. His grandfather's wisdom and counsel over his lackluster preaching ability was an unexpected and undeserved blessing. It was as if the older preacher could read his mind and see the frustration and doubt that troubled him so much. He realized Deborah Lynn didn't have the years of common sense his grandfather had, but even so, some of her remarks on the train ride back to Pierre rankled him.

He thought of the conversation they had last night. Deborah Lynn and he were practicing for yet another duet with Mrs. Smith at the piano. A caller came to see Mrs. Smith, and for the first time in a long time, he and Deborah were alone. She laid her hand on his arm and gave him a dimpled smile.

"CJ, we simply must not let our differences come between us. I have feelings for you. I think you have some little feelings for me too, don't you?"

She looked incredibly beautiful in her green dress with a black velvet collar. Her hair was arranged in soft blonde tendrils around her face, and her eyes were begging him to understand.

He bent down to kiss her. She gasped and stepped back, which made him feel like a fool. He immediately straightened and walked over to the fireplace and stood with his back towards her.

She came to stand beside him and once again laid her hand on his arm. "CJ," she implored, "I have always said I would save my kisses for the man I was going to marry. And while I have these feelings for you, I'm not sure we are—I'm not sure we are on the same mindset right now. Oh please, please understand and don't be mad at me. Please, CJ."

"How will you know," he had asked coldly, "if you will like kissing the man you are going to marry unless you kiss him before you accept his proposal?"

"My dear CJ, you *are* mad at me, aren't you? I just keep saying wrong things to you. CJ. Oh! Are you going to propose to me?"

"No. I was going to kiss you and go home." He turned towards her and gave her a grim smile. "And now, dear Deborah Lynn, I will simply get my coat and go home. Tell your parents goodbye for me."

He quickly left and fumed all the way home. He hadn't slept well either. He wondered if she had.

Now he decided he had acted like a spoiled brat. The cold sent him hunting for the pajamas his mother had packed. Slipping into the soft flannel, he decided he had better make amends to Deborah Lynn before this new fellow decided he also might have "feelings" for her.

As he pulled the covers up around his chin, he asked himself if he just had feelings for Deborah Lynn, or if he was falling in love with her. Did he really want to marry her, or did he think they were mismatched? Did he like her as a dear friend, or did he want to be her lover? Did—he yawned and rolled over on his side—did it make any difference? God most likely would work out His own plan.

Eight

December 15, 1898
Pierre, South Dakota

Dear Isaac,

You and your teacher both deserve an A+ on the very nice letter you wrote me. I'm glad you like the books, and will tell my mother that your teacher likes the fabric they were packed in.

Having your aunt Joanna for your school teacher would certainly be, as you wrote, "good but hard." I'm sure no other little boy your age could write such straight and careful letters.

Yes, Miss Smith and I are still singing together, and a Reverend Drew Wilson from New York State is helping Reverend Smith. Besides his many other duties, Drew takes time to sing with us, and it has been a learning experience to be in a trio.

We have had snow also and a lot of wind. Thanks for the advice to dress warm. My landlady, Mrs. Ordin, dragged out a huge buffalo coat that belonged to her first or second husband (she couldn't remember which one) and convinced me to buy it from her. It is wonderfully warm. Very heavy, but warm. I wear it when I work outside at the lumberyard. I keep the business books there, so am putting all the ciphering I learned to good use.

I want to wish you and your father and your aunt Joanna a blessed Christmas on the prairies of Dakota!

Your friend,
CJ Crezner

While CJ was folding up his letter and placing it in the envelope, he glanced at the thank you note he was sure young Isaac had been made to rewrite many times. CJ could almost picture his sturdy little form at the kitchen table, struggling to get every letter perfect on the pencil-lined paper. He was also mailing a small tin of hard candy along with assorted nuts and peanuts. He wondered what the folks out on the lonely prairie did for Christmas cheer.

"CJ?"

The light tap on the door was Drew Wilson. The two men were going to the Smiths' for some practicing for their Christmas Eve presentation. Of course, the two bachelors had been invited for supper.

To his great chagrin, he had discovered Reverend Drew Wilson was an extremely likeable guy. His good humor plus his extensive biblical knowledge and outgoing personality made him an instant hit with the congregation.

"Come in. I'm almost ready." The door opened to reveal Drew Wilson in a natty double-breasted wool coat. His gloves and hat were in one hand, and his silver-tipped walking stick was in the other. From the top of his thick auburn hair to his well-fitting boots, he was the picture of confidence.

CJ tied the addressed envelope to the square tin with grocery string. He would mail it on the way to the Smiths.

"A Christmas present?" Drew asked him as CJ struggled into his heavy buffalo coat.

"It's for a family out on the prairie." CJ gathered his own hat and gloves before the two men headed down the stairs. No walking stick. No well-fitting boots. Mrs. Ordin's advice on footwear had been taken. He found his four-buckled overshoes from the jumbled assortment on the rag rug in Mrs. Ordin's kitchen and quickly shoved his slightly scuffed boots into them.

He liked the piercing coldness of the December air. The walk to the post office was a comfortable paced gait, with neither man attempting more than casual conversation. Once inside the small and drafty building that housed the United States Postal Service, CJ took off his gloves and handed his package to the postmaster.

Within minutes, it was weighed, paid for, and ready to be sent to Stearns. "Oh, by the way, Reverend Wilson, here's a letter for you—are you sure you don't want to get a postal box rented?" The portly postmaster peered over his spectacles at Drew.

Drew took his letter and gave his usual warmhearted smile. "It's a good idea, but I'll wait a while." He quickly opened the envelope and read the note inside. When he looked up, CJ thought his smile was a trifled forced.

"You remember the young lady I was telling you about?" He asked CJ as they left the building.

"Your fiancé, ah, Mabel Noja?" CJ had been very happy to hear about Miss Noja. It meant Drew was unavailable to Deborah Lynn. At least, he hoped that would be the case. Drew and Deborah Lynn seemed to have a lot of mutual admiration for each other.

"Yes, that very one. She has written to tell me her mother is doing well enough for her to leave and come here. I'm pleased she will be here for Christmas, and the Smiths have already graciously insisted she stay with them."

"Well, that's quite a trip for her. How long did you say the two of you have been engaged?"

The wind was gathering strength as they headed up the hill towards the Smiths' home.

"We've been engaged for three years. Her mother is in very poor health. Mabel believes it's her God-given duty to take care of her."

"And what do you believe?" CJ couldn't help but ask.

"The same." Drew's answer was firm.

CJ thought if he loved a young lady and she loved him back, he would never wait three years for a wedding.

❧

CJ met Miss Mabel Noja at the Smiths' the day after she arrived. He wasn't impressed. She spoke in a quiet monotone, and she stressed repeatedly the trip was very difficult for her. She claimed she was totally exhausted and would look away with a long, suffering sigh. Her brother had escorted her on the journey and he looked ill at ease.

Brother and sister sat together on the settee while Drew, Deborah Lynn, and CJ went through the songs they were going to sing at Christmas Eve service. Neither made any comment aloud, but instead held a whispered conversation behind their hands.

It was quite distracting and rude, CJ thought, and he noticed Drew was unusually quiet. Deborah Lynn used all her charms and tactics to include them but the Nojas remained aloof during the practice. Mrs. Smith, as was her custom, played the piano with vigor, and when the last Christmas carol was sung, she applauded with gusto. Her two guests on the settee looked shocked.

At supper, the conversation, which usually was punctuated by bursts of laughter and animation, dragged dismally. Finally, Reverend Smith cleared his throat and asked Miss Noja how her mother was. It opened a floodgate of sighs and words, all pointing to Mabel's unending duties of care giving and catering to her mother's desires, and once having gained everyone's attention, she continued without ceasing.

It was boring to the point of nausea, CJ mused and looked covertly around the table to see how the others were responding. Mrs. Smith was smiling and nodding her head, her eyes were slightly glazed. Reverend Smith wasn't smiling, and Deborah Lynn repeatedly yawned, with her mouth politely closed. Only Drew made sympathetic remarks, while the brother's eyes shifted back and forth like a caged rabbit.

"Well." CJ finally interrupted the tirade, "Mrs. Smith, this was a delightful meal, as usual. I'm sure the young ladies will help you clear off the table, but as for myself, I must get back home." He stood and smiled at his hostess. "Thank you so much for your gracious hospitality."

"Oh, dear me, yes, CJ." Mrs. Smith cast him a grateful look. "Yes, of course, you're welcome. And now, Deborah Lynn, if you'll pick up the plates, I'm sure Miss Noja will bring the silverware, and we'll get started on cleaning this up."

Miss Noja looked quite pained, but slowly picked up several forks. Drew's complexion looked rosier than usual as he began to help his bride-to-be.

CJ and Reverend Smith both made a quick escape to the hallway, and while CJ labored with his heavy coat, Reverend Smith leaned confidentially towards him and whispered, "Thank you and praise the Lord, brother CJ."

The Nojas had planned to stay for three weeks. However, during the second week, a telegram from New York arrived, saying they were to come home. Mother was ill again.

CJ didn't bother to wish them well on their return trip. He didn't even bother to see them before they left. He decided he was sadly lacking in Christian charity for not liking the Nojas. Mrs. Ordin agreed he was, and so did Deborah Lynn, but at least, as he reminded both ladies, he was not a hypocrite. They also agreed on that.

January and February descended with cloudy days, snow, and wind. CJ didn't mind the weather, but the despondency of Drew began to bother him. As if Drew's quietness wasn't bad enough, there was CJ's added concern about Deborah Lynn's behavior.

She seemed to withdraw into herself as the weeks rolled along. She also began to make excuses for not being able to practice songs with CJ and Drew. Her lively chatter and animation was strangely muted. CJ asked if he had offended her again in some manner. She looked startled and quickly assured him that wasn't the case. He tried to question her further, but she laid her hand on his arm and softly told him, "You mustn't ask me any more questions, CJ."

The answers to all his questions bounced against him the first Sunday afternoon in March. He and Mrs. Ordin were sitting at the big dining room table having a companionable cup of coffee together. The rest of the boarders and Mr. Ordin had left to try ice fishing on the Missouri River and Drew had gone back to the church.

From their vantage point by the dining room windows, they saw Deborah Lynn walking with her bonneted head down. They also saw Drew coming from the other direction. When they met at the yard gate, Deborah Lynn gave a startled jump, quite like a fawn that's been surprised, CJ noted.

"Those two are a-lovin' and a-hurtin'." Mrs. Ordin clucked sympathetically.

CJ's raised coffee cup stopped in midair. He gave a puzzled glance at his landlady.

"A-lovin' and a-hurtin'?" He shook his head. "What does that mean?"

"Trust a man not to know." Mrs. Ordin snorted in disgust. "Can't you tell, CJ? He's a-lovin' her and is all tied up in knots 'cause he's engaged to Miss Noja, and he's a-thinkin' a man of the cloth shouldn't love a woman when he's engaged to another. She's a-lovin' him and is all tied in knots 'cause she's a-thinkin' it's wrong to love another woman's man."

CJ set his cup down and stared at the couple outside the window. They weren't touching each other. Both were looking at the ground, and upon closer examination, both looked extremely vexed.

He slowly straightened in his chair and looked at his landlady. "How do you know this?"

"Ain't it plain as the nose on your face that Mabel Noja is not the right woman for Drew? Any fool can see it."

"Well. I even thought that."

"That's what I said. Any fool could see it."

Before CJ could respond, the young couple entered the porch, and when Mrs. Ordin called "Come on in," they opened the door to the dining room.

As CJ stood to acknowledge Deborah Lynn's presence, he noted her cheeks were much redder than what the crisp March air would have given her. Drew, on the other hand, looked pale.

Deborah Lynn seemed to have a great deal of trouble gathering her thoughts, and when she did, she issued a jumbled invitation to CJ for supper that evening, pausing repeatedly, as if she couldn't remember what she had even come for. She turned to leave and murmured goodbye to both Mrs. Ordin and CJ. Drew said to no one in particular that he would walk her back home. He had left something at the church, he said, and followed her into the porch.

"See? Ain't they just a sorry lot?" Mrs. Ordin sniffed and dabbed at her nose with a well worn handkerchief. They watched as the couple walked past the window, carefully not touching each other.

"Well." CJ slumped down into his chair. "Well." This was a fine state of affairs. What were Drew and Deborah Lynn thinking of? A-lovin' each other when they shouldn't.

Mrs. Ordin was silent as she took a drink of her coffee. Suddenly, she set her cup into its saucer with a thud. Her blue eyes snapped as she looked at CJ.

"The way I see it, CJ, you're the one who's got to talk to Drew."

"Me?" CJ yelped. "Why me, of all people?"

"'Cause Drew Wilson is a nice guy. He comes here, not meaning to cause any stir. He starts a-singing with you and Miss Deborah. The next thing that happens is the poor little mouse of a Mabel comes, and I know what you think of her, but you ain't altogether right on it, 'cause I had a visit with her, and she ain't so bad, just sorta under her ma's thumb is all." Mrs. Ordin's earrings were bobbing in unison as she paused for breath.

"But Drew and Deborah Lynn have common ground on serving the Lord. It sure brought 'em together, sorta like, and after Mabel left, and her a-giving everyone a sour taste in their mouth so to speak, I think Drew realized Mabel wasn't the one for him. But how does he tell her that? And,"—Mrs. Ordin pointed her finger at CJ—"Deborah Lynn sure enough likes you and you like her, but now she knows you ain't the one for her."

CJ stretched his long legs under the table, leaned back in the chair, and folded his arms across his chest. With raised eyebrow, he asked with a great deal of sarcasm, "Just what am I suppose to tell Drew?"

"I'm a-thinkin' you tell him two things. One,"—Mrs. Ordin held up her forefinger—"tell him to break off his engagement. Give him good reasons. You know, good Bible reasons." She held up a second finger. "Two, tell him to go to Reverend Smith when the time is right and ask if he can court Deborah Lynn. That-away, you sorta give him the go-ahead to take your special gal."

"What if I don't want to give up my special gal?" CJ glared at her and clenched his jaw.

Mrs. Ordin looked at him steadily. "'Cause CJ, you and me both know you ain't suited for one another."

He looked away from her honest gaze and stared out the window. His grandfather had told him the same thing, in less blunt terms. He himself had wondered about it. Yet now, when the time had actually come to make the decision, he wanted to procrastinate and give the relationship more time.

He sighed and reached for his nearly empty coffee cup. "When am I to make this grand speech to Drew?"

Mrs. Ordin's features softened. She patted his arm and picked up her coffee cup and saucer. "Well honey, he's a-coming up the walk. I'm heading to the kitchen, and you may as well tell him right now."

The late March sun was playing peek with the clouds. One minute it felt like spring, the next minute it felt like winter. CJ left his buffalo coat in his room and swung down the steps with a light jacket on.

He had been summoned to the Smith home. A short note asking him to come as soon as he was off work had been delivered by a bashful little boy.

After his talk with Drew, CJ had buried himself in the work of the lumberyard. He even missed church services a time or two. He had said his piece to Drew and wanted to be left alone. Sometimes, he wondered how he was able to talk as fluently to Drew as he had that fateful afternoon at Mrs. Ordin's table. Yet, the words had flowed out smoothly, easily. In retrospect, he decided the Holy Spirit guided him, and it was a humbling experience for CJ.

The spring air made him yearn for something he couldn't quite put his finger on. He found he envied the men who came to build their homesteads and needed boards for their shacks. They had a dream; whether it would work for them or not was in the future. He felt as if he must be missing something, but just what it was he was missing, he didn't know.

He knocked softly on the front door of the Smith home, and within seconds, as if she had been watching for him, Deborah Lynn was there to usher him into the sitting room.

Her eyes were unnaturally bright when she turned to face him. "CJ, how can I ever thank you enough for what you've done?"

She was beautiful, he had always thought so. "Well." He needed to say more. He took a deep breath.

"Drew received a letter from Mabel Noja." Deborah Lynn continued in her slow drawl. "She returned his ring and—well, I don't know what all she wrote, but the crux of the whole matter is that Drew would have never written to her in the first place if you hadn't told him he must."

She clasped her hands in front of her. "I—we—that is, Drew and I—CJ, we never meant to fall in love. It happened so gradually, and then, it was so painful because I—we…both felt like evil traitors to you. You were, and still are, a special friend to both of us. And we didn't want to hurt Mabel." She paused and looked away.

"Deborah Lynn, stop." CJ smiled at her. "I heard all the same things from Drew." He put one hand into his pocket and looked down at her with the same smile on his face. "In the first place, I didn't do anything that great. In the second place, I'm happy for both of you."

Amazingly, he thought to himself, it was true. He was happy because they were so happy. "I can truthfully say I will never live the kind of life you and Drew want to have. I don't have the passion you two have. I have faith, but not the passions to preach and witness that you two have."

"Now *you* stop, CJ!" Deborah Lynn's hand was on his arm. "Daddy and Drew were talking about you last night. You should know what they said." She took a deep breath. "Not all believers are called to preach. You know the scriptures, CJ. So do I, but I forgot something important. Daddy said you are an Andrew, the quiet one who always brought people to Christ, the behind-the-scenes person. And it finally hit home to me! Your witness is just as important as Drew's and mine, but where Drew is a Peter, so to speak, the one who is in front of the crowd, you are the Andrew, the one in the back. And,"—she withdrew her hand from his arm—"it was always you, CJ, who got our music to the stage, arranged the chairs for us, provided the necessary things we needed. Drew and I were the prima donnas who showed up at the last minute to perform."

Her gaze left his face and traveled to the floor. "I never thanked you. I took it for granted that you would do all the preparation for me, for us. Last week at church, when you weren't there, Drew and I planned on singing a duet. We both forgot the music. Momma went to the piano expecting us to have placed her music on the rack like you always did, and it wasn't there." She looked up at him and he noticed a faint blush on her cheeks.

"It was a *most* embarrassing moment, CJ."

He smiled at her and couldn't help a smothered chuckle that escaped. He reached towards her with his free hand and squeezed her shoulder. "Do you think you can learn to live without me?" he asked with feigned innocence.

"CJ, I'll always have a little spot in my heart just for you," she said softly.

He withdrew his hand and looked searchingly at her. Beautiful and kind Deborah Lynn. A one-in-a-million kind of lady. He would always have a spot for her in his heart also. God's wisdom seemed to decree their relationship wasn't to be anything other than friendship.

"I'm satisfied with that." He said it with the conviction of one who doesn't like the inevitable, but acknowledges it.

She wanted him to stay for coffee and visit with her parents, but he politely declined. There were tears in her eyes as he left the house.

He slowly strolled down the sidewalk towards the river. There was a range of emotions in his chest, and he didn't bother to identify them. One thought, however, held dominance. If he was, as Deborah Lynn suggested, more of an Andrew than a Peter, it would explain so many of his failures, and as the thought took hold, there was the promise of peace of mind to know that, indeed, he hadn't failed the Lord as dismally as he had believed.

An Andrew. Not a leader, as the scripture said his brother Peter had been. Not a writer, not a speaker. The quiet guy who shared Jesus with whoever came to him. The organized one, who brought the fish to Christ. The one the Greeks came to when they wanted to talk to Jesus. Perhaps his grandfather was trying to tell him that when he suggested CJ search the gospels.

He let out a pent up breath and looked around him. He could see the ferry taking its load across to the west bank of the Missouri River. He could hear all the sounds of a busy, bustling frontier town. The evening breeze held mysterious promises that tickled his imagination.

He felt the old yearning for an undefined dream rumble deep inside him. He began to walk a little faster towards the river, as if his feet had a mind of their own. If Deborah wasn't the deciding factor in his life, and if preaching wasn't what he was called to do, that seemed to indicate for the first time ever in his life, he was free to follow wherever God directed him. But where would he go and what would he do?

He felt the western breeze waft over him and heard the rustle of leaves along the road. And he knew. Just like that he knew he wanted to stay on the prairie where he could be independent of his family. He loved every one of them, but he needed space from them. He needed to be where he could hear God's voice and be what God created him to be. He needed to be----he wanted to be-----what?

He stopped at the edge of the Missouri River bank, and looked wistfully toward the setting sun. He was independent and free and in God's grace. He could be patient. The answers would come.

Nine

April 20, 1899
Stearns, South Dakota

Dear family,

Much has happened since the last time I wrote about Deborah Lynn discovering her soul mate. They tell me a wedding is being planned for next year. Reverend and Mrs. Smith, Deborah Lynn, and Drew are busy getting the new church building finished and organizing a congregation. They said that was the first priority.

Earlier in April, my friends from Stearns, Simon and his son, Isaac, were at the lumberyard. Simon was to meet a relative who was going to homestead on a quarter near Simon's. The relative failed to come, and Simon had two wagonloads of lumber and supplies ready to take back to his place. Of course, Isaac is too young to handle a team and wagon; the idea had been for the relative to drive the other wagon.

Wanting a chance to see the prairie in spring, I volunteered to take the extra wagon. Simon was grateful, and then he had another idea. Why didn't I file on the hundred and sixty acres the relative had planned to? I had a hundred and sixty reasons why not. Simon was convincing, and for that matter, Mrs. Ordin, my landlady, also thought it was a good idea.

We compromised. I signed up for the hundred and sixty acres, but kept both my bookkeeping job at the lumberyard and my room at Mrs. Ordins'. Mrs. Ordin decided that was "a right good idea, (honey)," so she lowered her rent on my room with the idea that if someone desperately needed a bed, they could use mine while I was gone.

My new twelve-by-fourteen-foot home is built on a small knoll by the creek. Simon had the spot picked and knew how he wanted it built. It has one door, three windows, and even boasts a wood floor. Simon built it on skids so he could move it after I proved up. Will write more details later.

I was sorry to hear Grandmother Crezner had fallen on their porch steps. I've written to her, but please also share this letter with her and give her a hug for me.

Always grateful to hear news from home!

Love,
CJ

It had been a week since CJ had finished his letter, and he still hadn't made the ten-mile ride to Stearns to post it, nor had he been back to Pierre to do the bookwork at the lumberyard.

Springtime on the prairie had completely captivated him. After Simon and he had finished the shack, he had found all sorts of excuses not to leave it. He borrowed a walking plow from Simon and, with the gentle workhorse, made several furrows in the virgin prairie for a garden. This morning, he thought of his mother while he planted it— she loved to garden. He thought she would love the peace and quiet of the country, where the meadowlark sang its song repeatedly and the blackbirds gathered in the high tree branches to serenade whoever stopped to listen.

"Thee-J! Thee-J!"

He glanced up in alarm as he heard the thin piping voice of Isaac and saw the little guy running towards him at full speed. Isaac generally ran, CJ mused as he stood up. With his two front teeth missing, Isaac's speech had turned into a comical lisp, which amused all who heard him. Isaac handled his new speech impediment with good humor, but, as he confided to CJ, "whith theeth teeth would hurry up an pop in."

"Is everything okay?" CJ asked as Isaac came to an abrupt halt at the edge of the soon-to-be garden.

"Yeth thur! Aunt Jo 'n me ith goin' to Stearnths right away 'n thee wanth to know if you need thingths!" Isaac puffed out his information with great importance.

"Well. Well, yes, my good man." CJ smiled at the earnest little messenger. "I have a letter that should be mailed." He started into his shack with Isaac close behind him. In short order, he found his letter and some money and quickly jotted down a few items on a piece of a paper.

He decided to take it to the Swanson's himself, not—he assured Isaac—because he didn't think Isaac would lose anything, but because he wanted to visit them before they leave.

"Dad thnot goin'. Juth me 'n Aunt Jo. Dad'th hithin the buggy up right now."

"Would you like to hitch a ride on my shoulders?"

"Yeth thur!" Isaac's eyes sparkled as CJ knelt to the ground. He quickly clambered on board, and with the added advantage of higher ground, he kept a running commentary on the sights and sounds of the April spring morning.

Brave Bull Creek meandered through the middle of the land where the Swansons had homesteaded. Joanna had the house built on the south side of the creek on her quarter; Simon had taken the rougher hills and had put his shack close to the line of Joanna's quarter. CJ's quarter was east of Joanna's, and his dugout was also along Brave Bull Creek, but on the north side. Less than a quarter of a mile separated them, and Isaac soon had a grassy trail to CJ's dugout.

He had seen very little of Joanna. However she continually sent Isaac over with food of some sort—extra cookies, half a loaf of bread, small jars of soup for him to heat up, fried prairie chicken. Whatever she sent was delicious, and appreciated.

"Did you hear Aunt Jo thooten lath night?" Isaac asked as they crossed the creek. It was barely flowing, but Isaac had decided to put rocks in strategic places so he wouldn't get his shoes wet when he visited CJ.

"I did. What was she shooting at?"

"A big fat thnake wath in the tree where the robins are nethting." Isaac was clinging to CJ's shirt collar as CJ trotted up the gradual sloping bank.

"Did she kill it?"

"Yeth thur! One shot from Thmokey's pithtol 'n the thnake wath very, very dead."

"Really?" CJ was impressed. "Did you say Smokey's pistol?"

"Yeth thur! Thmokey gave it to Aunt Jo and thee alwath hath it."

Maybe that's why Simon wasn't worried about leaving her alone while he and Isaac went to Pierre, CJ thought as he neared the house.

Simon had the light buggy hitched to a mare he called Dolly. She wasn't exactly a good-looking mare with her Roman nose and smaller ears, but she was strong and sensible. CJ unloaded Isaac into the buggy and idly watched Joanna as she marched from the house. He thought she always seemed to marching with her quick, determined steps.

"Oh good, Isaac, you're back," she exclaimed and nodded at CJ. She briskly climbed the steps into the buggy before either man could help her.

"By jingles, little sister, you be careful now," Simon cautioned her.

She flashed Simon a smile as she took the reins. "Did you need anything, CJ?" She swept him a glance, which seemed to indicate if he had any instructions for her he better be quick about saying them.

"I wrote a few things down, no big deal if you can't get them. I gave Isaac some money for them."

"We'll be back in good time this afternoon," she said, slapping the reins gently on Dolly's back. Isaac waved goodbye until they were halfway up the big hill to the south.

"Let's have a cup of coffee." Simon was already walking towards Joanna's house.

"Maybe we should—ah, not have coffee in her house while she's gone," CJ said, feeling uncomfortable about entering the queen's domain without her consent.

"She said she'd leave the coffee pot on," Simon said over his shoulder and held open the door for CJ.

"Do you, ah, worry about her when she goes by herself?"

"Yup."

"I could have watched things around here if you wanted to go with her."

"CJ." Simon poured two cups of coffee and set the cups on the immaculate table top. After he had gotten comfortable on his chair, he continued, "Joanna is the last child in our family. My mother used to say Joanna was born stubborn. For sure, Ma and Joanna never got along. I guess they're both stubborn." Simon started to say more but suddenly stopped as if he thought he had said enough about stubborn women. "Anyway, when she makes up her mind to do something, she does it." He sat back in his chair and stretched his feet out in front of him. "She knew I wanted to start plowing today, and rather than wait until I could go with her, she decided she and Isaac would make the trip. She's been looking at the *Old Farmer's Almanac* and says there's a storm coming through in about a week. For that matter,"—Simon looked at CJ and grinned—"she says you better get back to Pierre before it hits and you're caught in the middle of it.

CJ scowled into his cup. Leave it to Joanna to try and tell him what to do. "Where are you farming at?" he asked.

Simon pointed to the north. "There's a nice flat spot there that I reckon might make a good grain field. There's a few spots on your quarter that'd be good too. Want me to work 'em up?"

CJ nodded. The deal between Simon and himself was simple. He filed on this piece of ground with the idea that Simon would buy it from him when he had proved up. Simon wanted land to farm and raise cattleand CJ wanted the adventure of being a homesteader.

"Do you think the range cattle will bother the grain when it comes up?" CJ reached for an oatmeal cookie in the tin that Simon set on the table.

"By jingles, leave it to a cow to find a grain field." Simon chuckled and dipped his cookie into his coffee. "I'm thinking I might have to string a two-wire fence around the field. 'Course, Isaac and his little pony can keep an eye on things."

The coffee was good. The cookies were even better. CJ reached for another one. "Isaac is a little go-getter." He grinned as pictures of Isaac running here and there to help all of them flashed through his mind.

"He's been quite a blessing," Simon said quietly.

"I, ah, I was sorry to hear about his mother's passing. It must have been quite a blow."

Simon nodded. "It was a strange sickness. One minute she seemed fine, the next she was laboring for breath, and well, in two weeks she was bedridden, and about a week later she died." A shadow flitted over Simon's face, and there was silence in the little kitchen.

"Isaac must have talked to you about Mary?" Simon finally asked absently as he poured the rest of his coffee into his saucer.

"He talks about her a lot. For a little guy, he has a host of memories. He misses her."

"I know." Simon picked up his saucer and drank his cooled coffee. "We all do. Joanna worked around the clock to save her. We had a doctor come—" Simon looked down and shook his head. "It's something I don't figure out, but I leave it to God." Simon slowly stood, and CJ quickly drank the rest of his coffee.

Both men tidied up the kitchen before they left and the conversation was back to farming and weather.

CJ helped Simon hitch the work team to the plow, and as Simon began his farming project, CJ started again to plant his garden. It didn't take long before the wind was beginning to gust, and CJ found himself looking southward. It was way too early for Joanna to be coming back and he was disgruntled with himself for watching the road like a nervous old hen with one chick missing. He ate an early dinner and then walked over to the corrals near Simon's barn. Quickly, he caught and harnessed the other work team and headed to where Simon was plowing.

"By jingles, CJ, you must have read my mind!" Simon exclaimed as CJ pulled the team to a stop beside him. "I was just thinking' it was time for dinner—my belly sure thought so too—and the horses need a break."

Before long, CJ and the fresh team were working the hardpan ground while Simon and the other team headed home. The hardpan grounds were spots along the prairie where nothing seemed to grow except cactus and sparse grass. Simon had hauled some manure onto this spot, and when the plow worked the manure into the poor soil, it was hoped the mixture of good and poor dirt would create better soil.

He was almost finished with the small field when he glanced to the south and saw Joanna's buggy clipping down the hill. Beside the buggy was a rider on a buckskin horse.

By the time the last furrow was done, Isaac was running down the trail towards him. And by the time CJ stopped and pulled the plow out of the dirt, Isaac was there to help. He was bursting with his adventure to Stearns, and he lisped excitedly, "Thmokey came home with uth!"

CJ decided during supper that while it was good to see the flirtatious Smokey again, it was also a bit wearing to listen to his constant stories. Mainly because as each tale progressed into another, Smokey's heroics also increased. Isaac listened with wide-eyed appreciation, but Joanna seemed to have little patience after the first several yarns. She finally interrupted Smokey in mid-sentence. She asked if he was staying at CJ's or Simon's house for the night.

"No offense, CJ," Smokey accepted the interruption with hardly a break in his monologue, "but I don't cotton to sleeping on the floor, and I don't expect you to give up your cot. I'll chase Isaac out of his little nest and sleep there tonight."

"Then, Isaac, you can stay here," Joanna said and brushed aside a wisp of hair that had fallen over her forehead. "What time are you two going to leave in the morning?" This was directed at CJ and Smokey.

CJ looked blank.

"Our friend CJ doesn't know that I'm going to Pierre with him." Smokey laughed. "I plum forgot to mention it, CJ. We got to looking at your shack, and then it was time for supper, and we didn't wanna keep the lady waiting."

"I didn't know I was leaving in the morning." CJ scowled at Joanna. She had to be the bossiest woman he ever knew.

"Joanna thinks the weather is going to change. She doesn't want us to be two little frozen lumps on the prairie." Smokey put down his knife and looked at CJ. "Maybe I better ask if it's okay that I ride in the wagon with you. Don't want to offend anyone."

"Of course, it's all right. I just didn't know I was leaving in the morning." CJ smiled in an attempt to put some humor in his words. "What time are we leaving?" He directed his question to Joanna and tried to keep the sarcasm out of his voice.

She sat up a little straighter in her chair and, with decided irritation in her gesture, brushed the aggravating strand of hair away from her face again. He noticed a triumphant glint in her eyes. "You may leave whenever you wish, but I'll have breakfast for all of you at first light."

CJ raised one eyebrow at her. Slowly, he turned to the worried looking Isaac and winked at him. He straightened a little in his chair and studied her as she tried to tuck her hair into her braid. Finally, he bowed slightly in her direction. "We'll head out right after breakfast."

Ten

June 15, 1899
Pierre, South Dakota

Dear Granddad,

Just a few thoughts. I'm grateful Mom telegraphed me in early May concerning Grandma, and how she had contracted pneumonia after her earlier fall. All the way to Missouri I prayed about her. When I saw how weak she was, and how Doc Regis was sure she had suffered more from the tumble then anyone realized, my selfish thought was to spend as much time as possible with her. I hope my constant hovering didn't distract the precious time between the two of you.

I remember how she corrected me when I sang a wrong word as we went through the hymns she wanted for her funeral and how we all laughed at that. She gave us that little three-cornered smile she saved for those occasions when she was pleased with herself. She has left us a great legacy, and even though I know she is in Paradise waiting for all of us, I again, very selfishly, wish she was still here.

I'm heading back to the homestead tomorrow with a load of supplies. When I left in April, things were just starting to green up. Now it looks like spring has definitely burst through, with creeks running and trees leafed out. We had a serious storm in April after I left the homestead, and I was glad we got to Pierre ahead of it.

I'm thinking of you all. I'm thankful I could be in Missouri with family, and I'm honored Grandma and you wanted me to sing at her funeral.

Love,
CJ

Death had been no stranger in CJ's life, yet saying goodbye to his grandmother left him in a melancholy mood. She had always been a support and pillar in his life. He felt bereft, as if a small part of him had disappeared without warning.

It was hot in his little room at Mrs. Ordin's boarding house. He put the letter in its envelope and decided he may as well get it mailed. The walk to the post office would be a welcome breath of fresh air.

He waved at Mrs. Ordin as he left the yard. She was weeding her garden and her round face was flushed in the late afternoon heat.

He wondered if the whole summer would be as hot as the last couple of days had been. This country seemed driven by extremes. When he and Smokey left his homestead in April, it had been a beautiful morning. He had felt rather foolish putting his buffalo coat below the seat in the wagon, and silently blamed Joanna for making him nervous about the weather.

He and Smokey had rattled along in the wagon, with Smokey's horse tied on behind, neither hurrying nor dawdling. The next morning had dawned cold and misty, and they began to think seriously of moving faster. By the time they got to Fort Pierre, CJ had his buffalo coat on while Smokey huddled beneath some blankets. They crossed on the ferry, and after the horses were tended to and they made the trek to Mrs. Ordin's, it was a full scale South Dakota spring storm—wind, sleet, freezing temperatures.

Mrs. Ordin had been greatly amused to hear Smokey tell about Joanna's faith in the *Old Farmer's Almanac*. Smokey elaborated at great length about CJ leaving even earlier than what Joanna expected him to, just for spite. They both had pooh-poohed about her storm during the first day when it was shirtsleeve weather. He said if CJ hadn't worn the old buffalo coat, he would have froze driving the team when the temperature dropped and the wind rose. Mrs. Ordin especially loved to hear that part. Her earrings made little bounces as she nodded her head and told CJ he could thank her for that great warm coat.

After CJ posted his letter, he wandered to the lumberyard to recheck his wagon. He had a full load and it would be slow going if the next couple of days were as warm as it had been the past two days.

After he had returned from Missouri, he had plunged into bookwork, scarcely taking time for anything else. Several businessmen had approached him about working for them, and their offered salaries were tempting. He had told them, however, that while he was on his claim, he wouldn't be available for the extra work. Maybe after he had proved up and Simon bought him out, he would be ready to settle down and put his mind to figures.

"CJ!" He knew the voice and his heart sank. He had not exactly been avoiding Drew and Deborah Lynn, or the rest of the Smith family for that matter, yet he had made no effort to see them. All of them were strolling down the sidewalk and he wondered why on earth they would have chosen the lumberyard to stroll to.

"CJ Crezner, you are one hard fellow to track down." Deborah Lynn's voice hung in the heavy air.

"Hello, everyone," he greeted them warily. Being tracked down by the Smith family might involve being asked to sing—and he had no time right now to duet or trio or whatever.

"Drew has been telling us that you've been using the midnight oil to get the business work done," Reverend Smith said as he approached CJ. "Surely you're not working on books on a Saturday afternoon?"

"No, sir, just out checking the wagon. I'm leaving early in the morning to go back to my homestead."

Mrs. Smith laid her hand on his arm. "CJ, we've wanted to have you over for supper, but my goodness, every time we get ready to send the message, we discover you're out of town, or you've eaten early, or some such matter. Are you avoiding us?"

CJ knew he looked guilty. "Well, actually no, but I have been busy. Ah, thank you for the note you sent after my grandmother died. She remembered both of you ladies when you visited last fall."

Mrs. Smith patted his arm with her gloved hand. "And we, of course, remember her very well. She was a charming and gracious lady."

Mrs. Smith casually linked her arm in CJ's and asked as she propelled him forward, "Are you going back to Mrs. Ordin's now?"

"Well. Yes, ma'am, I am."

"We will walk with you. We've just come from there and she is putting the finishing touches on fried chicken and gravy over biscuits. It smelled absolutely divine and she said you had better get there on time or else she was going to whop you!" Mrs. Smith laughed. "We thought we better escort you back with no delay, especially since she told us she had made your favorite pie, which I believe she said was chocolate cream."

CJ smiled at her. It would be rude to point out that with their leisurely gait, it would take twice the time to get to the boarding house as he had planned—even if they took the cut across.

Reverend Smith was on his other side, and Drew and Deborah Lynn walked behind them. They made desultory conversation concerning the weather, the heat, and the variances of South Dakota temperatures. But Mrs. Smith finally had enough of chitchat.

"CJ, we want to hear about your grandmother and, of course, your homestead."

"How is your grandfather?" Reverend Smith asked quietly.

"Well, he misses her, but he plans to continue ministering. I suppose the first year without her will be difficult."

"Yes. They were a devoted couple," Mrs. Smith murmured. "A fine example for all of us."

"We hear from Aunty that you sang at her funeral," Deborah Lynn said from behind him. "Aunty said you had everyone in tears and she said she'll never hear "All the Way My Savior Leads Me" without seeing you standing at your granddad's pulpit singing so wonderfully."

"Well…" CJ floundered for words.

"She also wrote that both your parents were crying when you started singing "Pass Me Not, O Gentle Savior." She said you sang so well that she completely forgot to cry herself and just immersed herself in the words. She said Mrs. Kraft told her afterwards that you didn't need to preach with a singing voice like that, and she is making plans for you to sing at her own funeral."

"Well." CJ took a deep breath. "I guess sometimes the Holy Spirit takes over when we aren't up to the task."

Drew spoke up emphatically. "You're right! But we won't admit it and we take the glory for ourselves." In a softer voice he admitted that he especially was guilty of that.

CJ stopped and turned around. "I doubt it, Drew."

"Yes, now we mustn't make you late." Mrs. Smith took his arm to head him the right direction and resumed walking. "You have such a good voice, CJ, and I feel positively embarrassed that we didn't have you sing more solos. We were wondering if you would sing solo at church—that is, when you aren't at your homestead. And speaking of church, when you come back, you must come to services and have dinner with us afterwards. You've been a stranger far too long—oh my sakes! Where are you taking us, Reverend Smith?"

CJ was surprised himself. Reverend Smith had turned all of them onto the short cut and was walking a bit faster.

"Mrs. Ordin will whop all of us if we don't hurry." The Reverend chuckled.

They all laughed and increased the pace.

"Now quickly, CJ, tell us about your homestead," Reverend Smith said.

"It's a tiny little shack along a creek. When I left, the plum blossoms were blooming. I really hated to leave! Smokey and I headed out at dawn, and the sights and sounds that morning were beautiful. I'm anxious to get back."

"Is it dreadfully isolated?" Deborah Lynn wanted to know.

"No. You remember Simon and his son, Isaac? They're just across the creek."

"You mean the Swansons?" Deborah Lynn's voice was incredulous. "You mean Joanna Swanson is your neighbor?" She tripped on the uneven boardwalk. Drew murmured something to her as she resumed her balance.

For some reason, CJ felt a small tinge of revenge. "Yes, ma'am, and she is as good at cooking as Mrs. Ordin." He wondered where that remark came from. He hadn't consciously even considered it.

"We have delivered you in good time," Reverend Smith said as they neared Mrs. Ordin's yard gate. He stopped and thrust out his hand. "Take care, and as Mrs. Smith said, don't be a stranger!" His handshake was firm.

Both ladies bade him goodbye with little pats on the arm. Drew shook his hand and said, "I'll see you later this evening." Like a flock of beautiful goldfinches, they seemed to suddenly take wing and only the sounds of their conversation lingered in the air.

CJ went up the steps, but paused before he opened the door. He could hear snatches of conversation. "Looks tired…working too hard…Joanna Swanson."

"CJ, you never hear any good about yourself when you listen at the keyhole." Mrs. Ordin's voice came softly from inside the house.

CJ had no idea he was harboring a stowaway in his wagon until he was far from the Missouri River.

The morning sun had peeked intermittently from lazy clouds until midmorning. He decided to stop on a rolling hill to enjoy the scenery and give the horses a rest from their heavy load.

When he turned around on the wagon seat to take a sandwich from the tin Mrs. Ordin sent, he yelped in surprise. Lying on top the tarp, with its scruffy head resting on the tin, was the sorriest dog CJ had ever seen. One ear was tan, the other was black, and the rest of the hair was dusty brown. But the most noticeable thing was the emaciated look of the creature. Frown lines creased CJ's forehead as he studied the dog for several seconds. "Who do you belong to?" he finally asked.

The dog sat up and her cocklebur encrusted tail thumped on the tarp.

"I don't need a dog on my homestead." The dog's tail thumped even faster.

"I was thinking of eating, if you don't mind." He picked up the tin and pulled off the lid. In one jump, the dog was sitting on the seat beside him, panting in his face.

"You are the skinniest dog I've ever seen. Did you know that?"

If she knew, she didn't care, and watched him closely as he took out a sandwich. He laid part of it on the wagon seat. The dog gazed at it for several seconds and then swallowed it with one gulp.

"Didn't your mother teach you to chew slowly?" CJ leisurely took several bites while the dog edged closer to him. "I already shared. Don't look at me like that."

He wondered if she would take it right out of his hand if he looked away. Not wanting to chance losing both sandwich and fingers, he quickly stuffed the rest into his mouth. Her reproachful look embarrassed him.

He muttered while he took another beef sandwich from the tin. "Here. Just take it all. Don't let it bother you that I'm hungry too." Apparently she didn't think he needed food as badly as she did and quickly devoured his offering.

"You could eat a man out of house and home," he muttered as he stepped down from the wagon box and found the oat bags for the horses. The dog jumped down and followed him as he walked to the front of the team. By the time he was ready to leave she seemed to think they were good friends and jumped onto the seat to sit with him.

"Who are you?" he finally asked after they had traveled a couple of miles. She closed her mouth, swallowed, and then licked his hand. "Hmm. Coy and mysterious," CJ muttered as he wiped her dog slobber on his pant leg.

By the time the day was getting ready to slip into evening, CJ had covered a lot of miles. The dog had intermittently slept with her head on his lap or jumped into the back of the wagon and snoozed.

He camped in a secluded area, and after he had taken care of the team, he started a small fire and cooked a frying pan full of bacon to go with Mrs. Ordin's biscuits. Coffee and cookies finished his simple meal in fine style he decided, and said as much to the dog as he fed her the leftovers. She had stayed close by him, stopping to sniff the lazy breeze, finding smells that tantalized her, but never getting more than a couple of yards away from him.

"If you're still here in the morning, I'll give you a name." The dog raised her ears and looked at him soberly. "So, what kind of dog are you?" He studied her closely and decided she might have some Labrador in her genes, but she also had a mixture of other dog identities.

He took his knife and knelt beside her. Maybe he could cut some of the burrs out of her tail. She didn't like it. They were so embedded into her hair that he had to cut close to the skin. Finally she got up and walked a short distance away and lay back down.

"Well. I don't know how you'll get 'em out if you won't let me help." She gave him a steady gaze that seemed to beg him to understand that her burred tail was the least of her problems.

Pass me not, O gentle Savior; hear my humble cry;
While on others Thou art calling, do not pass me by.
Savior, Savior, hear my humble cry;
While on others Thou art calling, do not pass me by.

The song he had sung at his grandmother's funeral flowed spontaneously as he neared his homestead. Burr was seated beside him, and occasionally she laid her head on his shoulder. As long as CJ didn't mess with her tail, the dog seemed to think he was an all right fellow.

It was mid afternoon and huge cumulous clouds floated serenely under the deep blue sky. The air held a promise of showers, but for now, shadows and sunshine dotted the prairie. It had put CJ in a melancholy mood. He wondered what his grandma would have thought of his homestead if she had had the chance to come out west and visit. Probably an isolated piece of land in the middle of nowhere wouldn't have appealed to her. Sometimes he wondered why he was so fond of it. Maybe it was the sense of independence and freedom that he found so attractive.

He sang more of the song, and could make out a little form running from the barn to the creek. Isaac was already at the shack by the time the wagon rattled to a stop.

"Hey, Isaac!" He was surprised at how glad he was to see his little friend.

Isaac hurtled himself into CJ's outstretched arms and hugged him tightly around the neck. "Ith that your dog?" he wondered as Burr bounded out of the wagon and barked at the two of them.

CJ put Isaac down, which seemed to suit Burr better, and gave introductions.

Isaac gently patted Burr's head, and Burr, fickle creature that she was, licked his face in adoration.

"How are things going, Isaac?" CJ started untying tarp strings.

"Oh—" Isaac shrugged his thin shoulders, and CJ noted there was a definite droop in his bearing.

There was no usual Isaac chatter as CJ unloaded several items at the dugout. He cast a worried glance at the little boy.

"Well. Now I'll head your way and unload the rest of the wagon. There might be a few surprises for you in here." There was no reaction. That, CJ decided, was cause for major concern.

He boosted the quiet Isaac up onto the wagon seat, and Burr jumped in the back, pushing her face between the two of them.

"What's wrong here?" CJ asked quietly as the team started down the trail.

"Today ith my mother's birthday. Aunt Jo wath crying." He looked at CJ with pleading eyes. "Don't tell her I thaid that!"

"I won't say anything," CJ promised.

"Aunt Jo thaid thee withed we could put flowerths on her grave, but ith clear far away."

They rode in silence while CJ pondered the situation. Suddenly he stopped the team.

"Isaac, even if there isn't a grave here, we can still pick some flowers for your mother. We can put them in some water and put it on your aunt Jo's table, and we can say this is your mother's birthday present from all of you. I think she would like that."

The wild flowers grew in jumbled perfusion across the prairie, and in a short time CJ and Isaac had plenty of spiderworts and wall flowers mixed with dainty bluebells and pointed phlox. By the time the wagon clattered into Joanna's yard, Isaac was grinning from ear to ear as he clutched his bouquet with both little hands.

"Aunt Jo!" Isaac began to climb over the wagon wheel. Joanna reached to help him, and he talked excitedly as she lifted him to the ground.. "Flowerth for Mama! Thee-J and me, we picked 'em for Mama becauth ith her birthday! They need water." He was running towards her house before she had a chance to comment.

She blinked several times and looked down, as if to compose herself. "It's Mary's birthday today," she finally said softly.

"That's what he said. He's pretty excited about having flowers for her birthday."

She nodded and looked up into the happy dog face of Burr.

"Good heavens! What is this?"

"This, Miss Swanson, is Burr. Burr, meet Miss Swanson." CJ had already warned Burr that Joanna would probably not like her.

The two looked at each other in silent appraisal. Whatever they thought of each other, they kept it to themselves. Burr jumped off the wagon, and her tail slapped against Joanna's skirt.

"I see where you got the name," Joanna said dryly, as cockleburs raked across the fabric. "Where on earth did you find him?" The breeze was blowing strands of escaped hair across her eyes, and she impatiently tried to tuck them back underneath her braid.

"Her. Burr is a her."

Joanna raised her eyebrows at his unintended rhyme.

"Actually, she found me. She was a stowaway, and I didn't know it for quite a while." CJ stepped down from the wagon seat.

"Thee? Thee? Ain't they nieth?" Isaac was running towards them with the flowers jammed into a cup of water.

CJ held his breath. The flowers looked quite bedraggled in the white cup. Joanna usually had wild flowers arranged to perfection on her table. He hoped she wouldn't scold Isaac for being careless.

"They are very—nice." Joanna took the cup from Isaac. "Your…Mama…would love them." Her voice broke slightly, and CJ noted the trembling lips and moist eyes.

"Mr. Isaac, we better find your dad and get this wagon unloaded, don't you think?" CJ thought a diversion was necessary.

"By jingles, I thought I heard some commotion out here!" Simon was hurrying from the barn, and CJ thought his voice sounded too hardy, as if he were trying to convince them it was just an ordinary day.

After Simon heard about the flowers and met Burr, the two men decided to unload the lumber at the barn. Joanna's list of items, which were at the front of the wagon, would be unloaded last.

"I'll have supper ready by then," Joanna said, "and CJ, I'm expecting you to eat with us."

He nodded and absently noted that dark strands of her hair had escaped the braid bondage and were once again tweaking her face in the breeze. He could see she tried, without success, to push them into place as she walked into the house.

Eleven

June 24, 1899
Stearns, South Dakota

Dear folks,

I'm thinking of all of you and wondering how Granddad is. It's hard to think of him without Grandma. They were always together.

I'm back at the homestead and have been helping Simon put up hay. We have cut some good creek bottoms and have several stacks made. I decided it might be worth our time to fence them from the range cattle. I don't know why cattle like to eat cut hay rather than fresh.

I have acquired a dog, and young Isaac and the dog "Burr" have become inseparable. I'm hoping Burr will stay at the homestead rather than come back to Pierre with me. However, the dog has a mind of her own, and she does whatever she feels like. I don't understand dogs or women. Burr would not let me remove the hundreds of cockle burrs in her tail. However, Joanna took the scissors and cut every last one of them out. Burr lay perfectly still for her.

June 27
I will finish this quickly. This morning our neighbor Tom rode in and said if we had any mail he could take it to Stearns. He and his wife and little daughter live farther down Brave Bull Creek.

I will be back in Pierre in a couple of weeks.

Love,
Your son, CJ

The letter was hastily addressed and stamped. If someone was kind enough to stop and take the mail, CJ didn't want to keep them waiting.

However, when he got to Joanna's house, Simon, neighbor Tom, and Joanna were visiting over coffee and cookies, and no one seemed to be in any kind of hurry.

"We could use you this fall when we gather up cattle, are you interested, CJ?" the neighbor asked as CJ sat down in a chair. As usual, Joanna's table was immaculate, with a fresh bouquet of wildflowers in the middle.

"Well." CJ had never thought about helping with the roundup. Every fall, the open range cattle were gathered, and the owners took their herds closer to their ranches for the winter. It would be a good way to earn some extra cash. "Sure." He smiled at the young rancher. "Let me know when you're starting, and I'll be there."

"I don't know how many more years we'll be doing the roundups. The country is getting more and more settled. And when those trains go through to the Black Hills, they'll bring all sorts of people out here."

Joanna shuddered, and a strand of hair danced over her eyes. "And there goes our lovely and quiet little neighborhood."

The men laughed. "Well, Joanna, you and Clara and Mrs. Anderson have kept all the bachelors fed and towing the mark on Brave Bull for a couple of years now," Tom said with a chuckle. "And if those Addison brothers ever get married, there'll be a couple more young ladies on the creek to keep us in line. Who knows, we might have to start a Brave Bull society!"

CJ couldn't tell if Joanna liked that idea or not. She smiled at all of them and tried to tuck the errant piece of hair back into her braid.

❧

Simon and CJ worked long days cutting and stacking hay from the creek bottoms. The last day of June was hot, and by late afternoon, thunderheads were building up in the west. The air was heavy, and both CJ's and Simon's shirts were soaked with sweat. Topping off that misery was the constant whine of mosquitoes around their heads. Men and horses alike were wondering if this was an example of hell.

When they saw Joanna's buggy coming over the hill, they pulled out of the thicker grass on the creek bottom and headed the teams over to a knoll that might catch a hint of breeze.

The horse, Dolly, was breathing heavily from the humid air. Joanna looked out of sorts as she poured some lemonade into tin cups and handed them some oatmeal cookies. Her misbehaving strand of hair had sneaked out from under her straw hat and was hanging in her eyes.

Both men expressed gratitude for the break, and all of them swatted mosquitoes.

"Isaac!" Joanna grumbled, "quit scratching those bites! You'll have scars all over your arms!"

"They itth, Aunt Jo! Thumthin awful!"

Dolly let out a whoomph and hurriedly put her nose on the ground. They could hear the buzz of nose flies and soon the teams started snorting and stomping the ground.

"By jingles, CJ, let's finish up that last stack we're working on and call it a day. We can start early in the morning when it's cooler and get the rest of it put up."

CJ nodded. At times like this, he wished he was sitting at a Ladies Aid meeting being a helpful preacher.

Joanna made an irritated swat at her hair. "Well, if I'd known you were going to quit this early I wouldn't have come out."

"Did you get all your washing done?" Simon asked her.

"Yes." Her answer was short and clipped. "And I had to take time out to hunt firewood along the creek. When we have time, we need to cut wood."

"Burr and I helped." Isaac offered, still scratching.

"Where is Burr?" CJ gave a worried glance in all directions. Usually the dog and the boy were inseparable

"He was mud from head to paw, and I wasn't about to let him ride in my buggy."

"She. Burr is a she." CJ said gruffly. It was a constant source of irritation to him that Joanna kept calling Burr *he*.

A low rumble from the west caused them all to scan the sky. A dark blue band was visible beyond the thunderheads.

"Let's get headed for home in case we get some weather here," Simon said and put his cup in Joanna's buggy.

CJ hurriedly did the same. He had no desire to be sitting on metal machinery during a lightning storm.

Joanna and Isaac made short work of getting the rest of the items in the buggy, and soon Dolly was headed back to the comfort of the barn.

CJ unhitched the haying equipment from his team, and Simon did the same. They each sat on a workhorse on the ride back to the place. Before they got there, the thunder had grown increasingly louder, and the wind began to whistle over the prairie.

By the time they trotted into the yard, a few drops of rain splattered on them, and the wind had changed from a whistle into a brass band.

"CJ!" Simon hollered at him. "Help Joanna get her clothes off the line and I'll take care of the horses."

CJ jumped off the broad back of his horse and headed towards the clothesline where Joanna was wrestling with the wildly waving laundry. Isaac was chasing down her straw hat and also the clothes basket that was rolling towards the barn.

In short order, they formed a team, and while he grabbed clothes off the line, she followed behind with her arms outstretched, holding onto the clean laundry and telling him to hurry.

An extra loud burst of thunder boomed as he tore the last pair of overalls off the line. Joanna made a wild dash for the washhouse as the splattering of rain became a torrent. CJ was right behind her, and another clap of thunder boomed as they darted into the little building.

"Whooh!" Joanna said as she dumped her heavy load of clothes onto the table. CJ shut the door and tried to peer out the window.

"I wonder where Isaac is," he worried, pacing to another window to see if he could catch a glimpse of the boy.

"Isaac, Simon, Burr, and my clothes basket are all in the barn, along with Dolly and the buggy. Where my stupid hat is would be anybody's guess." Her hair was hanging over her eyes and she impatiently pushed it. "Oh! This blasted hair anyhow! No matter how tight I braid the stupid stuff it always gets loose!" She stomped over to a hook on the wall and grabbed a pair of scissors.

"Cut it, CJ." She handed him the scissors and plopped down on a wooden stool. "I don't care how you do it, just cut it!"

"Well." He looked at the scissors and wondered if she knew he had never in his life cut anyone's hair.

"Just cut this top part." She jerked the offending hair and held it straight up. "Just whack it off. I don't care anymore how it looks, just so it isn't in my eyes!"

He walked over and scrutinized the misbehaving handful of brown strands she had wadded in her hand.

"Mmm. I think you should, ah, unbraid all your hair so I can get a better idea of what to cut."

She dropped the offending hair, and in seconds, the unbraided tresses floated over her shoulders.

With his fingers, he parted off the amount he was to cut. If he "whacked it," as she suggested, it would look terrible.

"Here, hold some of this," he said as he parted half of it and guided her fingers to the belligerent hair.

"Try not to make a big mess on the floor."

He smiled at her and realized she probably couldn't see him with her hair hanging down to her chin. "I'm more worried about making a mess of your hair."

She was silent as he studied her. Humming softly, he began snipping. Humming turned into a song he remembered from his childhood.

Do your ears hang low, do they wobble to and fro—

"What kind of song is that?" Her cut hair began to fall onto her lap.

"I think I learned it at Bible camp," he said absently, snipping across her forehead.

Can you tie 'em in a knot, can you tie 'em in a bow—

"I would hope it wasn't a Lutheran camp. What a silly song."

Outside, the wind and rain was in full force, and CJ was grateful they were inside.

He reached for her ear and studied it seriously before continuing his song.

Can you throw 'em over your shoulder like a continental soldier?

"Let go of the hair you're holding," he said with a small chuckle as she looked at him in disbelief. Once again, her eyes were covered as the escaped hair tumbled to her chin.

He let go of her ear and studied the best way to blend the uncut hair into what he had already trimmed. He combed through it with his fingers, and taking up his song and his snipping, he continued on.

Do your ears—hang—low.

"I'll bet it was a Methodist camp."

He grinned at her. "I don't remember. It was a long time ago and I haven't thought of that song for years."

"Well, I hope my ears didn't remind you of it," she said tartly.

This time he laughed out loud. Her eyes were beginning to appear through the curtain of hair, and he observed the humor flashing from them.

More hair fell on to her lap, and she began picking up the strands. "Hold still, Joanna, or this will be all crooked."

"Are you about done?"

"Almost." He began absently humming again, and then stopped with scissors in midair. "No, your ears don't hang low. I would say they probably hung about right."

"What a relief," she muttered dryly.

"Okay. Oh, wait a minute." He snipped a little more. He hummed a little more. Finally, he said, "Now, you can check it out. Do you have a mirror in here?"

He backed away from her and surveyed his handiwork. Not bad. Not especially good. Passable.

She stood and carefully lifted up her apron so no hair would escape and walked to a crate she used for a wastebasket. She shook the apron, and then she ran her fingers through her newly cut bangs to get the little snips and pieces out.

"Oh boy," she murmured. She looked slightly concerned as she went over to a curtained alcove and pushed the hanging muslin fabric back. CJ watched as she walked towards a standing mirror in an oval frame. She said nothing as she studied her reflection. Finally, she started braiding the rest of it into one long braid that trailed down her back.

CJ came a little closer and with one swift glance realized the alcove held a metal bathtub, a few hooks with some of her clean skirts and waists, a low chair, and, of course, the mirror.

"Well?" he asked, meeting her eyes in the mirror's reflection.

"I think you missed this little piece over here." She held up a wayward strand.

He reached over and with one snip it was subdued. He took her by the shoulders and turned her around to face him. Maybe it was more than passable, he decided. He brushed his fingers through her new bangs.

"Hmm. Maybe I should hire out as a barber."

"Maybe you shouldn't."

He noticed her eyes were dancing mischievously.

Lightning whipped through the air and the instant cracks of thunder made both of them flinch.

"That was close," CJ said and hurried to the window.

"I hope it hit a tree and not a building. Do you see anything?" Joanna was right behind him. They both peered through the gloom as rain pelted the wooden roof with fury.

"If it struck a building, I would guess the rain would put the fire out." CJ resisted the urge to put his arm around her and instead sat down on the stool she had sat on while her hair was being cut.

Joanna wandered over to the table and started sorting through the laundry. "CJ, you really did do a good job on my hair," she said over her shoulder.

CJ stretched his feet out and leaned against the wall. "At least, it won't be in your eyes now."

She was hunting for the mate to Isaac's sock and nodded absently in acknowledgement. "And I never told you how much I appreciated you helping Isaac pick flowers for Mary. That was such a bad day for us, but after you came, it was easier."

He folded his arms across his chest. "She must have been a fine lady."

Joanna looked up quickly. "She was absolutely the most wonderful woman that ever lived. She made every day special, but when it came to birthdays, she made them extra special. We always had so much fun celebrating. I guess that's why her birthday is hard."

CJ gave a sympathetic nod.

Joanna started a pile of clothes that needed to be ironed. She worked swiftly in the gloom, not looking at him. "You're a preacher, CJ. Tell me why these things always happen to good people."

He gave a sigh and unfolded his arms. "I truthfully don't know the answer, Joanna. There's a lot of things I don't know. I guess that's one reason I didn't feel like I'd be a good preacher. But, I believe God works in our lives and has a perfect plan for each of us. Personally, I'm beginning to think, as Romans eight verse twenty-eight says, 'All things work together for good to those that love God.'"

"Mary loved God," Joanna stated flatly. "She died praising Him. Can you tell me what possible good it was for her to die and leave a husband who will mourn her all his life and a little boy who—" Joanna stopped abruptly and shook her head. "I know I shouldn't question this. God's will and all that. It's just…" She turned to CJ and said in a broken voice, "I needed her so bad. She was my lifeline, CJ. Everything that my own mother was not, Mary was, and much more besides. I just wished…I could have…saved her." She pressed her hands against her forehead and gave a ragged sigh.

The least he could do was lend her a shoulder to cry on. He stood and reached for her and slowly gathered her close to him. She was trembling. Suddenly she laid her head on his chest and he could feel the warmth of her tears through his thin shirt. He wanted to run his hands over her hair and say comforting things to her, but no words came to mind. The rain pelted the wooden shingles for several minutes while they stood there in commiseration. She took several shuddering breaths as if willing herself to gain control of her emotions.

"I'm sorry." Her voice was muffled against his shirt. She sniffed and reached into her apron pocket for her handkerchief.

"It's all right to cry once in awhile Joanna," he told her softly.

She dabbed at her eyes and wiped her nose, then gave him a searching look. "Did you cry when your grandmother died?" Her voice was husky.

"Yes I did. We all cried. Even though we know she's in Heaven, we cried because we will miss her."

"Yes. Well," she squared her shoulders. "I generally don't cry, you know." She shook her head, and another tear trickled down her cheek.

"Are you lonely, Joanna?" He didn't know why he asked that.

"Sometimes."

"I know. Sometimes, I am too. Especially when we get a full moon. It would be nice to share it with someone special."

"What happened between you and Deborah Lynn?" She brushed at her eyes to tidy up any other tear that might be ready to trickle down her face.

"Nothing. Nothing happened. She's beautiful, and she's a good woman, and she's not the one for me." He ran his hand over her back and found a place to massage.

She stiffened instantly in his arms. "So, are you saying you need a homely and a bad woman?"

He let out a hoot of laughter and held her at arm's length. "I don't think I said *that,* Joanna! Where do you come up with this stuff?"

"Well, if a good and pretty woman isn't for you, isn't it logical to figure you want a bad and ugly one?" She looked miffed.

He started to laugh and couldn't quit. He also couldn't resist giving her a brief hug. Even when he could tell she didn't appreciate his humor, he still chuckled. "You are a delightful crabby woman!" He smiled at her broadly and released her. "I used to have a cat that would get the same irritated look on her face that you have sometimes."

"I guess if I can't be lovely and good, I can at least be crabby," Joanna said with a slight toss of her head. She looked past him and announced, "Simon is carrying Isaac to the house. We may as well head over there too."

"Okay. I'll carry you so you don't get your dainty slippers wet."

She hoisted up her skirt a trifle and looked at her sturdy work boots. "Ha! I know your kind. You'll dump me in the biggest puddle you can find!"

"I will not." He grinned at her.

When they stepped out the door, he swooped her into his arms and started the short distance to the house. It was still raining and Simon was coming at a slow trot from the barn.

"I have issues with you, Joanna," he puffed. She was heavier than he thought she'd be.

She grabbed hold of his neck as if she expected him to literally throw her into a puddle. "What? What issues?" she demanded.

"You must never again in my presence say another word about not being lovely or good. I take offense at that." He smiled down at her and noticed her eyelashes were long and thick. Funny, he had completely missed seeing that before.

"Aw, CJ." She gave his neck a quick hug. He noticed she was smiling when he sat her down on the back step of the house.

Twelve

August 15, 1899
Pierre, South Dakota

Greetings Winn,

Thanks for the note about joining the roundup this fall. I've signed on with a neighbor, so hope to see you. Will you be doing some cooking?

I've just returned from Missouri again. My grandfather died unexpectedly the early part of July, and I rode the train to get there in time for the funeral. Missouri in the summer is hot and humid. I knew that, but wasn't quite prepared for it. Am anxious to get back to the homestead, but am finishing up some bookwork at the lumberyard first.

Glad the cattle we trailed from Fort Robinson last summer wintered well. Wasn't surprised to hear Smokey lost most of his. He and I were together in April for a couple of days, and he was vague when I asked about his cattle.

Hope to see you soon. It will feel good to trail cattle again.

CJ

CJ read his note in the late afternoon at the stuffy office of the lumberyard. The big temperature gauge outside read a hundred degrees, and there was not a single leaf moving on any tree in the neighborhood.

My grandfather died unexpectedly. Winn would probably never know how he struggled to write those words. He had reacted quickly when he'd received the telegram from his parents saying Grandfather

Crezner had died. He caught the next train out of Pierre and within two days he was in Missouri. He sang the same songs for his grandfather's funeral as he had for his grandmother's. His parents comforted one another by reassuring each other and everyone else that Carl Crezner was in paradise with his beloved wife. They said he was extremely lonely without his helpmeet. They noted he had seemed tired the last couple of days of his life, and a little confused. His heart attack came quickly; he died in his bed.

CJ hadn't meant to stay so long, but there seemed to be no end of duties to take care of. He helped sort through his grandparents' personal belongings and then helped his cousin and family move into the parsonage. He sat down with his mother and began the task of answering and thanking all those who had written notes, all the bearers of food, all the ones who helped with the funeral. The list seemed to go on and on and on.

The humidity had him drenched in sweat every day, and he began to feel as listless and lethargic as an old dog in the summertime. When his parents asked him to consider coming home for good, he sadly shook his head. He yearned for the open prairie more than he wanted to admit.

Back in Pierre, he worked long hours to catch up with the lumberyard's business. He was tired and numb. And he felt guilty. He should have gone back last fall to spend his grandparents' final year with them. Even his guilt, however, wasn't enough to make him consider leaving the life he had in South Dakota and minister with his parents in Missouri. He hadn't prayed for direction in his decision. He was afraid to. He was pretty sure God would direct him to a life he didn't want, in a place he didn't want to be. He only asked for comfort for his parents and the rest of the family and left it at that.

"Oh, wretched man that I am," he muttered under his breath as he sealed and addressed his letter. His mind quickly knew the scripture he quoted. "'But I see another law in my members, warring against the law of my mind—'" His grandfather and father had both preached sermons on Romans seven.

"Talking to yourself again, CJ?" The owner of the lumberyard, Jim O'Reilly, came into the room with his usual swift gait. "Man, it's a sweat box in here!"

"Well. Yes."

"You better quit for today. John Ordin is watching the store while me 'n some of the guys are going down to the river for a swim. You come with us. Boss's orders."

CJ stood up and towered over the short O'Reilly. He stretched his cramped muscles and gave the matter brief thought before he replied, "Sounds good. I'll mail this letter on the way down."

"You know, CJ, you don't look so good." Jim said as they started walking towards the post office. "You look haggard-like."

"Haggard-like. That sounds about right," CJ answered with a slight smile. Jim O'Reilly was little and scrawny and drank enough beer to drown a draft horse, but he was an honest boss and a hard worker.

"My missus says I'm working you too much after all the funerals in your family."

CJ shook his head. "I'm just catching up for all the time you let me be gone. I appreciated that, Jim. Did you know your boy has been helping me some?"

Jim stuck out his chest a little. Everyone knew Jim's wife and six kids were important to him, but their crippled son, Mickey, held an extra tender spot in Jim O'Reilly's heart.

"He ain't bothering you, is he?"

"He's a big help. He's good with figures. I wouldn't be surprised if he could take over some of this bookwork if we helped him a little." CJ made a quick detour into the post office while Jim waited for him outside.

"You really think so? I mean, I sorta thought it, but you know, I'm partial when it comes to that kid." O'Reilly took up the conversation again when they resumed walking. "But I ain't got the patience to help 'im with those blasted books. You'd have to do 'er for me, CJ, and I don't know when you got the time."

"Well. If it's okay with you, I'll take some time tomorrow to get him started. We can see how it goes while I'm gone. I think he'll do just fine." CJ watched the heat shimmer off the buildings and heard the lazy drone of flies.

They passed the saloon, and for a moment, CJ thought he might lose his boss behind the swinging doors. Jim's gait slowed momentarily as they walked by, but the thought of swimming in the cool water seemed to propel him onward.

When they neared the river and the other men, Jim slowed down considerably. "You know, my missus and Missus Ordin were talking about you." At CJ's surprised look, he hastened to add, "Well, darn it all, you seem a little peaky, if you know what I mean, an Missus Ordin tells my missus that your just a-warrin' with yourself."

"I'm a-warrin' with myself?" CJ was surprised to hear those words again.

"Ah, yeah. A-warrin'. You know, parts of you wants to be on the homestead and away from everyone, and parts of you knows you need the money from your job. A war going on in your mind, you see. Missus Ordin sez that, and I think she be right on target, you know what I mean."

"Well, A-warrin." He *was* at war with himself he realized, but he also knew there was probably more to it than a war between Pierre and prairie. The real battle, he decided as he stripped down to his shorts, was the battle between living life his way or God's way.

The heat of the day was grudgingly lessening as CJ walked slowly back to Mrs. Ordin's boarding house after his swim. The water had felt wonderfully cool, but now his tiredness crept over him, and it was all he could do to put one foot in front of the other. He wished he could find a shady spot and have a long and uninterrupted sleep. He supposed Mrs. Ordin would have the whole town out looking for him if he didn't show up for her supper sandwiches, as she called it.

When he reached her house, he could hear Mrs. Ordin's voice on the east side porch, where she often sat and rested from the heat and her many chores.

"We're over here," she called out as she heard his footsteps on the wood planks.

He came around the corner and nodded at her before he realized she had a visitor.

"Hello, CJ. You look terrible."

He recognized the voice immediately, and his heart began an uncomfortable pounding. For the life of him, he couldn't think of why Joanna Swanson sitting on the old battered wicker settee should cause such a commotion in his chest.

"Joanna." He walked over to her and crumpled onto the settee beside her. It felt so good to sit. He didn't have the energy to say anymore.

Mrs. Ordin clucked her tongue and swiftly rose. "Did you eat anything today, or did you just pour over those blamed books?" She entered the house before he could answer.

Joanna shook her head at him. "Here, silly one. Put your head on my lap before you keel over."

"Sounds good," he muttered, and slid down to rest one arm and his aching head on her lap. "Just for a little while." It seemed the most natural thing in the world to do. Her hands were cool on his face. He closed his eyes and was asleep instantly.

❦

"Grandfather's death…looked tired…they insisted…early church…sing…should have slept…doctor?" He heard Mrs. Ordin's voice fade in and out.

He felt a light-handed touch on his hair and a gentle massage on his shoulder. Joanna's voice was softer, nearer. "Fond…grandfather… hard…" Her voice faded completely away. He drifted into nothingness and had no concept of time or conversation. He didn't know how long he had slept, but gradually bits and pieces of talk came again. He knew he needed to ease their concerns about him and sit up. He could do it, but just for the moment he would lay with his head on Joanna's lap and enjoy her tender touch.."He probably just needs food and sleep."

"Right." CJ patted Joanna's skirted knee and sighed. "Lots of sleep." He slowly sat up and ran his hands through his hair.

"You also need a haircut." Joanna smiled at him and straightened her wrinkled skirt.

"You've been out like a light for the past half hour." Mrs. Ordin checked her watch. "I was beginning to think I should fetch a doctor." She tilted her head back and her earrings bobbled busily. "Joanna said some lunch and sleep was probably all you needed."

He looked at Joanna and couldn't help ruffling her bangs. He noted she didn't seem to mind. Smiling lazily at her, he said, "I normally don't swoon when I see a lovely lady."

"Sure. I bet you tell them all that." She looked at him anxiously. "CJ, you really did worry us."

"I'm sorry. I think I swam too long. The water was cool and felt good, and then we started racing each other. I had to show off, you know. Couldn't let anyone beat me." He smiled apologetically at both of them.

"We waited to eat our own supper until you got your beauty nap." Mrs.Ordin set sandwiches and lemonade on a low table beside them. "Now you just stay put," she instructed CJ as he began to rise to lend her a hand. "for once, quit being so blamed helpful."

He sank back down on the settee beside Joanna. "She's a very bossy landlady."

"Honey, I boss those I like." Mrs. Ordin swatted his arm. "Joanna, would you please say grace." It wasn't a question.

It was while they were eating he found out Joanna and Isaac had come with the team and the wagon to get supplies. They were hoping he could drive the loaded wagon back to the homesteads for them. He was relieved when she informed him several neighbor families had made the trek together. He was irritated to hear Smokey was along and had driven the team for her most of the way. He also found out Joanna had come to the boarding house in the late afternoon to leave him a note, and Mrs. Ordin convinced her and Isaac to stay for supper.

"And where is Isaac, anyway?"

Mrs. Ordin shook her head. "John couldn't wait to take him fishing. They left about an hour ago. I'm just a-hopin' they can catch tomorrow's dinner."

As Joanna and Mrs. Ordin began to remove their supper dishes, running footsteps were heard.

"Thee-J!" Isaac bounded up the back steps and made a flying leap onto the settee and CJ's lap.

CJ gave him a bear hug. He had missed his little friend.

"And Burr hath puppies! Thixth of 'em! And—"

"Whoa, whoa, whoa!" CJ looked at Joanna in alarm. "Burr has puppies?"

Isaac put two fish-smelling little hands on each side of CJ's face and turned it to look at him again. "Yeth thur! Thixth little bitty puppies. In the barn! Dad thtayed home with 'em cauth he worried 'bout coyoths and—"

"Burr has puppies?" CJ asked again incredulously. Joanna nodded her head.

"And I want 'em all, but Dad thayth we have to give thum of 'em away. And—"

"Well, no wonder she hitched a ride out of town with me," CJ interrupted. "Six of them. For crying out loud."

"They're really, really cute! All thixth of 'em! And—" Isaac stopped and frowned. "Thee-J, you don't look tho good." Isaac's face puckered into worried concern.

"Well, I'm thinking of those six extra mouths to feed," CJ said lamely. He tried to put some energy into his wink and smile. The way everyone was looking at him convinced him that it was a strong possibility they might cart him away to the nearest doctor.

Thirteen

September 5, 1899
Stearns, South Dakota

Dear Mom and Dad,

Sorry I haven't written for a while. Hope you all are well. I can only imagine the void you feel without Granddad. I was glad to hear that Cousin Kentworth has been to see you with his family. Also that Uncle Henry and Aunt Edna have decided to come back to Springfield. You will enjoy family being close.

I'm back at the homestead for a while and will be going on the fall roundup pretty soon. I've had a chance to delegate some bookkeeping duties to the boss's son Mickey. I think he will do fine. He is crippled with a club foot and gets around with crutches, but a more cheerful or intelligent young lad would be hard to find. The days before I left Pierre were filled with showing him the details of my bookkeeping. That and church and some meals with the Smiths. They wanted to meet Joanna and her nephew—Joanna had brought a team and a wagon to Pierre. We loaded it with supplies for the winter, and I brought it back to the homestead.

The weather has cooled down a bit. Fall is in the air. The birds have flocked together and seem to be waiting for the signal to head south. I still plan to divide my time between the here and the lumberyard, but seem to find it more and more difficult to want to leave the homestead.

Thanks for all the letters; I really enjoy hearing the home news! Stay well.

Love,
CJ

CJ leaned back in his chair and rested his arms on its wide wooden arms which two badly carved lions held firmly in place. He had found the upholstered rocking chair in an obscure corner of the lumberyard and brought it into the office for extra seating. Jim O'Reilly shuddered when he saw it. He claimed the gaudy red fabric gave him the "creepers." When CJ was loading the wagon with supplies, Jim tossed the chair none too gently into the back of the wagon and hurriedly covered it with the tarp.

Joanna called it beastly and gave him a strange look when he placed it in his shack. But CJ called the red eyesore comfortable, and it had become his favorite place to sit.

In fact, he mused as his glance traveled around his shack, his little homestead brought him a strange contentment. Contentment, he decided, must be a giant step towards better health. The prairie also contributed its own antidote to tiredness. He left the windows open at night, and the fresh air settled as lightly over him as a feather filled blanket, lulling him to sleep instantly.

The late afternoon breeze nudged the flour sack curtains Joanna had hung on the windows. CJ gave a great sigh of satisfaction and let his mind settle upon her. She was continually busy, somewhat crabby, delightfully fun, and amazingly astute. How a person could be both crabby and fun was a mystery to him. Joanna was a mystery. They had shared confidences on the journey to their homesteads. The wagon had rattled over bumps, Isaac alternated between sitting between them and snoozing on the tarp, and together Joanna and he had observed the prairie, its habitants, the weather, and life in general. She loved the openness of the country, she said. And the thought of people swarming in and settling all around them bothered her. She dreaded to think of it, and dreaded to hear talk of the trains connecting their patch of prairie to the rest of the world.

He had seen very little of her after they arrived. She seemed to think the few days she was gone contributed to an overload of work when she returned. For that matter, he and Simon had also been busy. Simon constantly dwelt on improvements to the homesteads—all three homesteads. His pace was slow and steady, his plans were made in advance, and he was usually well prepared for the next day's work. CJ had learned a great deal from Simon during the short time they had worked together.

A movement outside caught his attention. He stopped rocking and peered out the window. He grinned to himself. Joanna was striding across the prairie with her clean skirt swishing demurely over her boots and her beribboned straw hat firmly on her head. She was carrying a basket, and his mouth started watering as he thought of what delectable's she might have stashed in her wicker basket.

He left his chair and hurried to the screen door. Opening it wide, he greeted her with enthusiasm. "Joanna! Fancy seeing you over here!" He reached to take her basket and was surprised at how heavy it was.

She stopped and looked at him intently. "You're looking better. Baching must be good for you." She swept past him and entered his domain. "I hope you didn't mind that I put curtains in here while you were gone."

CJ shut the door and placed the basket on the table. "I believe I already told you, Miss Swanson, they look very nice. Thank you, ma'am." He gestured towards the rocker. "Have the best seat in the house."

She eyed the rocker skeptically. "I'll sit on this other chair." She untied her hat and laid it on his bed before she sat down. "Simon and Isaac left to take laundry and eggs to the Addison brothers. I decided to fix us some supper and come over to, ah, visit." She looked slightly flustered and gave him an uncertain smile. "Hope I didn't catch you at a bad time."

He lowered himself leisurely into his rocker. "Perfect timing, Joanna. I didn't have a clue what I was going to fix to eat. What did you bring?" He was suddenly famished.

"Oh, just some cold chicken, a little potato salad, and a pie."

"Is that all?" He raised his eyebrow and gave her a slow grin.

She suddenly smiled at him. It was like sunshine on a cloudy day. Unexpected and appreciated.

"Some cucumber pickles, bread—do you have coffee?"

"Yes, ma'am, I do."

"Fresh, or three days old?"

"This afternoon fresh. Is that good enough?"

"Maybe." She began to take the food out of her basket, along with plates, flatware, and, to his amusement, napkins.

"I see you smirking." She tapped him lightly on the arm. "We can have class on the homestead—use your napkin, sir, and not your sleeve, if you please."

"I'm too hungry to smirk. I didn't even think about food until you came, and now all these good smells make my belly growl."

"Oh. I thought Burr was in the house. Again." Joanna was not a fan of dogs in the house.

"She was here a little while ago, but I guess her maternal instincts got the better of her. I imagine she went back to her puppies."

"You shouldn't let her in here. She probably has ticks and worms and fleas and you name it." Joanna shook her head at him and lifted a beautiful rhubarb pie out of the basket.

"I know." CJ watched her carefully set the pie on the table, and he practically drooled thinking about it. "She likes to come and have a little petting and a snack. She tells me she's as clean as a dog can be."

"Did she tell you who fathered her children?" Joanna asked archly, with her eyebrow raised.

"I don't believe she mentioned that." CJ stood and pulled the rocker to one side and brought up his other straight chair to the table. "I can eat better sitting on this chair," he explained to Joanna.

"I would think so." She shook her head at the rocker. "Good grief, CJ, that's an ugly chair."

"You should sit on it. You'd forget all about how ugly it is." He smiled at her and reached for her hand. "I'll say grace, and we can eat."

His family had always held hands while they prayed at the table. He forgot that wasn't a custom of the Swanson's. Joanna looked startled when he took her hand, but quickly bowed her head when he began to pray.

When he finished, he gave her hand a gentle squeeze before he let go. Joanna's hands should have been rough and calloused from all the work she done; instead, they were strong and firm. Gloves, she informed him once when he had commented on her hands. Rubber gloves to do laundry, garden gloves outside. Protected the hands. Kept slivers out of them when she carried wood.

CJ piled his plate high with food. He remembered to correctly unfold the napkin and place it on his lap. Joanna beamed approvingly. She had barely made a dent in her smaller portioned meal when his first plateful disappeared. After he watched her eat for awhile, he decided he needed seconds of everything.

"Do you like to cook, Joanna?"

"I like to cook. I don't love to cook, but I enjoy seeing hungry men get filled up. You're eating like a man again. Not like a finicky old woman picking away like you did in Pierre."

CJ paused with his buttered roll halfway to his mouth. "Finicky old woman? Thanks a lot!"

"If you don't mind, I think I'll make fresh coffee for our pie." She stood and peered into his blue enameled coffee pot. "Yes, we definitely need fresh." After she had thrown the brackish-looking coffee out the door, she went over to his pail of water and quickly dipped water into the pot.

"Grounds?" She inquired, looking at his cupboard.

He pointed to a jar half full of ground coffee beans.

"Basket?"

"I just throw the grounds into the water."

"Good grief, that's uglier than your chair." She shook her head at him and found the new-looking basket roosting in a corner of his open shelves. Her movements were swift and fluid. Within minutes she had stoked the fire in the little camp stove and set the coffee pot on the burner.

He buttered another roll and put a heaping teaspoon of jelly on it. "Is this your chokecherry jelly?"

"Yes, but it didn't set as good as it should have. It's a little runny."

"It tastes just fine."

"Well, you should know. That's the fourth roll with jelly you've eaten, but who's counting." She shrugged her shoulder and gave him another smile. "Did you save room for pie, or do you want to wait a while?"

"If we wait, I'll have to take a nap. We could sit on the shady side of the house, and I could put my head on your lap." He raised his eyebrow at her. "That was certainly pleasant, Miss Swanson."

"How would you know? You were conked out and snoring within seconds."

He tilted his chair back and studied her for a few seconds. "I'd like to know how many fellows you offer your lap to." He raised his eyebrow again.

"Apparently one too many." She huffed as she checked the coffee.

"Well." He pushed back his chair to stand up. "You are the feistiest woman I've ever been around." He stepped closer to her and reached into his cupboard for two cups. And since she was trapped between him and the cupboard, and since he already had his arms partially around her, and because she looked so madly adorable, he kissed her.

He soon discovered kissing Joanna was unlike kissing any other woman. She melted against him and wound her arms around his waist. And she kissed him back.

The sound of coffee boiling brought him back to reality. He quickly grabbed a pot holder and after wrapping it around the handle, he moved the coffee pot to the back of the stove.

"Now," he murmured softly against her hair, "where was I?"

She opened her eyes. "Did you kiss Deborah Lynn like this?"

"Like this?" He kissed her again, slowly.

She took a deep breath and nodded.

"No." He had to ask. "Do you kiss Smokey like this?"

She pulled one arm away from his waist and wound it around his neck. "Like this?" he heard her say as she pulled his head towards her.

"You better never have kissed anybody like this, Joanna," he muttered seconds later, holding her closer. "And if you have in the past, you better not ever let me catch you kissing anyone else but me in the future."

She buried her head into his chest. "I don't make a habit of kissing anyone, CJ." Her voice was muffled. She raised her head and looked at him searchingly. "Smokey is an outrageous flirt. I've never even *wanted* to kiss him. He goes to places he shouldn't—" She shook her head. "But—darn you, anyhow. You bother me, and I can't get you off my mind."

"Good." He ran his hand over her back. "I mean, good that you think about me. Not good that I bother you." She fit very nicely in his arms.

"This is *not* good," she said sharply and quickly moved away from him.

"What isn't good about it?" he demanded, more than a little miffed. "I sure thought it was all right!"

"It isn't good because we aren't right for each other." She backed into the table and stood with her hands on her hips.

He grabbed the two cups out of the cupboard and slammed them down on the table. What in tarnation did women think of, anyway? Not right for each other. Always not right for each other.

"CJ—" Her voice was subdued. "CJ, don't be mad at me."

He turned and glared at her.

"I'm—I'm not good enough for you, can't you see that?" Her voice pleaded with him to understand.

"You let me decide if you're good enough for me. Joanna, I don't ever want to hear that again. Don't think it, don't say it. Don't kiss me like you just did and then tell me it isn't good." He reached for the coffee pot.

"You're going to burn your hand," she warned him. She grabbed the scruffy potholder and held it out to him.

"I am not!" He grabbed the handle and released it just as quickly. For a long moment, he looked at her. Finally, he took her by the shoulders and guided her to a chair. "Sit."

Her eyes widened as he pushed her down. He took the pot holder she was still holding and used it on the coffeepot handle.

When he poured two cups of coffee for them, he sat down himself.

"Why don't you cut the pie?" he said brusquely.

She unclasped her hands and slowly pulled the pie towards her. She glanced at him. "I didn't know you had a temper."

He brought his gaze from the window to her face, and then back to the window again. "It's a closely guarded secret," he muttered grimly.

She reached for a knife and evenly divided the pie into six. When she laid the knife down, their eyes locked in silent combat.

"Okay, just listen to me." She said it firmly. "I have…faults, CJ. I get mad too easy. I get aggravated when things don't go right and fly off the handle and say things I shouldn't—and I usually regret that later on." She took a deep breath. "You know all that. There's more about me, but, what I'm trying to say is, I would be a disaster as a minister's wife."

"I know that," he answered shortly. Her eyes narrowed, and he interrupted her when she started to say more. "I know that," he repeated. "I would be a disaster as a minister. I think we've talked about this coming home from Pierre."

"But you said your family had been preachers for generations. What about that?" She reached for the desert plates.

"My family now knows everyone isn't cut out to be preachers. Look, Joanna, isn't it enough that the two of us are good, responsible citizens who try to help people? The world can't be all preachers. There's got to be some sinners to preach to, for crying out loud."

She slapped a piece of pie onto a plate. "That's silly and you know it. You told me coming back from Pierre that everyone has a calling, you just weren't sure what yours was yet. I thought you meant—" She paused and looked at him. "You meant, I presume, that God has a plan for your life. A plan, CJ, not just to fritter your time away sinning in the middle of the prairie."

"I didn't know eating pie was sinning."

She looked down at the pie and gave a smothered chuckle. "Oh, silly one. Here, I have some cream in the basket to pour over it."

He watched while she hunted for the small jar of cream and decided out of the blue he could easily love this crazy woman. He wanted her. He was happiest when he was with her, and most miserable, he realized, when he was away from her. It was ridiculously absurd—just a year ago, he was sure Deborah Lynn was the one for him.

As if she read his mind, she suddenly asked, "What happened between you and Deborah Lynn? Oh, here it is!" She triumphantly found her jar of cream and handed it to him.

He took his time answering. After he generously poured cream over the rhubarb pie, he set the jar down and picked up his fork. "She fell madly in love with Drew Wilson, and he fell madly in love with her. End of story."

"No, it's not the end of the story. Where do you fit in?"

He put his fork back down. "That's just it, Joanna, I didn't fit in at all. I couldn't be what she wanted me to be. I didn't even want to try to be what she wanted me to be. She and Drew fit like hand and glove. They both have this passion to bring the gospel to everyone, to preach, to sing at tent meetings, to be active leaders in the church." He took a sip of coffee and set his cup down thoughtfully. "I finally realized, and so did Deborah Lynn, that I'm not capable of serving the Lord in that manner. I'm...more the behind-the-scenes kind of servant."

"You're an Andrew." Joanna stated flatly.

He looked at her in surprise. "Exactly."

"But what I don't understand," Joanna mumbled as she poured cream over her own piece of pie, "is if two people are madly in love, why are they waiting forever to get married? I sure wouldn't. Good grief, what are they waiting for, anyway? It sounds like they're not planning a wedding until a year from now."

"I don't know." CJ shrugged. "I don't figure it out myself." He took a bite of pie and sighed blissfully. "Joanna, this is wonderfully good pie! I believe I'm in love with you, and we better get married right away."

Joanna stopped eating and looked at him in disbelief. "Why, so I can cook for you and do your laundry?"

He took another sip of coffee and winked at her. "That too."

She took a bite of pie and watched him through narrowed eyes as she chewed. "CJ, are you madly in love with me?"

"A little while ago, I was madly in love with you. Now, I'm just in love." He grinned at her.

"If this isn't the most absurd—I've never had such an outrageous proposal!"

"How many times have you had a marriage proposal, anyhow?"

"Couldn't you have asked me under a full moon or something romantic like that? Good grief, here we are, stuffing our faces, and you come up with this." She shook her head at him and took another bite.

"Well, I tell you what. When the moon is full, I'll ask you again, Miss Joanna Swanson. What do you think about that?"

Fourteen

October 10, 1899
Pierre, South Dakota

Dear Mom and Dad,

We hit Pierre yesterday with over a couple thousand head of beeves and have spent most of this day loading them onto rail cars. The critters belong to several ranchers and are sorted by brands.

We have spent the past weeks gathering them from White River to Bad River. The roundup isn't finished yet, but we were told to start trailing this bunch into Pierre, and I would imagine there will be a great many more coming in. Another town, by the name of Evarts, farther north, usually gets the most cattle. They seem to have quite a setup there that can easily handle the huge herds.

It seems like western South Dakota is divided into several areas for the roundups, and each area has a wagon boss. Ours is our neighbor Tom Jones. He has good men with him, and they work well together. They tell me these roundups take place in the spring, when they gather all the cattle and brand the calves, and then again in the fall, when they sort out the steers and old cows to sell and drive the rest of the cattle back to the home ranges, where each ranch winters their own herd.

We've spent long days in the saddle, but it has been interesting watching the men work together and, of course, seeing the prairie and all its variances.

Simon keeps a close watch on his bunch and tries to keep them herded closer to the homestead. He and I brought them home before the roundup started and put them into a small pasture we had fenced out for the purpose of keeping them separated from the other cattle while they were being rounded up.

Some of the big cattle companies have thousands of cattle. I was surprised by their size and by the many men who ride for them. Most of them are owned by investors who live in other states and are taking advantage of free grazing.

Sorry I'm rambling on about all this. Hope all of you are doing fine. Will close and get this mailed. We will be heading out early in the morning to get back to the herds.

Thanks for your letters! I like to hear all your news.

Love,
CJ

He had written the lengthy letter sitting at a table in the post office. Quickly he sealed it and put the two cent stamp on it before thrusting it into the slot.

"CJ, I did remember to give you all your mail, didn't I?" The postmaster's eyes squinted from underneath his visor.

"Sure thing, I have it here in my pocket."

"Don't trip over those spurs," the postmaster murmured absently as CJ started walking towards the door.

CJ looked down in surprise. He had forgotten he had them on. "Well. I thought if I wore the spurs and chaps I might look like a cowboy." He grinned as the postmaster chuckled.

"I hardly recognized you with all the whiskers. You look all cowboy, CJ. Where's the six shooters?"

"In my saddlebag. Everyone thought the world would be safer if I wasn't wearing them."

This time the postmaster laughed aloud. "They probably thought you'd accidently shoot yourself!"

"That's about right." CJ chuckled and walked out the door accompanied by more laughter from inside the post office.

CJ learned from his first cattle drive that he may as well acknowledge he had limited ability on the range. While it was true he could rope, ride, even shoot with accuracy, he was always in awe of the men of the open range who knew instinctively where to be in a cattle situation and reacted with speed and dexterity.

He watched, he learned, but he felt the natural ability of the true cowboy eluded him. He was grateful he was accepted by the rest of the crew—mostly, he decided, because he volunteered for the menial tasks no one else wanted to do.

He entered the general store with purposeful strides and headed towards the sock aisle. Acceptance or not, the boys were a rascally lot, and one of their pranks involved taking his clean socks and leaving their filthy ones. He didn't intend to furnish the bums with new socks, and he didn't plan on washing all their dirty ones. He did intend to have clean socks when he finished the roundup.

His next stop was the lumberyard. He and Mickey O'Reilly spent a pleasant hour going over the books together, and CJ was impressed by the young boy's diligence in recording expenses and income.

"You've done a good job. I think your dad probably doesn't need me anymore." CJ patted the boy's thin shoulder.

Mickey gave him a bashful grin and ducked his head. "I really like figures, CJ, and my mother tells me I have a gift, you know, to cipher and things like that."

"I agree with her. Not only that, but your numbers are all written good and clear. Makes for easy reading. Looks to me that your dad is one lucky guy to have a son like you."

Mickey glanced at the crutches resting against the desk. "I don't know if he's lucky about me." He sighed and shook his head. "But my brothers all get around good so Dad is grateful for that."

"Mickey,"—CJ pushed back his chair and stood up—"you hold a special spot in your dad's heart. Never doubt it; he's proud of your bookkeeping abilities and of you." CJ reached for his old Stetson. "I'll talk to Jim the next time I'm in town. You may as well take me off the payroll and put yourself on. If you run into a snag, let me know. I don't think you will, though. Looks like you have a good grasp of everything." CJ put his hat on and started towards the door. "I have a supper date, Mickey, and I better not be late. Tell your folks hello for me."

"Will do. CJ—you look like a cowboy."

CJ laughed. "Probably smell like one anyway." He touched the brim of his hat in a farewell salute. "Take care, young man."

He thought about Mickey and his deformed feet as he walked towards Mrs. Ordin's house. Surely, there must be doctors somewhere who could fix them. Such a good kid—maybe he'd mention something to Jim about looking into a medical solution. For that matter, Drew might know of some doctors back east who would be capable of corrective surgery. If he was at Mrs. Ordin's for supper, CJ would ask him.

The aroma of chicken frying wafted out to greet him as he neared the house. His belly rumbled and reminded him that his last meal had been a long time ago. He bounded into Mrs. Ordin's kitchen without knocking and greeted the lady of the house with a bear hug.

"CJ Crezner!" Mrs. Ordin sputtered. She backed a few steps away from him and shook her head. "I hardly knew who was a-hugging me!" She waved a spatula at him as her earrings bobbed gleefully. "Whiskers! Spurs! Now see here, sir, no spurs at my table!" She stopped abruptly and swatted his arm with her spatula. "I've worried about you for the past month, and now here you are, looking like a ruffian and a-grinnin' from ear to ear. I hope you're hungry 'cause I fixed all your favorites for supper."

It was unusually hot for the middle of October, at least that's what several of the riders next to CJ said. He didn't join in the conversation.

His feet were hot and sweaty. Dirty socks—someone had swiped his new ones, and also his clean ones. His knee throbbed because young Ira Nelson's horse was a vengeful devil and didn't like being roped. His whole being ached from the wild chase to re-gather the three and four-year-old steers that had stampeded. And he was irritated by the whole mass of riders who informed him he had made a serious breach of cowboy conduct by catching Ira's horse and helping the young boy gather up his gear.

He knew chasing steers was tricky business. They all knew that, including Ira. But the kid didn't realize when he reached behind his saddle to get some jerky from his yellow raincoat pocket that his horse would spook and start bucking. Nor could Ira have known the coat would start flopping and scare the herd, or that he would get bucked off right in the middle of the goofy critters as they started to scatter.

It was especially disheartening since they were only a couple of miles from Pierre when it happened, and all thoughts of getting the cattle across the river and into the stockyards at a decent time went flying out the window.

The guys rode hard and fast, and when the steers were re-bunched and headed once again in the right direction, CJ turned back to find Ira's horse. The guilty gelding threw his ears back when CJ found him a mile from the herd. As CJ approached, he noticed the reins were broke, and all signs of slicker and bedroll were gone.

"Whoa, boy." He hoped he could sidle up with his own horse and grab the longer rein.

The rascal would have none of it. As soon as CJ was close, he bolted and ran several hundred feet before stopping.

This happened several times before CJ decided the only way he was going to catch him was with his lariat. He was hot, sweaty, and his feet burned. He could feel his temper reaching a boiling point.

Many colorful metaphors were spoken before CJ finally caught the stubborn horse and snubbed him to his saddle horn. As if the whole episode wasn't enough, the horse rammed against the side of his horse with CJ's knee catching the brunt of the force. The ride back to the herd was swift and CJ wondered why a young kid rode such a mean-spirited horse.

Ira was on the cook's wagon, and his face was pale underneath his freckles. As CJ rode up with his horse, he heard Donavan, a young and cocky crew member, tell the young boy he wasn't sure if he'd kill him now or when they got to Pierre. Perhaps the man was joking, but Ira turned even paler.

"Better get back on this ornery devil and we'll find your gear," CJ said. Donavan snorted and rode away as the cook stopped the wagon. CJ kept a tight rope on the horse as the young boy remounted. If Ira was scared of getting bucked off again, he didn't show it.

It took a while to find the slicker and the bedroll. By the time they got it gathered up and tied to the back of the saddle, the herd was a couple of miles away.

"Well, we better get to moving and catch up with them. Are you okay, Ira?"

"Yeah. But I'm in big trouble with everyone."

"I know. It wasn't anything you done purposely though. Just say you're sorry and let it go at that. Accidents happen."

Ira sighed. They didn't say anything anymore as they loped across the prairie. The reaction from most of the men was cool as CJ and Ira took their places behind the herd.

Donavan made a point to inform CJ he should have let Ira catch his own horse and find his gear by himself. Maybe next time he wouldn't be messing around with his slicker and cause a whole blankety-blank mess. Several nodded their heads in agreement.

"Accidents happen." CJ's voice was clipped. "On the other hand, thievery is usually planned."

Nobody said anything for quite a while after that.

It was twilight by the time the cattle were safely in the stockyards at Pierre. Ira had made his apologies to all of them before he left for his grandmother's farm. The last bit of business between the representatives of the cattle companies and the buyers was finished, and a general round of back-slapping and hand shaking signaled everyone's satisfaction.

Gradually, the rest of the cowboys drifted back to Pierre until only CJ and the cattle buyers were left. Some of the reps would be riding with the cattle on the train to Chicago, but CJ's job was done. He walked wearily over to his horse and slowly mounted.

"Hey, white man." The voice came from behind him.

He turned in his saddle and could just barely make out the features of the two men on their horses. "Joker—why are you here?"

"White man must have shown a little temper today."

"What?" CJ squinted past Joker to the other rider.

"We thought we better fetch you and see that you had a good meal in your belly 'cause it sounds like you might have had a right aggravating day."

"Winn?"

"Sure. Me 'n Joker got here with an earlier bunch and were waiting for you to show up."

"Well. Good. I could eat half a beef and still not be full." CJ urged his horse forward and Joker and Winn joined him.

"Yup," Winn continued, "the fellows are saying your usually good nature is getting strained."

"They should know why." CJ snorted.

"Pro'bly more to story than what white men say." Joker reflected, looking at CJ with his expressionless eyes.

"Probably."

The three men moseyed away from the stockyards and headed towards Pierre's main street. The town was full of cowboys, and the saloons were doing their best to quench the thirst of every trail driver.

As usual, several show-offs were shooting their pistols in the air, and it was a loud boisterous affair. CJ and his friends rode quietly on the far side of the street with the intentions of finding a livery for their horses and a good place to eat.

"I said 'dance' and I meant you, kid!" A drunken voice roared above the rest of the bedlam. Several shots were fired and other voices were heard telling the drunk to leave the kid alone.

"Don't tell me what to do! I ain't listening to none of you. Now kid, let's see you hop to it. Move it before I shoot your foot instead of your crutch!" The threat was ugly and the bystanders started yelling at the drunk in protest.

"CJ, what are you doing?" Winn's voice was filled with alarm.

CJ was off his horse and running towards the middle of the crowd where young Mickey O'Reilly was trying desperately to stand on his crippled feet. His shattered crutches lay on the ground.

In a flash, CJ was in front of Mickey and facing the ugly sneer of the drunk. "Leave the kid alone." The coldness in his voice made some in the crowd back away.

"Hey, you just make me, mister do-gooder." The drunk belched insolently.

Maybe it was the whole day catching up with him, or maybe it had more to do with dirty socks than he realized, but CJ's temper took over. Without giving the matter a second thought, he kicked high and hard at the man's wrist. The gun flew into the air and landed with a metallic thud on the street. With unsuppressed fury CJ slammed his fist into the drunk's face. He took pleasure in hearing the sound of flesh against flesh, and with a flurry of well aimed punches he savagely pummeled the face and upper body of the drunken bully.

He was being cursed with every foul word the man could think of, but CJ didn't waste his energy responding. His goal was to teach this lowlife a lesson in manners, and he remembered every boxing move and step Doc Regis taught him. His anger was so great he scarcely felt the blows he was receiving. He didn't know if he was fighting because of Mickey or because of all the times he'd been harassed and bullied because he was a preacher's kid.

When both men lost their balance and fell to the street, CJ was pinned underneath the heavy weight of his opponent.

"You weasel! I'll make mincemeat out of you!" The man straddled CJ's chest and meant to hammer his face with serious intent of bodily harm. However, too many whiskeys had slowed his movements. CJ swiftly reached up to grab his shirt collar and with a strength he didn't know he possessed, shoved the drunk off him. Now he was on top, and with rage he slammed his fist into the man's flaccid face. He scarcely realized Joker was talking to him, or that Winn was pulling him off the man's slumped body.

"You better quit before you kill him." Joker had an iron grip on CJ's arm. He pulled CJ to a standing position and stood close beside him.

CJ took several deep breaths and his chest rose and fell with each one. His temper was still boiling. He glanced at Joker and looked at the stunned faces of the crowd. One face in particular was staring at him with a touch of panic written on his features. Purposefully, CJ strode over to Donavan.

"Take off your boots."

"Now, CJ, it was just sorta a joke." Donavan's voice was loud, but not blustery.

"Take off your boots."

"Look, I'll buy you new socks." There was a generally moving away from the two men by the rest of the crowd.

"Take—off—your—boots."

Winn's voice was coaxing beside him. "CJ, we'll make sure he buys you some new socks. Let's go get some supper."

The quiet voice deep in his heart told him to let it go. His temper was unwilling to listen, however, and for several seconds, he glared into the nervous features of Donavan.

"Come on, CJ." Winn said quietly.

Without a word, he turned away, walked over to where the drunk was half sitting, holding his head, and then to the small group around Mickey. Jim O'Reilly was there holding the broken crutches in one hand. With the other hand, he grasped CJ's bloodied hand and shook it gratefully. "I wished you'd made mincemeat out of him!" he roared along with some curses in an almost unintelligible Irish brogue.

"Are you all right, Mickey?" CJ asked the young boy.

Mickey nodded, but his face was pale and he was trembling. A team and buggy were coming swiftly down the street and stopped beside them. Young Mickey was helped into his mother's buggy, and with a curt nod, Jim was beside her. His wife made a U-turn and headed home without saying a word.

"All right, let's break it up." The authoritative voice of the sheriff boomed out, and the crowd began to drift back into the saloons. The drunk found himself helped to his feet by the strong arm of the law. He would spend the rest of the night in jail and part of his sentence would be to furnish Mickey with new crutches.

"Here." Joker handed him a wet rag. "White man looks red."

"White man isn't in good humor tonight, Joker."

"So I see. White man surprised the devil out of Joker."

Winn brought the horses over to them and they walked towards the livery with Winn leading all three tired animals.

"Ah, CJ, you're full of surprises, man. We didn't know you could fight like that. I mean, you're good."

"Well, I'm good and mad. I'm good and tired. I'm good and hungry. That's apparently not a good situation. Winn, you make sure Donavon buys me six new pairs of socks."

Fifteen

October 26, 1899
Stearns, South Dakota

Dear folks,

Several things are weighing on my mind right now. The first is I lost my temper and got into a fight with the man who was terrorizing a young friend of mine. Mickey O'Reilly had been working late at the lumberyard doing his father's bookwork. One of his younger brothers came to tell him the milk cow seemed to be dying and his mother wanted the dad home immediately. Mickey closed the lumberyard and moved as fast as he could to the saloons where he knew his dad would be. Before he could find him, a drunken bully broke his crutches and was harassing him. I saw Mickey trying to stand on his crippled feet. I guess I plunged in before I thought. It was a brutal fight.

Someone had notified Jim that Mickey was in trouble and he sent word to his wife to bring the team and buggy downtown on the double. I don't know how Mrs. O'Reilly accomplished that so fast, but by the time things quieted down, she was there.

I visited Mickey and the O'Reilly family the next morning, and new crutches had already been delivered along with a note from the drunk apologizing for his behavior. Jim said it was his fault that Mickey had been thrust into such a predicament. He promised us he was through drinking. I would imagine if he keeps that promise his wife and kids will be happy. I had spoken to Drew Wilson earlier about a medical solution for Mickey's crippled feet. The Smiths were also at the O'Reillys' when I was there and they said Drew has made inquiries back east. Hopefully some doctor will be able to help Mickey. You might remember the O'Reilly family in your prayers.

I should have handled the situation better and not charged in like a cranky range bull. I thank the Lord my friends Winn and Joker were with me. They kept me from making even more mistakes.

Another matter on my mind is—

Burr erupted from the front step with a frenzied barking. CJ stopped writing in midsentence and looked out the window in time to see Winn and Smokey slowly ride up to his hitching rail and dismount.

The letter was quickly put away, and by the time he got to the door, both men were coming up the pathway.

"Got a little something for you. Thought we'd drop by and deliver it sort of personal like," Winn greeted him as CJ opened the door.

"Well. Good thing I just made a fresh pot of coffee. Come in! Burr and I like visitors." Burr especially liked visitors if she was invited into the shack with them.

"Kind of a windy bugger out there today," Winn observed while he decided which chair to sit on.

"CJ, what are you doing with *that* chair?" Smokey was still standing by the door and he pointed vigorously at the gaudy red upholstered chair.

"I was sitting in it until you guys rode up, why?"

"Yeah, why? Other than being ugly, what's the matter with it?" Winn asked as he settled himself comfortably in a straight chair that faced the door.

Smokey muttered and walked over to the red rocker. "Same chair—has my marks on the lion's mane. I can't believe it."

CJ took the two cups of steaming coffee he had poured and set them on the table. "Where are you sitting, Smokey?"

Smokey took the other straight chair and slid into it with a smirk. "I believe I'll sit in a Christian chair, and not one that came from a house of ill repute."

CJ poured himself some coffee and sat down on the red chair. "A house of ill repute?" He rocked for a while before he asked, "How did you know that, Smokey?"

"Yeah, how did you know that?" Winn echoed with an innocent look.

"I know a lot of things you naïve children don't. The question is, how did this chair end up in your shack, Mr. CJ? You, sir, have some explaining to do!" Smokey gave a languid smile and stretched out his legs in front of him.

"Where did you get it from?" Winn took a slurp of coffee.

"I found it. It said it had repented of its former life and wanted another chance to be a good, decent chair. Probably another chance like the misguided gals in your house of ill repute are looking for."

Smokey coughed on his coffee. "Whoa, now, see here," he gasped when he caught his breath. "It ain't my bawdy house for crying out loud. What made you say that? I just said that's where it came from."

"One mystery solved then. I always wondered where it came from. Do you folks want to have supper with me and bunk here tonight?"

Winn nodded slowly. "Sure. Well, to be truthful, we'd rather eat Joanna's cooking than yours, but since we've already bummed off her before, maybe we better leave 'er alone this time."

The wind had switched directions several times during the day, and now a gust blew in from the northwest. It grumbled around the corners of the shack before it moved on.

Smokey nodded. "Joanna works too hard, you know. This miserable country makes old women out of young ones. Work, work, work. That's all they ever do. I told 'er to marry me. I said we could go back east in the wintertime and I could show her some theaters and good times."

CJ narrowed his eyes at Smokey for a split second. He didn't like Smokey's remark at all.

"What did she say to that?" Winn asked.

"Ah, you know Joanna. She likes to work, she likes the country, she don't like towns or cities. She likes the birds and on and on. Crazy."

"I like this country," Winn stated and leaned back in his chair. "Yessir. I like waking up in the morning and it's peaceful. I look east over my hills and maybe there's a mist in the air, and then I step outside and breathe in pure fresh air. Ain't nothing like it as far as I'm concerned."

"I look to the east and what do I see? Blah hills. Can't see to the south because of Bad River banks. Ugly black banks that cave in. I can't stand being there in the winter. I've asked a neighbor to watch the cattle, and I'm heading east before snow flies." Smokey looked at CJ. "If you were smart, an' you are 'cause you talk with book learning, you'd head back south to your family."

CJ took a while to reply. "Well. It probably isn't as much a matter of being smart, as it is being healthy. I feel better up here. Guess the air is drier."

Smokey shook his head and twirled his coffee cup on the table. "What kind of learning did you study for?"

CJ took a deep breath. "I'm an ordained minister."

The news seemed to be a revelation to Smokey, and for several seconds, he blinked in surprise.

Winn, on the other hand, merely nodded. "I sorta wondered if that wasn't the case."

"You're a minister and you fight like—well, like someone who sure enough has fought a few battles before. How did you learn to fight?" Smokey whipped off his Stetson and laid it on its crown on the floor and sat back with his coffee cup raised, along with his eyebrows.

"A preacher's kid isn't supposed to fight, so I learned to run really fast. Finally, Doc Regis got tired of seeing me streak through his yard, and with my dad's permission, he gave me some boxing lessons in his barn. Then he talked his brother Giles into letting me tag along on a few trail drives. I owe the doc a lot—especially since I have a habit every once in a while of losing my temper."

"Now, wait a minute." Smokey set his cup down. "If I was pegging you, I'd say you were an easy-going softie that never got riled." He paused thoughtfully. "'Course, after last week's fight, I've sorta changed my mind on that."

Winn spoke up. "For the record, CJ, and contrary to what Miss Deborah Lynn thinks, you did the right thing. You were the only one with guts enough to get it stopped."

Smokey looked instantly intrigued. "Really? Our lovely Deborah wasn't impressed?"

CJ spoke more heatedly than he realized. "She thought as a man of God I could have handled the situation differently."

"Which reminds me!" Winn drew out a dainty envelope from his shirt pocket. "She asked me to give you this."

CJ put the envelope in his own pocket and got up to refill their coffee cups. When he had poured all three of them another steaming brew, he set the empty pot at the back of his cook stove. "What's in this package of yours, Winn?" He settled back into the rocker.

Winn thrust a brown paper package tied with grocery string in front of CJ. "Open it and see."

CJ felt of it first. It had the unmistakable soft feel of socks. He began to smile and slid the string off. When he unwrapped the package, six pair of new, extra heavy, full, seamless wool socks lay on the table. Three pairs of blue and three pairs of natural gray.

"Nice. Real nice. Even better than the ones I bought. Did Donavan spring for these?"

Smokey started laughing. "The fellows in your roundup crew who snitched your socks for the last several weeks all went together with a little persuasion from Donavan. It seems like you spooked some goodness into them."

"Well, I handled that wrong too. I should have taken care of the matter before I simmered and got so mad about it."

"Ah heck, who's perfect, anyhow?" Winn said comfortably. "You did a good thing with Mickey, CJ. Let it go at that. Besides, the boys on the roundup needed a little lesson anyhows."

In spite of the fact the wind blew most of the night, the next morning dawned with hardly a cloud in the sky and with a promise of a crisp fall day.

After breakfast, Smokey and Winn leisurely saddled their horses. Winn was riding with Smokey to Stearns before he headed to his home on White Willow Creek, and Smokey was settling a few debts at his father's store before he rode on to Bad River.

CJ handed Winn the letter to his parents that he had hastily finished that morning and asked him to mail it. The men planned to stop at Joanna's to pick up some laundry she had finished for them.

For some reason after they rode away, CJ was at loose ends, and finally decided to have one more cup of coffee before he continued with his day.

It was while he was comfortably settled in his rocking chair and looking out the open door that he remembered Deborah Lynn's unopened letter in his pocket.

Their meeting and her remarks at O'Reilly's had irritated him worse than a sore tooth, he reflected. She and Reverend Smith had come with good intentions of delivering a message of hope, along with some ideas for a fundraising if Mickey could have surgery done back east. They had heard about the ruckus, but didn't have any idea of CJ's part in it.

When Mickey elaborated on the fight, Deborah Lynn refused to meet CJ's glance. Reverend Smith, however, had invited him for lunch afterwards, seemingly unaware of Deborah Lynn's disapproval. As they were walking on the planks that led to the O'Reillys' gate, CJ thought briefly of accepting if only to state his case. Perhaps pride was a factor, but for several reasons, CJ declined. As he opened the gate, he paused and looked down at Deborah. He noted the small frown on her face.

"I really think, CJ," she said softly, "that as a man of God you could have handled the situation differently."

He felt his face flush at the rebuke. With a curt nod of farewell to Reverend Smith, he untied his horse from the fence and swiftly swung into the saddle. He was packed and ready to leave Pierre and put the whole episode behind him.

Joanna was in a whirl of fall house cleaning when he arrived at his homestead. She had already heard about the fight and seemed to dismiss it from her mind after he gave her a few terse details. He and Simon were busy building a small barn for CJ, and somehow, time had slipped away.

Now he slowly looked at Deborah Lynn's envelope. May as well read it and get it over with. The stationery was as dainty as the envelope.

CJ,

Please forgive me for judging you before I knew all the facts. I know you are very angry with me, and I deserve that. I unwisely told your friend Winn the same thing I told you. I believe cowboys have a code of honor amongst you to not rebuke a lady, even when the lady is wrong.

Fortunately, my father sought out the sheriff to hear the whole story. The sheriff said you took care of an ugly situation before it became worse.

I also just found out from Drew it was at your urging he sent letters to doctors in the east inquiring about surgery for Mickey. I had assumed it was Drew's idea.

You have my deepest and most sincere apology for all past and present offenses.

I hope and pray we can continue to be friends.

Yours in Christ's name,
Deborah Lynn Smith

CJ read the letter several more times. She was right in thinking he was angry with her.

"Oh Lord." He took a drink of coffee and shook his head in exasperation. "Of course, You know I forgive her. But it isn't as easy to forget she is always quick to jump to the wrong conclusion about me. I guess that's why You brought in Drew Wilson. She seems to always want to think the best about him."

CJ poured himself the last bit of coffee in the pot. "And that brings me to the other matter on my mind, Lord. Joanna. Joanna. If it's Your will, I'm going to ask her to marry me—again. Under the full moon, which is tonight. I might have been infatuated with Deborah Lynn's beauty and charm, but I'm just plain in love with Joanna. I don't know why, either, Lord. There's just something about her that makes me want to be with her. Maybe it's because she doesn't have any airs. She's blunt about who she is and how she sees other people. Maybe it's because she seems to size up people and situations in a concise manner that has always eluded me. She thinks in practical terms. Probably You sent her to me because I don't think that way. I'm usually befuddled about what to do, except—I'm sure I want to marry her. The question is will she want to marry me?"

The moon hung like a brilliant orange lantern in the eastern sky as CJ walked over to Joanna's house. He had already convinced himself that she would say no. Darn woman anyhow.

She answered his knock almost immediately.

"Would you like to go for a walk this evening, Joanna?"

She nodded in a nervous manner and reached for her shawl.

He pointed to the moon as they started walking. "Full and beautiful tonight."

"Yes."

He reached for her hand and was surprised to discover it was cold as ice. It didn't seem like a good sign to him.

"Listen, CJ," she said, and began to walk a little faster towards the hill to the south. "I've thought about us every since the night I took you supper. And, I just have to—I mean, there are things about me that are—oh, I don't know," she burst out in exasperation.

"I know you are a bit opinionated." He was trying to be helpful.

"Oh, that too," she muttered, and her walking pace became even faster. "I'm selfish, bossy, and stubborn, just to list a few things."

"Who says that?" CJ was indignant.

"My mother. And the worst part of it, it's most likely true. Oh, Mary took a lot of the rough edges away, but basically, I'm sure I'm still all the things my mother said I was. I—I'd probably be after you all the time to do this or that, or I'd nag about you cluttering up the house, and if we had children, I'd probably be a shrew and make their little lives miserable. It's no good, CJ. And I'm just being honest now. Most of the time I'm a proud wench, you see, and as for being a minister's wife—the Lord himself probably shudders at that." She was walking at furious pace. "See, you don't even have any good answers, do you? Why aren't you saying anything?"

"Joanna." He gasped. "Stop. Whoa, girl! I'm out of breath trying to keep up with you."

She had slipped her hand out of his and was a good three paces ahead of him.

"Now." He caught up with her. "Now just listen to me." For several seconds, he stood looking at her while he caught his breath.

The moonlight danced on her shining hair, and her dark eyes were luminous with emotion.

He wrapped his arms around her and kissed her. He decided immediately it was a great alternative to walking. She melted against him and said something he couldn't quite hear so he kissed her again.

"Not fair," she whispered.

"I know." He held her close. "I don't wish to be disrespectful to your mother, but she told you things that aren't true."

She buried her face in his shirt. "Yes they are," her muffled voice insisted.

"If you can live with my faults, I can live with yours."

"But I can't be a minister's wife." Her voice held a trace of panic. Suddenly she looked up at him with fearful eyes. "I just can't!" She was trembling and he tightened his arms around her momentarily.

"Joanna, listen to me. I love you. I want to marry you. Soon. If and when the time ever comes the Lord decides he wants me to be a minister in a church, he'll give us both the grace and wisdom we need. Trust me on that."

She moved out of his arms and made a desultory step to distance the two of them. She twisted her hands in front of her, and when she spoke her voice was unsteady. "It's not a matter of not trusting you, or not trusting God. It's more a matter of not trusting myself to be a good wife or mother."

"Are you going to give those same silly reasons and say no to the next man who asks you to marry him?" He was beginning to get frustrated.

"I—I—what kind of question is that, anyhow? I'm not saying no! I'm saying you'll be sorry I ever said yes! And when you're wondering why in the world you ever married me I'll just remind you I told you so! So there." Her eyes were flashing little mirrors in the moonlight.

"Are you saying 'yes, you'll marry me'?" He wasn't sure how this argument was going.

She took a deep breath. "Did I say that?" She sounded scared.

Only Joanna could take a marriage proposal and make an argument out of it. The absurdity of it all began to amuse him, until he broke out in hopeless laughter. He reached for her and saw the surprise in her eyes. He quickly wrapped his arms around her waist and drew her close to him once again. He wanted to kiss her, but all he could do was laugh. She shook her head in disbelief and gave him an uncertain smile.

"Miss Joanna," he finally managed to gulp out, "will you marry me?"

"Oh, I suppose so," she muttered after a short pause. "But don't say I didn't warn you." He thought he saw stars reflected in her eyes.

He kissed her then.

"CJ," she said later, when the moon was higher up in the sky, "I was attracted to you the first time we met. After I heard you sing, I couldn't quit thinking about you, but I never thought we were right for each other at all." She traced over his cheekbone with one finger. "Even when I knew I was head over heels in love with you, I wanted to cry because—well, because I was sure you were just talking when you asked me to marry you the first time." The night breeze lifted her bangs slightly and ruffled them into disarray. "I've spent this past month in total misery! One minute I'd maybe you were serious and maybe marriage between us wasn't impossible, the next minute I'd think that I was foolish to even consider it." She shivered slightly.

"Let's walk to the top of the hill. We have some plans to make, and unless we start walking again, I'll just want to stand here and kiss you."

"And what's wrong with that?" She gave a merry chuckle and moved out of his arms. "One thing for sure, I don't think either one of us has a long engagement in mind."

Sixteen

October 30, 1899
Stearns, South Dakota

Dear Deborah Lynn,

Thank you for your letter. Of course you are forgiven.

This letter is short because we are extra busy here. Joanna and I are getting married, and I feel very blessed to have her as my wife.

Hope this finds you and your family well. Please greet them for me.

Sincerely,
CJ Crezner

November 3, 1899
Pierre, South Dakota

Congratulations, CJ and Joanna!

We all were surprised to hear you were getting married and want to wish you the very best in your future wedded state. If Momma or I can help Joanna in any way, please let us know. Drew and I would be honored if we could sing at your wedding, but of course that is up to you.

My father would also be honored if he could perform the ceremony, and what better place than the church you helped start? What fun Joanna and I could have picking out announcements and a wedding trousseau together! I'm so looking forward to your next visit to Pierre and want to make certain that you will plan to have dinner or supper with us.

Will your parents be making the journey to South Dakota for this wonderful and exciting event?

I will personally see that Mrs. Ordin knows of your plans. She always speaks so highly of you.

In Christ's name,
Deborah Lynn and family

November 18, 1899
Stearns, South Dakota

Dear Mom and Dad,

In my last letter, I closed asking you to pray for Joanna and myself, as we were talking about getting married. Thank you for being prayer warriors.

We were quite surprised to hear that a traveling circuit preacher was going to be at the neighbor's ranch last Sunday. We dressed in our best, took a wicker basket of food for the potluck dinner, and after a Sunday morning of worship and singing, everyone enjoyed a great meal. After that, the minister married Joanna and me, and because the wind was picking up, everyone hurriedly offered their congratulations and we all headed for home.

A snowstorm hit later that day, and Joanna and I decided our honeymoon at the homestead couldn't have been any cozier. I feel very blessed to have Joanna for my wife. She wryly tells me I probably won't say that for long, but God knows how much this woman has captivated my heart.

I'm anxious for you to meet her and she is eager to meet you also.

Love and prayers,
CJ and Joanna

Joanna read what he wrote as she leaned over his shoulder. Her face was inches from his as she quickly scanned the words. When she finished, her eyes were slightly moist.

"CJ, you write the nicest things." She turned to face him and ran a finger along his jaw before she kissed him.

"I take it this letter is 'Joanna approved.'" He gave her a slow smile as he pushed his chair back. Now there was room between him and the table to pull her onto his lap. She came willingly and settled comfortably into his arms.

"I think you forgot to shave this morning," she murmured as he gave her a gentle whisker rub.

"I think you forgot to put your shoes on," he said as she slid her bare foot down his leg and lodged a couple of toes into his boot top.

"I'm wondering something."

"What are you wondering now?" It was a game they started the days before they were married when they had so many questions for each other.

"I'm wondering if the Smiths and Drew are going to be a little put out at us for ruining all their wedding plans."

"We didn't ruin their wedding plans for us. We just had a different plan for our own wedding." CJ suppressed a smile as he remembered Joanna's reaction to Deborah Lynn's letter. He knew she was upset at all the suggestions, but she pursed her lips together and said very little. She didn't need words, the fire in her dark eyes expressed her feelings eloquently.

"And,"—Joanna sat a little straighter in his lap—"do you know that all the while I've been living on Brave Bull Creek, there has never, and I repeat, never, been a traveling circuit preacher. Never. Not once." She folded herself neatly against him once again. "I call that answered prayer."

"Well, it solved a multitude of problems." CJ sighed. "I suppose I better write and tell the Smiths we're married before the prairie grapevine reaches them."

"You do that." Joanna slipped her foot away from his boot. "I'll find my shoes and put on a fresh pot of coffee."

He let her go reluctantly. He wished he didn't always feel duty-bound to carry on correct correspondence.

He sealed and addressed his letter to his parents and, with a great deal of grumbling, started a letter to the Smiths. Several times he crumpled a paper and gave it a toss to Joanna's wood keg that doubled as a wastepaper basket.

Finally, Joanna set a steaming cup of coffee in front of him, along with oatmeal raisin cookies, and took matters into her own hands.

"I'll write it, CJ. It was because you knew I absolutely didn't want any part of a big wedding that you were so willing to get married last week." She smiled at him and took fresh paper, dipped the pen into the ink bottle, and began writing.

By the time he finished his third cookie, she was finished. She blotted and handed him the letter with a flourish and quickly grabbed an envelope to write the Smith's address on.

CJ raised his eyebrows at her and rubbed cookie crumbs off his fingers. With great pomp, he began to read out loud:

Dear Smith family,

CJ and I want to express our gratitude for your kind suggestions concerning our wedding. We appreciate them, and also our friendship with you.

However, we were pleasantly surprised at the arrival of Reverend Olson, who is a traveling circuit preacher, and last Sunday he married us after the church service at our neighbor's home. We have thanked the Lord many times for this unexpected visit. We feel blessed God led us to each other, and to our home on the prairie.

We hope you will visit us when weather permits.

Sincerely,
CJ and Joanna Crezner

"Well. Well." CJ was astonished. She had very quickly composed a good letter with gracious tact—and perfect penmanship.

"Very nice, Mrs. Crezner." He handed it back to her. "Put it in the envelope, woman. You have done a good morning's work."

"Horsefeathers." She snorted as she swiftly folded the letter and stuffed it into the envelope. "I haven't done a good morning's work since we got married. My work routine is pathetic."

"You can have the rest of our married life for your work routine. This will be our only honeymoon, unless, of course, we decide to get married again." He stood and reached over to ruffle her bangs. "Where do you keep the letters you want to mail?"

She pointed to a small wooden box nailed firmly beside the door. It also contained some pencils and paper for her lists, plus some hooks below it for her aprons. It was crudely made, he observed, but serviceable.

"Isaac made me that for Christmas last year and I let him decide where to put it. I thought it was very good for such a little guy."

CJ grinned at the mention of his little friend. "He wondered if he should call me Uncle CJ. He doesn't lisp so much now that his teeth are coming in. He's making good use of his vacation from the school teacher."

"I know." Joanna rolled her eyes. "I told him this week was all he was going to get. Next Monday classes resume. Honeymoon is over for both him and us."

"What a slave driver. Poor kid won't have any free time from now until Christmas," CJ gave her a lazy grin. Burr's barking drowned out Joanna's reply.

A grey horse trotted into the yard, and his rider was leading a packhorse. In one fluid motion, the rider dismounted and tied both horses to the hitching rail. CJ recognized him as one of the Addison brothers and he opened the door to step outside.

"Better come in and have some coffee!" he called out. Jake waved in reply and sauntered up the path. Like everyone who entered Joanna's house, he stopped before coming in to swipe his feet over the rug at the door.

A gust of cold air entered the house with him, and even if blue cloudless sky and sunshine dominated the prairie, the crisp freshness of the air reminded everyone winter was approaching.

"Wanted to congratulate the newlyweds." Jake shook CJ's hand and gave Joanna a hug. "You didn't waste time taking her away from us," he scolded CJ and winked at Joanna.

"I had too much competition to dillydally," CJ said, motioning towards a chair.

Jake sat down with a sigh. "Well, me 'n Otis are sorta bashful, we didn't want to seem pushy." Joanna pooh-poohed that remark as she set a cup of coffee on the table in front of him.

The conversation drifted towards weather and the recent snow. Several cookies later, Jake told them he was heading to Stearns for some supplies and wondered if they needed anything, or wanted him to mail letters.

While Joanna studied her list and wrote down some items, Jake and CJ's talk veered towards the roundup.

"I'm just afraid it's all coming to an end," Jake said wistfully. "The open range and our way of life is sure gonna change once the railroad comes through and all the homesteaders come."

"Do you think they can make a living on a hundred and sixty acres?" CJ asked.

"No! Biggest dang lie the government tells folks is that it'll be paradise, with their own land. Maybe in Iowa or even East River that worked. It ain't gonna work here. This country takes at least twenty acres for one cow. At the most, they could run seven to ten head on their hundred and sixty acres. Can't make a living on that."

"I think the railroad is as full of stories as the government." Joanna handed Jake a pile of letters and a short list.

"Yup, and nobody cares about the guy who brings his family out here in this country and tries to scrape out a living with the scorching heat in the summer and freezing cold in the winter. If they'd let 'em file on six hundred acres, it would make more sense," Jake said, slapping his hand on the table.

 CJ nodded. "I read someplace where a guy was trying to tell Congress the homesteads should be at least twenty-five hundred acres and should be surveyed by natural boundaries. I think he said each homestead should have bottomland for hay and a creek for water."

Jake stood up. "Now that makes too much sense for those eastern congressmen to understand. I'd like to shake that feller's hand!"

CJ snapped his fingers. "Major John Wesley Powell. That's who the article said gave the report to Congress."

"Any relation to Dan Powell?"

"I don't have any idea," CJ offered apologetically. "I don't know a lot of people around here yet."

Jake shrugged back into his sheepskin coat. "Well, I better hit the road and get to Stearns before dark. Dang days are so short now. I'll be back in the next day or two." He grinned at Joanna. "I think I have enough coffee and cookies to get to the next stopping place."

After Jake left, Joanna paced from window to window. Suddenly she turned to CJ. "I don't want this country to change, CJ," she burst out. "I don't want wall to wall people like they are back east. One of the best things about the prairie is its space—just grass and sky—and I want it to stay that way." She walked over to the stove. "I just don't want people all around me." She put her hand on her hip and tilted her head back defiantly. "If that train comes through here and there's going to be someone on every quarter, I'll move!"

"Well." CJ stared at her thoughtfully. "You probably won't see a lot of change until the railroads come in." He started to put his coat on to bring in more wood. "But, Joanna, I doubt we can stop what they call progress. Life always changes."

Seventeen

November 20, 1900
Stearns, South Dakota

Dear Mom and Dad,

Joanna and I celebrated our one year wedding anniversary with a short walk to the corrals to see the new horse I bought. After she had duly admired it, Joanna turned to me and said, "Saddle up this foxy horse and ride over to Andersons. Tell Josephine our baby is most likely on the way."

I hate to admit the complete ineptness on my part after that announcement. While she walked back to the house, I stumbled into the barn with great haste. I became tangled in the cinch as I hurried to saddle up and ended on the ground, much to Isaac's amusement. I couldn't believe Mrs. Anderson's complete calmness and, may I say, her absolute pokiness in coming back to our house. It seemed to me both Joanna and Josephine moved in slow motion, and finally, Simon (upon Joanna's suggestion) ushered me over to his house. It was a diabolical plan to get me out of the way for a while.

Nevertheless, in due time, our little son, John David, named after his two grandfathers, made his appearance at 11:45 p.m. on November 14th, and is at this moment nestled snugly in his mother's arms. Joanna would tell you the worst part of having a baby is trying to keep the father calm. A great exaggeration, of course.

We will write more later, but wanted to let you know all is well with both mother and son.

Love,
CJ, Joanna, and John David

CJ sat back in his chair and gazed reflectively at Joanna. He decided his wife looked contented and motherly as she rocked their son. In the course of the preceding year, they both had their moments of discontent as they learned to adjust to each other's habits.

"He's a beautiful little guy," she murmured absently and looked up to meet his gaze.

CJ nodded. "I suppose all parents think that about their kids." He paused and watched her rock back and forth. "Pretty good rocking chair, right?"

She tossed him a bemused grin. "I can't believe you and Simon and Isaac worked your rocking chair over. Except for the silly lions, no one would even recognize it."

CJ was proud of his gift to her on their anniversary. It was a pride he shared with both Simon and Isaac, as the three of them had spent the better part of a month painstakingly sanding off the black finish of the notorious rocking chair. Solid oak was underneath the layers of lacquer, and several clear coats of varnish brought out the grain of the wood. They had taken off the raucous red upholstery and replaced it with green printed velour. It was solid and comfortable, and in CJ's imagination, the rocking chair was probably quite happy to lose its bawdy house reputation.

"You have no idea how hard we worked to get the finish off those lions. We even thought of taking them out of the chair all together, but Isaac liked them so they stayed."

Joanna's expressive eyes softened. "Isaac brought me another bouquet," she murmured, pointing to the dried gumweed arrangement on the table.

"I see. He's pleased over his new cousin. Simon is proud as punch too. You done good, Joanna." CJ hesitated, knowing he was walking on thin ice with his next remark. "Are you going to write to your mother about our little boy?"

Joanna and her mother had a precarious relationship. After they were married, she waited a couple of weeks before she wrote to tell her mother and she included the note with a set of handkerchiefs she had embroidered for her mother's Christmas gift. Several months passed before they received an answering letter. It was a tersely written short note, expressing sympathy for any man who married her daughter Joanna. An equally brusque thank-you was included for the handkerchiefs. Joanna's gift from her mother had been a tasteless pound cake, sent in a crate with Simon's and Isaac's gifts.

Joanna had handed him the note and busied herself by sweeping the floor while he read it. He was caught off guard by the tone of her mother's letter and had looked at Joanna in puzzlement. She snatched the note from his fingers and threw it into the stove where it quickly disintegrated into ashes.

Her eyes had been unnaturally bright. She had turned from him and muttered over her shoulder, "She always manages to hit me where it hurts the worst."

He had taken the broom from her and held her tightly. "She's a very misguided woman and apparently doesn't know her daughter Joanna is considered the cream of the crop out here."

Joanna's voice had been muffled against his shoulder. "You know what really makes me mad, CJ? I still care what she thinks, and I want her approval."

"I guess no matter how old we get, we want our parents to support our decisions." CJ kissed the top of her head.

"I refuse to write another word to her. I'm done. And I'm done working all fall trying to make the perfect embroidered handkerchiefs. Done. Finished. She won't hear another word from me and she won't get another gift from me either." Joanna had looked up at him with flashing eyes. "And this time, I mean it!"

And, so far, she hadn't written a word, or prepared a gift. She seemed to have erased her mother out of her life and been the happier for it. CJ wanted to question Simon about the strained relationship, but for some reason, he couldn't seem to bring the subject up. Instead he prayed for the mother and the daughter and figured God would nudge someone into action in His own time.

Joanna rocked in silence as she studied her baby. Finally, she answered, and her words were softly spoken. "I've prayed about this, CJ. I know it isn't natural to feel all this irritation about a parent. I loved my Pa. When he died, my life fell apart. I had to get away from her, I just had to. That's when I went to live with Simon and Mary.

Everything Ma wasn't, Mary was. Kind, and gentle, and—" Joanna took a deep breath and rocked a little faster. "I haven't seen Ma for several years. Truthfully, I wouldn't care if I ever saw her again." Joanna looked up at him. He couldn't read her expression.

"And," Joanna continued with a mirthful snort, "she feels the same way about me." She looked away from him. When she spoke again, her voice was strained. "CJ, if I ever act like a witch to my kids, please straighten me up. I don't want to repeat family mistakes."

He stood up and walked towards her. "I promise. I'll straighten you up so fast you won't know what hit you." He leaned over and kissed her and nuzzled the head of the sleeping baby.

"I'm serious, CJ."

"I'm serious too. And I'm not worried about you treating your kids the way your mother has treated you. It's not your style. You'll love them and correct them, like you do with Isaac."

"Ah, my little man, Isaac." There was a strange melancholy note in her voice. CJ surmised it was because she was thinking of Mary.

❧

After weeks of unsettled weather that brought snow to the prairie, December twenty-third dawned with the promise of sunshine. Despite Joanna's protest that the almanac was predicting a fast and furious storm over the northern plains, CJ quickly harnessed his strong swift team to the sleigh and headed towards Stearns.

The breeze carried a harsh bite of cold, and more than once CJ debated with himself the wisdom of the trip. Ten miles of travel in the winter might not be purty. However, some supplies were needed, and no mail had been sent or received for three weeks. He kept to the ridges, and his sleigh seemed to glide over the crusted snow. The bells on the team's harness made a cheery sound as he hastened along.

He pulled in front of the general store by midmorning. The little settlement was strangely quiet. Before he could tie up his team to the hitching rail, Smokey poked his head out the barely opened door.

"CJ, get in here before you freeze your southern hide!"

CJ felt like his face would crack from the cold if he smiled. Once inside the store, prickles of feeling began to dance over his features.

Smokey handed him a cup of hot coffee, along with several choice words of condemnation for being out in the freezing weather.

"Well. You sound like Joanna. And merry Christmas to you too." CJ took a drink of coffee and drew out his list to study it.

Smokey smiled and shook his head. "Sure, sure, merry Christmas. Listen, southern boy, I'll get your mail and packages together while you get your stuff. We better get you loaded and out of here before another storm hits."

CJ was surprised at Smokey's genuine nervousness about the weather. He began to wonder if his friend knew something he didn't, and that thought sent him hustling around the store to grab things while he hurriedly drank his coffee. It didn't take long for him to get all the items he needed plus some fabric for Joanna. While Smokey's father figured the bill, Smokey packaged and loaded everything under the tarp on the cutter.

"Now listen, don't waste time getting home, new daddy. Give Joanna a hug from me." He gave CJ a swift handshake. "How is everything on the Bad River?" CJ asked as he pulled down the earflaps on his Scotch cap.

Smokey shrugged. "So-so. Maybe when we got more time I'll tell you about it."

CJ heeded the advice about not wasting time. His team wanted to be home as bad as he did.

As he left the White River breaks, the northwest wind became stronger. He was glad the snow was settled and not drifting. He was also grateful for his buffalo coat. Nevertheless, by the time he had gone very many miles, he drew another thick robe over his lap to break the cold.

He could see the dark blue band in the west racing towards him. As if they sensed trouble, the team trotted faster and would have broken into a gallop if he had let them.

A mile from home the wind hit with a furiousness that almost took his breath away. His eyes watered from the cold and the tears froze on his face. When he crested the hill overlooking the homestead, the wind-driven snowflakes increased and felt like tiny bullets. It was as if a huge bucketful of white fury was being thrown from heaven, and within seconds, the landscape became obliterated.

CJ had been saying prayers for the last mile. He became disoriented when the world changed from landmarks to a white nothingness. He knew his best chance would be to let the horses find their own way. He relaxed the reins. They didn't change their pace but instead kept a steady gait.

It can't be much farther. I wonder if the horses went past the place and we're heading into—no, I'm sure we haven't crossed the creek. Father, please watch after this fool.

He thought after what seemed an eternity that he saw a dim glow, and as the horses headed towards it, he realized it was lanterns in all the windows of the house.

"Thank you, Lord!" he exclaimed, and his voice sounded muffled in the storm. *And thank you, Joanna, for lighting the lanterns in all the windows so I could see them.* He guided the team as close to the back door as he could.

Simon bustled out the door as CJ clumsily tried to climb out of the sleigh. He was amazed at how stiff he was.

He warmed up a little as they hurriedly unloaded everything, and he found time to scold Joanna for trying to help them instead of staying in the house where it was warm.

He and Simon led the team to the barn and unharnessed them. "I think they deserve a little extra oats," he muttered to Simon as they rubbed them down.

"By jingles, CJ, that was a close one. We were just plain worried." Simon's usual jocular voice was strained.

Simon had taken extra precautions and had run a wire from the barn to the house just before the storm struck. It was a reassuring guide for the two men as they headed into the wind and snow to get back to the house. Even so, the short distance seemed to take forever. At times the gusts were so strong it became a struggle to stay upright.

The sweetest sound he thought he ever heard was John David crying as they entered the back door. He was home. Safe. Joanna would tell him, he knew, that once again the almanac was right, and he should pay more attention to it. He looked across the small back room at the woman he loved and smiled at her. At least, he tried to smile. His face seemed stiff and motionless. She was beside him in a flash, helping him take off his heavy coat, telling him she had been worried out of her mind, scolding and laughing with relief at the same time.

Eighteen

December 7, 1900
Springfield, Missouri

Dear Joanna, Carl John, John David, Simon, and Isaac,

What a precious blessing to get your letter and packages! We are thrilled to hear John David has made a safe arrival, and both mother and son are doing well. My John has practically popped all his buttons thinking he has a grandson named after him. I'm sure your father, Joanna, would be equally as proud.

Isaac, we have enjoyed the card you sent us with a tracing of John David's foot and hand, and it holds a special place of honor on the bureau in the parlor. Thanks also for including the date and weight and height of your new playmate!

Joanna, I especially enjoyed your letter that included details we women love to hear. I appreciate that note and cherish it. I was as excited as a child when I saw the package from you that said "Open before Christmas." How I love the handkerchiefs you embroidered! I've never had a set of poinsettias, cedar boughs, holly leaves, and wreaths. You sew beautifully, and the corner crochet below the embroidery is a work of art! Thank you so much! The ladies of the congregation have admired my Christmas handkerchiefs and tell me I'm very blessed to have a daughter-in-law like you. John and I concur wholeheartedly.

The other packages are under the tree and will be opened on Christmas Eve. We hope the crate of gifts and this letter will reach you before Christmas.

Reverend Drew and Deborah Lynn Wilson were in Springfield in early November with a visit to her Aunt Coramae Rovey. They had pictures of their wedding, which included one of you, Carl John. They said they had to twist your arm to persuade you to sing at the wedding. They both told us your song was very good! Deborah Lynn was under the weather while they were here. Miss Rovey just told me last week that a little one will be coming to their home in early summer.

Your cousin Kentworth and his family seem quite settled in your grandfather's church, and he and Drew both preached at your father's church last month. The two preachers almost got into an argument over some bit of theology, and finally your father told them they must agree to disagree on that particular subject.

John and I are discussing the possibility of a trip to your homestead this summer. We would like to see the prairie, and most of all, we would love to see all of you. I know none of you like the thought of trains hooting across your prairie, but wouldn't it be nice if John and I could ride in a passenger train all the way to your homestead?

Give our grandson hugs and kisses. What a precious gift Our Lord has given all of us with this little child.

May the joy of Jesus Christ bless you this beautiful Christmas, and may the love of Him guide you throughout the coming year.

Love,
John and Charlotte

CJ rocked his little son in silence after Joanna finished reading his parents' letter. Isaac was sprawled under the Christmas tree, looking longingly at the unopened packages, and Simon was sitting in the old comfortable wing chair by the bookcase.

Outside, the fury of yesterday's snow storm was still creating havoc with the freshly fallen snow, but this Christmas Eve afternoon, the inside of their home was filled with quiet contentment from all of them.

Joanna skimmed through his mother's letter again, reading it in the fading afternoon light. She looked up to catch CJ's gaze and smiled at him.

"Your mother writes beautiful letters," she said softly as she slowly folded the letter and laid it on the table.

"Now can we open presents?" Isaac inquired with a wistful air.

"No, let's have your dad read the letter from—" There was a slight hesitation before Joanna continued, "From your grandmother."

"Well, I'd rather hear you read it, but we'll give 'er a whirl." Simon dug out some reading glasses from his shirt pocket and opened the sealed envelope with his knife.

He gave a great sigh but when he saw the enclosed note, he brightened considerably. It was very brief.

Christmas greetings,

This will be quite short as I'm very busy and not feeling the best. My doctor told me I worked too hard for too long and needed a change. I've been offered a good price for the farm and will be selling, unless you think you can match it and move back here. Also, I'm going to have a farm sale in the spring. If you want something, I think the only fair way is to come and buy it.

There is a nice home in town that I'm going to buy when the sale goes through. I've already spoken for it, and it comes furnished so I won't be taking any of the junk from this house.

Mother
PS. Glad the baby is here.

Simon looked up at Joanna and frowned. He slowly read the letter aloud once more as if he couldn't quite grasp the meaning of it.

"Did you want a chance to buy the farm?" Joanna asked him after he finished the second time.

Simon was silent for several seconds while he scratched his chin. Finally, he shook his head. "No. It would cause too many problems with everyone. May as well let her sell it to whoever she wants, but by jingles, she can always shock a person, can't she?"

"Oh yes," Joanna said adamantly.

"I sure don't wanna move back there," Isaac said stoutly. "I need to stay here and be John David's best cousin."

CJ glanced at his son's sleeping form and nodded agreement. "We couldn't begin to manage this place without you and your dad," he said. "When your aunt Jo and I decided to get married, your dad and us agreed that we'd share in everything, and as far as I'm concerned, there couldn't be better partners than Simon and son."

"Amen." Joanna smiled at both Simon and Isaac. "But maybe you need to think about this, Simon. I know you worked like a dog on that place."

"So did you, little sister. All of us kids worked hard. While Dad was alive, we always felt it was worth it. After he died, I guess we could all see the handwriting on the wall. Mother was a different kind of task master." Simon put the letter back in the envelope and stood up. "Let's open up the barrel that came from the family. Maybe Bertie might have sent a letter in there."

Isaac brightened considerably. He found a claw hammer for Simon to pry the lid off and could hardly contain his excitement as Simon slowly pulled out the nails. Simon was right, his sister Bertha, always known as Bertie, had placed her letter on top of the packages.

"You read it," he said, handing three pages of soaring script to Joanna.

Isaac sat down as close to the barrel as possible and gave a resigned sigh. Bertie's letters were long and rambling and hard to decipher. It would take a while to wade through the thing. CJ raised a sympathetic eyebrow at him.

The afternoon was already casting long shadows. Joanna lit the lamp on the table before she started reading.

Dear family, and hugs and kisses to the little one. Joanna, thanks for remembering Dad in your babe's middle name. He would be so pleased as you and he were always best buddies and you took it so hard when he died. Ma is so wrapped up in her "business" that she had me buy all the presents for the whole family, and let me tell you I had all sorts of instructions on how much to spend so I finally told her that it was too big a hassle to get each one a gift from her and from me too, so I would just combine the whole thing and get each family one gift from both of us. Good grief, I have my own kids to make gifts for, and now that Charlie and Willie are both married and with their own families and I'm a grandmother four times already, I have about all the hassle I can handle. But try to tell Ma that someone besides her is busy—she's sure she's under the weather all the time, but I think it's just Ma feeling sorry for herself again. This deal about the place being sold has caused quite an uproar with our other brother and sister, and don't think they haven't all been coming here along with the in-laws to yowl and howl about it. I'm so sick and tired of the whole mess I'll just be glad when it's all done. And of course, she probably has wrote you that she ain't giving anybody anything, so if we want some of grandma's dishes or furniture, we'll have to bid on it. Well, I have always wanted grandma's rocking chair, and I told Ma that for ages, but oh boy, no sirree. It was all going to the auction. I was pretty sore about it, and then I find out that brother Wilbur's wife, who never lifts a finger ever to help anybody, wants the rocker too. I said no sirree, that rocker means a lot to me, as grandma used to rock all us kids in it, and it sure can't mean that much to Wilbur's wife. Anyway, it's been a big mess, and of course since you two are in that "God-forsaken-place" as Ma says, it's all fallen on the three of us here to help her out. Of course, we can't please her, so sometimes things just get pretty tense. Remember the fit she had, Joanna, when Pa gave you the little chest of Grandma's? She still says she should have had that and not you, but remember how Pa for once stood up to her and said he wanted you to have it because you reminded him so much of his mother, course that sent Ma into another tizzy because she couldn't stand Grandma . But I'm glad you at least got that. Don't look like you're going to get anything else unless you come here to the auction and bid on something you want. Running out of paper. Love, Bertie, Joe and family

Joanna shook her head and frowned. A heavy silence fell onto the room. It was finally broken when CJ stood up with his precious bundle and handed John David to his mother.

"Isaac, let's see what's in this barrel. Looks like your aunt Bertie packed it to the brim."

Isaac whooped softly and quickly reached into the barrel and brought out a package wrapped in an embroidered dish towel. It was tied with grocery string, and it was for Joanna, from "Ma and Bertie's family." It was round and heavy, and CJ groaned inwardly as he remembered the weighty pound cake from last year's Christmas. He placed it on the table beside her, and they flashed sympathetic smiles at one another.

Next came a softer package with Simon's name on it, another similar package with CJ's name, a paper sack full of nuts and hard candy which made Isaac grin from ear to ear, and finally, a box marked " Isaac," wrapped in a baby quilt.

Isaac and CJ carefully unwound the quilt from the box, and when it was free, CJ held it up for Joanna's inspection. It looked warm and serviceable, with brown- and cream-colored squares, and Bertie had pinned a note to it which read, "John David's quilt came from two wool shirts of Pa's that has been in a drawer at my house all these years. Ma paid for the flannel on the bottom side. Hope it keeps the little guy comfy warm."

"Very nice!" Joanna exclaimed and ran her hand over the wool fabric. "I remember Pa wearing these shirts when it was really cold out. Do you remember that, Simon?"

Simon nodded. "He said they itched, but they sure kept him warm."

CJ folded it up and laid it on the table. "What's in the box, Isaac?"

"I dunno know! Can I open it now?"Simon's nod was the signal to take the top off the sturdy wooden box, and Isaac almost trembled with excitement.

Inside the box was a pair of socks. "New socks! Brand new socks, and a good box! I can put all sorts of stuff in here!" Isaac beamed with happiness and then let out a girlie squeal. "There's more! There's more! Look at—what is this?" He slowly lifted a brightly colored object from the box.

"Hey, boy! Isaac, it's a windup toy!" CJ was about as excited as Isaac. In Isaac's hand was a perfect miniature donkey cart with a driver. The wheels of the cart were brightly painted, and the little donkey's ears pointed forward with a perky air.

"See the key on the bottom of the cart? You can wind it up, and it should go forward on its own." CJ pointed to the key and would have liked to take the toy and wind it up himself.

"Good grief," said Johanna. "What will they think up next?"

"Do you really think it'll go?" Isaac was astonished.

CJ moved the empty barrel to clear out a space. "Let's see if it does. Wind it up."

Isaac's thin fingers gave a twist to the key and he quickly set it on the floor. A few whirrs on the part of the toy, a tiny step forward, and then the donkey and cart stopped.

"Even if it don't go like you said, it's still super!" Isaac declared as the little donkey refused to budge any farther.

CJ picked it up and wound the key several times before he set it down. The donkey and the cart started forward and soon ran into Simon's foot. Simon turned it another direction and it started back towards Isaac. Suddenly, the Chinaman driving the cart leaned back with the reins, the donkey kicked up, and the whole affair started moving backwards.

"Wow! Wow! Look at that!" Isaac shouted, and the others were equally excited.

The whoops and hollers of everyone soon had John David awake, and after a few startled bleeps, he watched CJ rewind the toy.

"But you might wear it out!" Joanna cautioned; however, her eyes danced with merriment as she settled the baby in her lap so he could watch the amazing toy.

This time CJ put the toy down where it would have lots of room for its antics. Once again they watched the donkey move forward. When the Chinaman, with his tasseled cap, leaned back and pulled the reins, the donkey kicked again and started moving backwards. Isaac clapped his hands with glee and Simon's "by jingles" was drowned out with the laughter from the rest of them. Several times it was repeated, but finally, the little donkey whirred to a stop.

"This time you wind it up," CJ told Isaac.

"One more time, and then you better put it up so we don't break it," Joanna added.

Even though they knew what to expect by now, it was still a novelty to them. After the toy performed its tiny act again, Isaac obediently put it on a bookshelf and gazed in wondrous admiration at it.

Joanna leaned back in her chair. "What a fun gift! What do you have in your package, Simon?"

Simon was still chuckling at the little donkey as he unwrapped his gift. A pair of wool socks was proudly displayed. CJ had the same thing in his package. Joanna's gift was in a decorated tin and was the usual pound cake. However, after sampling a tiny bite of it, her eyes widened in surprise. "Hey, this is actually good!"

"Bertie must have made it," Simon said with a grin.

"I think she made the dish towel, too. It looks like her fancy stitching."

"Your sister Bertie must have been a busy woman if she put as much work into everyone else's gifts as she did ours," CJ said.

"By jingles, Bertie always can talk as fast as she works, and she works all the time. Even when she was little, she could talk a leg off anyone who'd listen." Simon pulled Isaac onto his lap and ruffled his hair. "I'm thinking we should eat some of that soup I'm smelling and have some of those rolls and get ourselves rested up to open some more gifts, what do you think?"

They all agreed that was a fine plan, and while Joanna took care of John David, the rest of them set the table. There was, for a change, no hurry in their routine. The outside evening chores had been taken care of, and the weather determined no one would be coming or going from the isolated homestead.

By the time Joanna had the baby snuggled in for a slumber in his cradle, CJ had the beef stew ladled into their bowls. While the lamp reflected its soft glow from the middle of the table and the aroma of

Joanna's cooking wafted in the air, CJ's mealtime prayer was grateful acknowledgement of their many blessings, and especially for the blessing of their new baby and for the baby Jesus born in a manger so many years ago.

Hearty amen's followed the prayer. Crackers in the glass bowl were passed around, Joanna's feather light rolls were buttered and big globs of chokecherry jelly were spooned onto them. The stew, whose aroma they had smelled all afternoon, was pronounced excellent and CJ refilled his bowl and Simon's several times.

"I think," CJ reflected, after he declared he couldn't hold another bite of anything, "that I have just enjoyed one of the best Christmas Eve meals in my life. Second only to last Christmas Eve," he quickly added at Joanna's raised eyebrow.

"I'm sure your mother had delicious meals," Joanna said as she buttered one more roll.

"Yes, she did. But Christmas Eve in a minister's family usually includes all sorts of people who are lonely. At least, in our family, it did." CJ smiled at Isaac, and it carried over to Joanna and Simon. "Call me selfish, but I like our little group just the way it is. I like being able to enjoy our packages by ourselves. I'm even grateful the storm has prevented anyone else being here for tonight."

"Well, call me selfish also then. I was thinking the same thing. This has been a perfect afternoon." Joanna finished her roll and sighed. "I'm just so thankful you are here with us, CJ, and not lost in the storm."

Simon and Isaac nodded agreement, and for a few moments, the only sound was the whistle of the wind around the corner of the house.

"Well, the Lord sends His angels to watch out for fools. I thought when I left yesterday morning that the weather was tricky, but I sure didn't think it would blow in that fast." CJ took a drink of coffee. "It's a good thing Smokey loaded all our freight up as fast as he did."

"Is Smokey an angel?" Isaac wondered.

The rest of them laughed.

"Smokey acted like an angel yesterday," Joanna said, "which is a lesson that reminds us everyone has some good points now and then."

"Yeah, even our mother, Joanna," Simon said.

Joanna only shook her head and smiled at his remark.

CJ decided the men should help clean up the kitchen, and in short order, the table was cleared off and the big tea kettle was filled with water and set on the stove to heat. Joanna put an apron around CJ's waist, which caused no end of cackling from Isaac and Simon, and with CJ washing dishes, Simon wiping them, and Joanna putting everything away, they were soon ready to begin the rest of their evening.

The big crate from CJ's family was pulled into the middle of the room. When it was opened, a collective chorus of enthusiastic remarks was heard. Once again, Isaac was the designated handler, and the first package he lifted out was to John David. Joanna told him to open it. Inside the folds of paper were several pairs of infant night wear plus a handsome little suit.

"Beautiful!" Joanna was ecstatic over the gift.

There were books and pencils, shirts for the men, a silk waist for Joanna, and a warm jacket for Isaac. A quilt with a log cabin design was brought out for Joanna and CJ, another quilt with patchwork design for Simon, and wrapped snugly in that was a slate and chalk for Isaac. In every available nook and cranny were bags of corn to pop, dried fruit, hard candy, and walnuts.

"I've never in my life had a waist like this! Look at it, CJ!" Joanna held the turquoise blue blouse in front of her. "Look how it buttons down the front, look at the tucking and the little buckles, look at the wide cuffs, it's just beautiful! Oh, I hope it fits me! Even if it doesn't, I'll still wear it!"

CJ walked over to her and kissed her flushed cheek. "It's for a beautiful woman." He knew his mother would be pleased at Joanna's obvious delight.

The next half hour was spent in admiring the books, making letters on Isaac's slate, trying on the shirts and jacket. Joanna disappeared into their bedroom and came back beaming. She had twisted her hair into a high pouf that threatened to tumble down at any moment, and with the high-necked collar and snug fit of the waist, she was stunningly attractive.

"Aunt Jo!" Isaac gasped as she twirled in circles around them.

"You may touch the sleeve if your hands are clean," she said haughtily, her straight nose tilted high in the air.

Isaac touched it timidly. "Feels like Burr's belly," he said reverently.

Joanna dissolved into a fit of giggles and her pompadour tumbled to her shoulders.

"Looks like we can write to my mother and tell her she sent a perfect fit." CJ touched the shiny fabric on Joanna's shoulder. It was smooth and soft. He put his arms around her to experience the whole effect. "Very nice," he whispered in her ear, which caused her to blush.

"I better take it off," she said, laughing up at him and batting her eyelids. He released her reluctantly.

Finally, Simon decreed it was time to open their gifts to each other. Joanna had sewn each of "her men" flannel shirts; they were warm and practical, and much appreciated.

Simon had noticed CJ's bridle reins were riveted in several places. He and Isaac made new ones out of rich-smelling leather and had them oiled and ready to put on CJ's bridle. CJ, in turn, gave Simon a fish cord cinch he had made. Isaac had spent hours helping him tie the knots in the intricate pattern.

"Well, little sister, us three made something for you," Simon announced to Joanna when there was a pause in the festivities.

"Uh huh, I had that figured out." Joanna grinned. "Isaac isn't the only one who was looking at packages under the tree. When I didn't see my name on anything, I hoped it was because my present was too big to wrap!"

Isaac's eyes were sparkling. "You're really gonna like this, Aunt Jo!"

From the little back porch, and with a lot of grunting and puffing, CJ and Simon carefully carried in their gift and set it in the corner opposite the old wing chair and overflowing bookcase.

"We decided, with all the books we all like to read, you needed this," CJ said. "And if you aren't the hardest woman to keep a secret from! Every time we started to sand or lacquer, you were coming out to the barn for some darn reason or another!"

Joanna's eyes sparkled as she carefully pulled off the blanket that covered the bookcase. "This is perfect! And you built it the right size to fit in this corner between the wall and the window! Look at all these shelves, just in time to put all the new books in!"

She waltzed merrily around CJ and gave him a swift kiss, Simon got a hug, and Isaac was the recipient of both a kiss and a hug.

When all the excitement of the bookcase died down, Joanna put the coffee pot on and declared it was almost time to sample the pound cake.

"Are there any packages left?" CJ looked at Isaac.

"By jingles, I guess there's just the one I saw in the porch," Simon said as he reached for cups to set on the table.

"Better get it, Isaac," Joanna said nonchalantly

Isaac ran to the porch and, in a flash, returned with a long, thin package. "It's got my name on it!" he shouted.

He carefully set it down in front of the tree, and though he tried to take his time and not tear the wrapping paper, his fingers worked faster than his brain. Within seconds, paper flew off to reveal a long wooden box.

"Oh boy! Oh boy! You reckin' the lid is nailed on?"

Simon crouched down beside him. "Nope. You can just lift the lid off."

CJ put his arm around Joanna as they watched Isaac open his gift from the three of them. The wonder on the boy's face as he peered into the box was something CJ would treasure the rest of his life.

"Pa..." He breathed. "Oh boy, Pa, maybe you better take 'er out for me. I might drop 'er."

Simon chuckled and slowly lifted a gleaming Stevens Favorite 22-caliber rifle out of its box. "Here she is, Isaac, the one you've been pouring over in the Sears catalog for the past year. It's from all three of us."

Before Isaac took his new rifle, he gave Simon a bear hug, and then he jumped up and ran over to CJ and Joanna and threw his thin arms around both of them. CJ noticed Joanna's eyes were brighter than usual, and after she had hugged him and planted another kiss on the top of his head, she turned away muttering something about the coffee boiling over.

The three males of the household did what all men do when they look at a new rifle. They worked the bolt, held it to their shoulder, and looked down the barrel; they examined every inch of the walnut stock and pronounced it just fine.

By the time Joanna had slices of pound cake on a plate and coffee poured for each of them (even Isaac had his cup with a swig of milk); they had already taken out the set screw to remove the barrel and had put it back together again.

Isaac reluctantly put the rifle back in the box. CJ thought he had never seen anyone so proud to own a gun.

"Before you shoot it," Joanna cautioned, "there better be some rules laid down."

"Yup, Aunt Jo. I know all the rules. CJ and Pa tell 'em to me all the time."

"This is good pound cake," CJ said, taking another piece.

"CJ." Simon took a sip of coffee while he looked at CJ over his raised cup. "I knew you made that trip yesterday mainly to get this rifle—"

"Have some more cake, Simon. We are very blessed this evening." CJ understood the emotion in Simon's voice. It was a fool's mission, perhaps, and it could have turned out to be a tragedy. But this evening, seeing the look on Isaac's face, was worth the long cold ride. Praise God.

John David reminded his mother he was famished. Once again, the kitchen was cleaned up, treasures were admired, and while Joanna nursed their son in the rocking chair, CJ opened the Bible to Luke's Gospel.

He looked at his wife and thought motherhood had softened her. Simon sat in the wing chair; Isaac was scrunched in beside him watching the silhouette of the fire in the stove make dancing shadows on the wall.

Contentedness washed over him. Even if he was only blessed with the joy of it for this evening, he would remember and be grateful. After he adjusted the lamp, he began to read aloud.

"And it came to pass in those days, that there went out a decree from Caesar Augustus, that the entire world should be taxed..."

Nineteen

May 15, 1901
Stearns, South Dakota

Dear folks,

Sorry I haven't written sooner, but like I said in my last letter, Simon decided to help his mother get ready for her auction in Minnesota, and I have a new appreciation for all the work my brother-in-law does around here!

We are in the middle of calving right now, and looks like we're going to have a good bunch of calves. The spring storms were numerous and wild in March, but by the middle of April, the weather settled down, and by the time our first calf was born, spring eased into fair weather with a few showers to start the grass growing.

Joanna and Isaac are both glad "school" is dismissed! She is a strict task master, but we are proud of the way Isaac knows his numbers, and also how well he reads. He keeps us on our toes with his many questions, and that makes us extra grateful for the books you have supplied us with.

Simon returned last week, with quite a surprise for us. His two nephews came with him, each driving teams with two wagons hitched together, and those wagons were full of building supplies, plus some items from his mother's sale.

He had gotten quite a bargain on the lumber because his brother-in-law (Bertie's husband) runs a lumber mill. He thought Joanna and I should build a bigger house. I had been thinking along those same lines. In fact, I had sketched out some house plans, and when I showed them to Joanna, she rearranged a few walls on paper, and knew exactly where the new house should be. We began digging a basement, and have made good progress. When we move into the new house, Simon and Isaac will live in Joanna's old house.

We always look forward to your letters. Whenever we get one, we gather around the table and Joanna reads them aloud. Isaac thinks Missouri must be a beautiful state, but he is sure he'll never want to live anywhere but South Dakota. (We must have influenced him unwittingly!)

We are beginning to see a few more people staking out homestead claims. Our cattle got into the garden of one family, and the woman used strong words to us about the damage. We try to keep our cattle herded in a different direction now.

We are counting the days until your visit in September!

Love,
CJ, Joanna, and John David

"Do you want to read this before I seal it up?" CJ asked. Generally Joanna read his letters over his shoulder, but this evening, she was busy taking care of a fretful baby.

"No. When I get this little rascal settled down, I'm going to bed. I'm more than bushed."

"Want me to take him for a while?"

Joanna handed their grumpy little baby over to him and wearily got up from the rocking chair. "If by some miracle he falls asleep, put him in his cradle. He's all ready for bed; he just doesn't want to give it up and go to sleep."

CJ had discovered that babies just naturally mold against the chest. He also discovered Joanna had a limit to her patience, and a household with both a mad mamma and baby was an unsettling experience. She had been particular upset over the incident with the cattle in the new homesteader's garden. She threatened to ride over and give the whole family a piece of her mind. He and Simon had finally persuaded her it would be better to let the matter rest.

He slowly walked around the table and then, on impulse, covered John David with a light blanket and stepped outside. The frogs along the creek were practically bursting with their croaking and the leaves were adding a soft rustling sound to the music. CJ started humming and walked slowly toward the new house site.

He walked, sang, and snuggled his little son absentmindedly. His thoughts were more on house building and the garden episode than on the baby he was crooning to.

CJ walked around the perimeter of where the new house would be built. It would have an east porch—he and Joanna both wanted that—upstairs bedrooms under the sloping roof, a small living room, a bigger kitchen and eating area, and the crowning glory, a laundry room for Joanna.

It was a bold move, he thought, considering the uncertainty of homesteaders flocking in after the railroad came through. They would take away all the grassland for the cattle, but until they came, free grazing was available, and while it was there, the early settlers would use it. His mind raced into the future where towns would probably sprout up beside railroads and every quarter most likely would have someone on it. The land couldn't handle it—he was sure of that. The government insisted every settler had to plow so many acres. Virgin grassland plowed under—he shuddered at the thought.

"John David," he whispered to the now sleeping baby, "if all the newcomers are like the family with the garden, it ain't gonna be purty."

The nephews were big husky Norwegian men from Minnesota Northwoods. They had a fun-loving nature, and their mother's ability to talk and work at the same time. Bertie's husband managed a sawmill, and their two sons, Willie and Charlie, knew lumber secrets and were good carpenters.

Their jokes and hearty laughter punctuated the spring air, and their appetites were voracious. They argued incessantly between the two of them about the best way to build a house and seemed to relish the ongoing debate.

The modest house seemed to spring up from the prairie overnight, and by spring roundup time, the finishing touches were made. Joanna had said she could paint the inside plastered walls, but her nephews, enamored with her cooking, insisted on staying another week to accomplish that job.

The day before they left was declared a holiday. CJ took them on a buggy tour of the homestead and beyond. While they agreed the prairie was wild and untamed, and a little bit nice, they were homesick for Minnesota and trees—and their wives and children.

"Yeah, time to go home," Willie said as CJ guided Dolly along a high ridge that opened into a panorama of wide open spaces. "Glad to come, glad we could build the house, and even if Charlie don't know beans about beams, we got 'er done."

"Hah!" Charlie snorted. "If it falls in around you some winter morning, blame Willie. I tried to tell him about braces." His nudge in CJ's ribs about took CJ's breath away.

"Yeah, yeah. Say, CJ, I don't figger something out." Willie leaned closer from the backseat. "This homesteading stuff—some say it's free land and some say you pay for it. It ain't clear in my mind, an' shut up, Charlie," he added as his brother started snickering.

"Well. It is confusing. The Sioux lands, which is what we are settling on, were opened up to homestead in '89, after the Indians each received their hundred and sixty acres. The first homesteaders had to pay a dollar and twenty-five cents an acre until '92. Then I guess it was seventy-five cents an acre until '94, and fifty cents an acre after that, until 1899. But after ten years, if there isn't claimed land and after you've been on a quarter for five years, all you pay is the filing fee." CJ noted Willie's baffled look.

"They keep changing the laws on it, Willie. What was so a couple of years ago has changed. I paid the fifty cents an acre after I was here for fourteen months. Joanna and I had gotten married after I first filed, and I didn't want to mess around trying to fill the requirements for five years to get it for nothing. I paid eighty dollars for the quarter."

"Aw, yeah, some things ain't all free 'n easy like it sounds." Charlie scratched his beard. "I wouldn't wanna be out here. Those Indians coming and going sorta bodder me."

"Well, sometimes when they come in without knocking they 'sorta bodder' me too," CJ admitted as he stopped the team and the buggy on top of a high hill to the west of their homestead. "Most of the time they just go about their business, and we go about ours. In fact, I have an Indian friend that is a good fellow to help you out in a pinch."

"You know what I don't figger," Charlie said, getting out of the buggy to stretch his long legs, "is why you're here grubbing out a homestead when you got an ed-u-ca-tion." He dragged out the word and shook his head. "Seems like you could be anywheres." He took a slow look in full circle where they had stopped. "Why here? Nothing but grass and sky. No towns. No trees. You know, I don't even hear many birds."

CJ leaned back on the seat and took in the vista of green hills, blue sky, puffy clouds and noted the slight breeze that had a hint of coolness in it. He decided if all that couldn't tell its own glorious story, nothing he could say would impress Charlie.

"I like it here." He had another thought. "And Joanna wouldn't want to live anywhere else."

"But there's no women here for her," Charlie mumbled.

"Aw, Charlie, there's women. There's the neighbors." Willie gave a short laugh. "Yeah, and there's the new neighbor woman that Joanna don't like much."

"Yeah, yeah. Joanna's friends are miles down this little dry creek. And that's another thing. Where's the water at in this creek?"

"Sometimes, there's water." CJ chuckled. "But I think Joanna has been praying for dry weather so you guys could get her house done."

Willie also climbed out of the buggy and looked around the same horizon Charlie had. "It's green and purty on these hills. But lonesome. Yeah, too lonesome. But Simon said he don't know if he could go back home with all those trees and people. And it don't hurt to have lotta miles between Grandma and Joanna."

"Oh boy, yeah. Before they came out west, Simon and Isaac and Joanna came to visit the grandma. So we're all there to give a big welcome home thing, and the first thing the grandma says to Aunt Jo is, 'Girl, you're as scrawny as your old granny Swanson always was.' Remember that, Willie?"

"Yeah. That was a bad thing to say. Aunt Jo got those two red spots in her cheeks that she always gets when she's madlike. You know what I mean, CJ?"

CJ nodded.

"Then Aunt Jo says, 'Mama, you're as big a butterball as your own dear mama always was,' an' the fight, she was on." Charlie rolled his eyes while Willie hooted with laughter.

"Well, there certainly seems to be a coolness between the two." CJ hesitated to say anymore.

"Grandma is a hard woman to understand a lot a time," Willie offered. "But we got her settled in her house in town after the auction." He gave a relieved sigh. "Maybe now our own mother can settle down."

"Yeah, now that Pa bought that wreck of a rocking chair for her," Charlie said. "Why she wanted that old piece of junk I don't figger out," He pointed a finger at Willie and added, "And you're wrong, Willie, to say Grandma is hard to understand a *lot* a time. I ain't *never* understood her!"

After paying Simon for the building material and the two nephews for their labor, CJ's rainy day fund had shrunk considerably. Still, he consoled himself, the land and the new house was paid for. And as Joanna pointed out, it wasn't a huge home, but big enough so they shouldn't have to add on if their family increased.

He was grateful both his and Joanna's parents had raised their children to be frugal and hardworking. He was also grateful he could earn some money at the spring roundup.

It didn't take long for Joanna to pack household items for the move. She kept them all busy emptying her house of furniture and crates. The little house was cleaned to her satisfaction, and finally, with eyes bright with excitement, she began the unpacking process.

The furniture that almost crowded them out of the little house became lost in the spaciousness of the new house.

CJ groaned inwardly and worried that she might want to splurge on more pieces. He should have known better. She soon had everything arranged in cozy fashion.

"I think, after we hang these curtains, you better get your bedroll ready for the roundup," she informed him several mornings later.

"What? Kicking me out of my own house already?" He grinned at her and was rewarded with a swat on his arm.

"Do you know what? I love those nephews of mine, but I am so ready to quit cooking for a while."

He noticed for the first time the dark circles under her eyes. "Joanna," he said, putting his arms around her, "when I'm gone, I want you to slow down, take care of John David, and not try to put in twenty-five hours of work every day."

"When you're gone." She sighed and leaned against him. "When you're gone I'm not going to cook one darn thing except for John David's eggs."

"When do you want me to come back?" He brushed a kiss against her forehead.

She looked at him for a second before a slow smile graced her lips. "When the moon is full."

❧

It wasn't hard to find the roundup crew. The dust from the milling cattle and the din of the bawling cows and calves was seen and heard from several miles away. By the time CJ joined them at the head of Dry Creek, they had already been gathering cattle for a couple of weeks.

Greetings were brief as he rode into camp. The cowboys were busy, and CJ was told to grab an iron and start branding. He could remember brands and who they belonged to, and his marks on the calf hides were easily read. Besides those facts, he thought with grim amusement, he just wasn't the greatest roper, and he may as well leave that job to the experts.

The roundup had started on the north side of White River, where it dropped into the Missouri River, and had worked its way west. It would continue in a huge circle, taking in the prairie between the Bad River and the White River, as far east as the *15* pens that were situated on the Little Buffalo. If CJ stayed with the roundup for the month remaining, he could earn almost forty dollars.

By late afternoon, the calves were branded and back with their anxious mamas. The cook wagon had already pulled out and was heading towards the east fork of Brave Bull Creek. CJ would only be a few miles from his own homestead, but he had already decided to leave Joanna to her privacy and would bunk down with the rest of the crew at camp.

Late spring sunsets over the grassland of Dakota was a lingering enjoyment. The new camp was only a few miles northeast of Stearns, and as the sky became a kaleidoscope of colors, both badlands and prairie were bathed in colors that lasted only seconds until another wave of the Master's paintbrush tinted the land with different shades.

CJ listened to the banter of the men as he filled his plate a second time and felt the contentment of good camaraderie. The food was good, coffee was strong and hot, and the wind had settled down to a gentle breeze.

"Life is good, ain't it?" Winn said as CJ crouched down beside him.

"Very good." CJ had decided God preached an eloquent sermon every time a Dakota sunset graced the land.

"So how is that little guy doing? I forgot to ask you that before."

"Growing." CJ took a sip of coffee and watched the sun sink a little closer to the horizon.

"I was wondering if you was gonna make it this spring. I heard you were house building. Plus being a family man and all that." Winn chuckled before he forked another pile of beans into his mouth.

"I think my wife is ready for some time to herself." CJ grinned at his friend. "You know Joanna. She cherishes her privacy."

"A rare and wonderful gem is our Joanna." Winn was reflectively. "Lots of women can't stand the loneliness out here. She ain't bothered by it." He pulled off his hat and set it on the ground beside him. "But

179

say, what about our purty Deborah Lynn and her baby—now that sounded like an ordeal."

CJ finished chewing his mouthful of biscuit and gravy before he answered. "Drew wrote to us that he was afraid he was going to lose both her and their little girl. Sounds like they're living with the Smiths while she and the baby recuperate."

"Good. She'll get lots of care from her momma."

CJ nodded. On one of his trips to get supplies for the house, he had stopped at the Smiths to visit both Drew and Deborah Lynn. He was shocked to see how frail she was. Their little baby girl was a month old, but looked as drawn and haggard as Deborah Lynn herself. He was irritated at Drew's hearty assurance that mother and baby were doing fine. They both looked near death to CJ. He had prayed about it all the way home.

Winn set his empty plate beside his hat and burped complacently. "Ain't nothing like good food after a hard day's work."

CJ raised an eyebrow at him. Winn was a rep for some of the bigger ranchers, and his job mainly consisted of making sure the right cattle were correctly branded for the ones he was representing. If Winn caught the look CJ threw him, he chose to ignore it and instead crossed his outstretched legs and gave a heavy sigh.

"You know, we best enjoy this grassland while we can. I'm seeing more and more little claim shacks around the country. It ain't purty."

"I know. We have a family that moved in a couple of miles from us. Name of Tinner. Nobody seems to know where they came from. They're not very friendly. In fact, there's something about them that makes a fellow a little nervous. I'm glad I've seen the open range before it all changes to a bunch of little places."

"Yessir. The railroad ain't gonna rest until it figures out a way to make money from these big cattle companies. It'll tell all sorts of tales about homesteading out here to lure folks to come, thinking they're in a place like Iowa. There ain't no water in these parts, no wood, no water, unless you're by a creek." Winn shook his head. "Aw, well, we've talked about all that before. I'm wondering if there's might be a piece of cake over there." He pointed towards the cook wagon.

CJ swigged the last drop of coffee down and stood. The sun had dropped below the hills to the west, and the breeze had an unexpected chill to it. He took his metal plate and fork back to the cook wagon, swished them in the hot soapy water that filled a washtub, and shook them in the breeze to dry. He was thinking of his bedroll and a good night's sleep. He was also thinking about Joanna and missing her more than he thought he should.

Twenty

June 27, 1901
Recluse, South Dakota

Dear Mom and Dad,

Don't know if you remember this or not, but almost three years ago, I mailed you a letter from the Recluse post office. It's still run by Wolfer Thompson and his wife, Ida. I'm on the spring roundup again, and today we gathered cattle and branded at the *15* pens. This brand, *15*, belongs to a fellow called Missouri John. He had the pens built along the forks of Little Buffalo Creek. There is one huge pen that holds about three thousand head, and two smaller ones. I'm told Missouri John lives along White River, and there seems to be quite a few colorful stories about him.

The land is a little different here than at Brave Bull Creek. We have more rolling hills, but here there is quite a lot of flatland, which breaks up into steeper hills the closer it gets to Bad River.

The new house is finished, and we are very pleased with it. It's not huge, but it sure is a big improvement over Joanna's little home. Simon and Isaac are happy to have the old one, and Joanna is busy getting everything settled into the new one. We'll have plenty of room for you when you come to visit us in September.

I think you picked a good time to come. The mosquitoes will be gone (hopefully) by then, and the days will be a little cooler. We are all very anxious to see you.

My friend Smokey was at the *15* pens today, and he had visited Deborah Lynn and her family in Pierre last week. He said she was as lovely as ever and has begun to feel much stronger. Her little daughter also seems to be gaining, and Smokey claims she will be as lovely as her mother when she grows up. I thought you might want to pass this information along to Deborah's aunt Coramae. Smokey also told me that Mrs. Ordin had given him orders to draw out a map to our homestead for her. She and Mr. Ordin are planning a visit the end of July. "Honey," she told Smokey, "we're a-comin' even if it's hotter than Hades," which it probably will be, but nevertheless, I know Joanna and I will both be delighted to see them.

I will catch up on your newsy letters when I get back home. I'm thinking that will be in a couple of weeks. I would really like to just ride home and forget the roundup, but money is needed this year, and I guess John David won't forget his dad in that length of time.

Love,
CJ

The twilight was almost gone when CJ finished his letter. It had been a hot and humid day, with little or no breeze. He was sweaty and tired, and the area was buzzing with the drone of mosquitoes. Sleeping wouldn't be good this night.

As he lay on his bedroll swatting the pesky insects, he began to wonder if the wages were worth the agony. Sheet lightning danced through the western sky and the night air was almost heavy enough to be suffocating.

It started sprinkling a little after midnight. If CJ had been awake, he would have made an effort to find a drier spot to sleep. Instead, he snored through the light rain and found himself alone when the early dawn crept into the eastern sky.

His companions had found wagons to crawl under, but from the mutterings coming from that direction, their sleep wasn't any more refreshing than CJ's. He dug out clean socks from his saddlebag, and in spite of feeling damp and bitten half to death, he grinned. No one ever messed with his clean socks.

He wiped the dampness from his bare feet, and by the time he pulled socks and boots on, coffee aroma permeated the air.

Grouchy mosquito-bitten cowboys swore softly as they grabbed platefuls of bacon, eggs, and sourdough biscuits. Roundups were enjoyable the first weeks, but the last days could be challenging as temperatures and tempers soared along with the persistence of mosquitoes.

Not a whisper of a breeze stirred the air as CJ and Winn left the crew behind. They had been entrusted with the mailbag and were making a quick detour to Recluse. The *15* pens were located a short distance from the Chamberlain to Deadwood trail, and as they headed for the trail's crossing on Little Buffalo, CJ looked at the valley that stretched before them. To the north, Stoneman rose majestically above the Bad River. The green ribbon of trees that marked Little Buffalo Creek and several draws that dropped into it wove its way through the prairie until it joined the Bad River.

As they followed the trail to the western ridge above Little Buffalo, Winn slowed his horse's gait until they ambled leisurely at a walk.

"May as well enjoy the morning's coolness, such as it is." He gazed around him thoughtfully.

"Good grass here," CJ said, feeling the first tickle of breeze.

"It should make a fine ranch for somebody someday." Win's blue eyes squinted as he tried to make out a moving shape far ahead of them. "Looks like there are already folks moving ahead of us. Is that oxen that's moving that freight?"

CJ admitted he couldn't tell. It was too far away. Within a short time, they were at the turnoff to Recluse and could see a thin vapor of smoke coming from the dugout's chimney.

Barking dogs announced their arrival, and Wolfer stepped out the door with a coffee cup in hand. In curt tones he ordered his animals to shut up, and they did so immediately.

"Ain't seen you in awhile, Winn," he greeted his friend as Winn dismounted.

The two men shook hands and complained about the weather as CJ swung off his horse, the mailbag firmly in hand.

"Remember CJ Crezner?" Winn asked, as Wolfer stared at CJ with an uncomprehending gaze.

"I remember a skinny guy named CJ. Not this bear."

CJ smiled through eight days of whiskers and offered polite greetings.

"Heard you married. She must be a good cook. You look like the fatted calf."

"She'll be pleased you noted her cooking achievements." CJ made a mental note to check himself in Joanna's mirror when he returned home. He didn't think he had put on *that* much weight.

"Better go on in and let the missus take care of all that mail. Stage should be coming today."

CJ nodded. He opened the door and wondered how many people stumbled down the three steps of the dugout. Whatever the accident rate, the Thompson dugout was wonderfully cool inside.

Ida Thompson's daughter was washing breakfast dishes. The other children were inside and outside doing various chores while Ida herself sorted mail in the corner which doubled as the post office.

"Hello," she greeted CJ without looking up. "Put your letters on the table here. Are you looking for mail?"

"Is there any for the roundup crew?" CJ asked as he pulled the letters out of the mailbag he had brought.

"Tom Jones roundup pool?" she asked.

"That would be the one."

She reached into a pigeon hole and quickly handed him several letters. He double checked to make sure he had emptied the mail bag and then placed all the letters she gave him back into the bag.

"Mr. Crezner and me need a cup of coffee," she said to her daughter.

CJ was about to say that wasn't necessary, but two cups of steaming coffee were already poured. Mrs. Thompson set her work aside and finally gave him her undivided attention.

"I believe we have a promise from you to sing, Mr. Crezner. Now I don't play the best,"—she motioned him towards the piano—"but I can play well enough for you to sing."

"Well." He took the offered cup of coffee and thanked the young girl.

Ida Thompson took her place on the piano stool and began to play a few chords. "I like 'Softly and Tenderly.' Do you know that one?"

CJ took a slow sip of her strong but good coffee and nodded. He hummed a few notes and she smiled as she found chords that would put the song in a comfortable key for him.

"Mrs. Thompson, did you know that a man named Will Thompson wrote this song?"

"Really?" She was clearly surprised and stopped playing for a moment. "Well, he must have been a true Christian fellow, 'cause the words are wonderful."

"Actually, I think he's still alive."

She pondered this for a while and then began an introduction for him. The piano was out of tune, but no matter, CJ had sung with far worse accompaniment. He liked this song. It was a gentle urging to accept Christ, and with that acceptance, the promise of eternity with him.

Softly and tenderly Jesus is calling, calling for you and for me
See on the portals He's waiting and watching, Watching for you and for me.
Come home, come home, Ye who are weary, come home;
Earnestly tenderly, Jesus is calling. Calling "O sinner, come home!"

His voice was a little scratchy, he thought, and took another swig of coffee before he started another verse.

He thought it was too bad there wasn't an alto voice to sing the extra notes of the chorus with him. However, Mrs. Thompson did her best to fill in with piano notes..

Time is now fleeting, the moments are passing, Passing from you and from me;
Shadows are gathering, deathbeds are coming, coming for you and for me.

Come home, come home, Ye who are weary, come home;
Earnestly, tenderly, Jesus is calling. Calling, "O sinner, come home!"

Mrs. Thompson paused and looked at him questioningly. He held up one finger to indicate there was another verse. She nodded and continued with some fancy chords that sounded very good.

O for the wonderful love He has promised, Promised for you and for me;
Tho we have sinned He has mercy and pardon, Pardon for you and for me.

CJ thought of his grandparents when he started the chorus. They came "home," and they were with each other for eternity. And even better than that, they were with their Lord on a heavenly journey that must be wonderful. He was unaware that his voice became almost caressing as he finished.

"Mr. Crezner," Ida's voice broke into his thoughts. "CJ, I hope you can sing that for me when I die."

"I would hope that will be a long time into the future," he said lightly. He would have said more, but was arrested by the seriousness of her demeanor.

"One never knows," she said softly.

He noted her hand trembled slightly as she drank her coffee.

Wolfer's voice had a strange timbre to it when he opened the door and announced the stage was coming in.

Immediately, Mrs. Thompson left the piano stool and stamped the letters lying on the table. With one deft motion, she placed them in the government mail bags, and by the time the stage rolled into the yard, Wolfer had the leather bag. He effortlessly tossed it onto the stage and caught a different one marked "Recluse." The stage made a circle and was gone within seconds.

"They don't waste any time, do they?" Winn's remark was more of a statement than a question.

"Nope."

CJ put the mail bag for the roundup crew on his saddle. He nodded goodbye to several of the children that milled around and, uncharacteristically for him, took Mrs. Thompson's hand and pressed it between both of his.

"Thank you, ma'am, for the coffee and the music. You play the piano very nicely."

She smiled at him, but the smile didn't reach her eyes. "I've always enjoyed music."

He released her hand and moved towards his horse. Winn and Wolfer were making small talk while standing beside Winn's horse. Suddenly, Wolfer came towards him with an amazing agility for a man of his size.

CJ barely had time to collect his thoughts when Wolfer's left hand grabbed his arm with a viselike grip and the right hand stretched out in an unmistakable gesture.

"Take care, sir," CJ managed as his hand was crushed in a firm handshake.

"Thanks for the song. The missus—" Mr. Thompson left the words unspoken and let his hands drop to his side. His piercing eyes sought CJ's, and for a brief moment, CJ glimpsed the tender side of Wolfer Thompson. He loved his wife and he was worried about her.

"Take care yourself," Wolfer growled softly.

CJ nodded and swung into the saddle. Winn was already mounted, and after a few parting words and waves, they urged their horses into a slow trot. The early morning sun already promised it would be another scorcher; yet, as CJ observed to himself, there might be worse things for a man than a hot day in the saddle.

"Heading out?"

CJ finished tying his bedroll on his saddle while his horse stomped impatiently. "Going home for a couple of days, Winn. Tom said tomorrow was the Fourth of July and he was giving the boys a break."

Winn nodded and pushed back his hat. "Yup. They need a little time to whoop 'er up. 'Course then they'll need a day or so to recover after the whooping."

CJ grinned while he fastened his saddle bags on. "What about you? Staying or heading out yourself?"

"Staying, I guess. Stopped in my place before we got here, looks like all is well there. I may as well enjoy the feed and the fun." Winn looked past CJ towards the north where two riders were coming in at a fast trot.

"Wonder who that is."

When the riders stopped before them, CJ noted they were young-looking and, unless he missed his guess, they hadn't eaten for a while.

"Is this Jack Dailey Creek?" asked the older of the two.

"Yup. Looking for someone?" Winn was eying the worn out horses.

"Yessir. We were looking for the boss. Heard he might be hiring."

"Well, now, he just put on some extra hands, don't know if he needs anymore."

CJ thought the younger boy looked even bleaker at Winn's remark.

"The other roundup boss over that-a-way weren't needing no one, he sent us here." The spokesman of the two slowly dismounted. CJ wondered how long they'd been riding on an empty belly.

"Why don't I go talk to him?" CJ offered, handing Winn the reins of his horse. "He might have a spot for you." He took some jerky out of his saddlebag and gave a few pieces to both boys before he headed to the cook's wagon.

Before long, he returned with a plate of food in each hand. "Mr. Jones thought you might be hungry." He watched the smiles of appreciation light both faces. "He also said he would talk to you after you ate." CJ gestured towards the cook's wagon. "He's sitting over there."

He saw the frown of puzzlement on Winn's face, and taking the reins of his horse, he motioned for Winn to walk with him a short distance away from the boys.

"CJ, what the heck did you do?" Winn asked softly. "I know for a fact Jones wasn't about to hire any more hands."

"Well. Well, I asked Tom if he would hire the two in my place. I need to be home, Winn. Simon shouldn't have to be doing all the haying and chores around the place. Besides, I worry about Tinner.

I've been hearing from the fellers that Zed Tinner can get ornery when he's drinking. I don't trust the guy. Anyway, I figured these boys need the work and the money a little more than I do. There's about two weeks left, everybody knows their jobs and it seems to be going good. Maybe you could sort of keep an eye on those two." CJ glanced at his friend's long face and started grinning. "Winn, they can do what I did plum easy, get wood for the cook, wash a few dishes, you know."

Winn was not smiling. "You know. You know darn good and well you do more than that. Shoot. Those two kids pro'ly can't do one thing except eat." Winn turned and eyed the boys as they walked towards the cook's wagon with the empty plates in their hands.

CJ swung into the saddle and leaned down to pat Winn on the shoulder. "Stop by sometime and see us. Joanna is one good cook."

He nudged his horse forward and chuckled as Winn shook his head and gave an exasperated wave. With a few more farewells to the men in camp, he turned his horse towards the south and home. It was almost time for the full moon.

Twenty-one

July 25, 1901
Pierre, South Dakota

Dear ones in Christ,

When Mrs. Ordin said they were going to visit you, I decided to hastily write this note and send it with them. If you are able to, please send a reply back with them.

Momma and I have wished so often that you could all come and visit us, and we were wondering if that visit would be possible when CJ's parents are here. Please feel welcome to come for dinner either when you are meeting them to take them to your ranch, or when you are bringing them back at the conclusion of their visit.

Joanna, thank you so much for your kind letters to us! Your amazing spirit and vitality always makes me feel better, and as one new mother to another, your observations are insightful.

Hoping to see you this fall.

Love,
Deborah Lynn

CJ read Deborah Lynn's letter in the fading twilight and laid it on the dresser in their bedroom. He studied his wife as she unbraided her hair in a leisurely fashion that was slightly uncharacteristic of her.

"I didn't realize you had written to the Wilsons and Smiths," he said.

"Um," Joanna replied, the hair pins in her mouth prevented her from saying more.

"She doesn't mention how she's feeling, but guess from what the Ordins said, she must be on the mend, along with the baby."

Joanna nodded and ran her fingers throughout her unbraided hair.

"Which time works better for you?"

She raised her eyebrows at him and took the hair pins out of her mouth. "I think when we take them back. CJ, what does insightful mean? I wish I had a dictionary."

CJ unbuttoned his shirt before he answered. The July breeze coming through their window was warm, but at least it moved the air and kept their bedroom comfortable. "Insightful? It's a compliment, Mrs. Crezner. It means you understand what she's going through as one mother to another. Something like that."

He walked towards Joanna and ran his hands over her bare shoulders. "Like, I have insight that you are purposely looking extra lovely tonight because Smokey rode in with the Ordins to visit us."

"Mr. Crezner, you silly man." Joanna wrapped her arms around his waist and gazed up at him. "Your insight is all wrong." Her long brown hair tumbled over her shoulders and he buried his face into tresses that smelled of soap and sunshine.

"I think I'm a jealous husband, Joanna, and it's all your fault." He growled and held her tightly against him.

"How come we're so jealous of each other?" she whispered and traced his beard and mustache with a gentle finger. "I didn't like the look on your face tonight at supper when we talked about Deborah Lynn. You looked all worried and upset." She grabbed some whiskers in mock anger and continued, "You didn't even look like that when John David was born."

He rubbed his whiskered face against the smoothness of her cheek and then kissed her. Kissing Joanna was one of the delights of his life. She was unabashedly affectionate and usually returned the favor with enthusiasm.

"Woman," he muttered after several passionate seconds had passed, "you made me lose my train of thought."

"Let's go to bed, CJ. Maybe you'll remember your train of thought after the lamp is out."

He seriously doubted any semblance of thought would occur when the lamp was out.

"Now, CJ, honey." Mrs. Ordin's earrings fluttered wildly as she rocked John David. "I don't want you to take offense, but I'm a-wondering how you're going to pay for this here house."

It was Sunday afternoon, and everyone, with the exception of Smokey who left early in the morning for Stearns, was comfortably ensconced in the living room. Joanna had cooked a bountiful noon meal and they had eaten in leisure. The kitchen had been tidied up, and with the languid summer breeze wafting through the room, the atmosphere was slightly drowsy, except for Mrs. Ordin's vigorous rocking.

"I'll make Joanna take in twice the laundry she does now," CJ replied, "and then she can sell some of her garden produce along with that." Joanna looked at him amusedly and shook her head.

"Oh sure, you will," Mrs. Ordin snorted. "And probably make Isaac break broncs for a little extra cash besides."

"Well, I hadn't thought of that." CJ reached over to Isaac and ruffled his hair. "Seriously, Mrs. Ordin, Simon got such a good deal on all the material, and his nephews worked for reasonable wages. It isn't an expensive house."

Mr. Ordin, who fancied himself a carpenter, looked approvingly at the finished product. "They did a good job. It should last you folks a lifetime."

"Good!" Joanna said and rescued her wide-eyed little boy from Mrs. Ordin's increased rocking speed. "It's time for this little guy to take his nap. I'll take him upstairs."

Mrs. Ordin abruptly stopped rocking and watched Joanna leave the room. When her earrings settled down, she tilted her head and gave CJ a searching look. "I didn't want to say anything while Smokey was here, but the rumor is that he's a-having trouble keeping his ranch afloat."

"I hadn't heard that, had you Simon?" CJ looked over at his brother-in-law. Simon had his eyes closed and was very comfortably settled in the big wing chair. He slowly opened his blue eyes and gave a nod.

"I'm not surprised. Smokey is a good guy, but this country bothers him. He told me once about a crossing they have on Bad River, where the Chamberlain to Deadwood trail is. They call it, 'baby crossing.' Said some people were crossing there when it was in flood stage, and the water tore a little baby out of his mother's arms and the baby drowned." Simon paused reflectively.

"It really upset Smokey. He said the poor mother had to bury her baby there on the banks and would probably never see the grave again."

"Well, now honey, bad things happen to good people all the time. It ain't just in this country." Mrs. Ordin was adamant. "Take Deborah Lynn for example. Now you all just tell me why she has had to suffer so much from having a baby. Lord knows she's gonna be a good mama, but she sure has had a struggle getting her feet back underneath her."

"But Smokey said she was getting better," CJ smiled at Joanna as she reentered the room. He hoped he kept the worried look off his face.

"Well, sure she is. She's gonna make it if something else don't get her. I know for a fact she's a-really looking forward to seeing all of you when your folks get here, CJ."

"Which reminds me," Joanna said as she detoured towards the bookcase, "would you give Deborah Lynn this letter when you get back?"

CJ looked at his wife questioningly. He wondered when she found time to answer Deborah Lynn's letter and what she had decided.

"I wrote that we would all be there when we took your parents back to Pierre after their visit." Joanna answered CJ's unspoken question as she handed Mrs. Ordin her letter.

⚬⚬⚬

The sun was barely peeking over the horizon the next morning when the Ordin's waved goodbye and started their journey back to Pierre. The hours had flown while they were visiting; CJ had forgotten how much he enjoyed their homespun wisdom and frank appraisal on any given subject.

"I love that woman," Joanna said, waving until the buggy crossed the creek and headed northeast. "She's honest. Sometimes painfully so, but she has a heart of gold. So does he."

"They did good to come all this way to visit. Hope they come again," Simon said, and CJ thought the same thing. "Well, by jingles, I guess we better get going on some of that hay that still needs cutting, don't you think?" Simon looked at CJ inquiringly.

"I'll get the team in. They've enjoyed a couple of days of vacation and should be ready to get back to work." CJ squeezed Joanna's shoulder lightly. "And what does the lady of the house have going on this morning?"

Joanna looked at him with raised eyebrows. "It's Monday, Mr. Crezner. What do I do every Monday?"

CJ grinned at her and started walking towards the barn. "Laundry," he said without breaking stride. "Every Monday Mrs. Crezner does laundry."

"What does Mrs. Crezner do every Tuesday?" She raised her voice so he could hear her.

"Ironing. Every Tuesday Mrs. Crezner irons." CJ hollered without looking back. He raised his arm in salute before he ducked into the barn.

Simon chuckled as he followed him. "Yessir. And Wednesday is mending, and Thursday is baking, and all the time she keeps us fellers in line."

"In a sensible and good way, of course." CJ grinned at Simon as he reached for the halter rope.

The August summer days seemed to fly by as they readied the homestead for CJ's parents visit and also for the coming winter months. Stacks of hay dotted the creek bottoms, Simon's grain crops were harvested, and Joanna put Isaac to work snapping green beans, a job Isaac detested but manfully endured without too much complaining.

CJ had thought they should share some of the green beans with the Tinners, even though he didn't think his cattle had hurt their garden as much as Tinners claimed they did. However, he changed his mind after he and Zed Tinner exchanged heated words in the Stearns post office one hot afternoon. The Tinners apparently never forgot a grudge, and when Zed saw CJ, he shook a dirty finger in his face and reminded him to keep the Crezner and Swanson cattle off his land. It rubbed CJ the wrong way, and he slapped the man's hand away from his face.

"It happened once Tinner. Get over it. We've herded our cattle the other direction every since."

Zed Tinner seemed to sense the ill will radiating from several cattlemen in the post office. He turned and left without saying another word, but CJ had a premonition their difficulties with the Tinners had just begun.

At last the day came when CJ stood near the Pierre depot and watched the train come chugging in. The passengers descended one by one, and finally, he saw his father step down and reach for his mother's arm to steady her as she made the last step.

"Did you have a good trip?" He asked as he walked towards them. He wasn't prepared for the startled look they gave him, nor for the silence. He had expected them to rush towards him with their usual enthusiasm and hugs.

"Mom?" He held out his arms in a gesture of greeting.

"Carl John?" She looked at him incredulously.

"The voice is familiar, but—" His father walked towards him shaking his head.

CJ started laughing as he watched the puzzlement on his parent's faces. "Hey, it's me. I haven't changed that much!"

His mother was in his arms by then and he gave her a gentle bear hug.

"Those whiskers make you looks so different! And you've grown, Carl." She gasped in breathless excitement.

CJ reached out to include his father with another hug, and for several minutes, the travelers marveled on his increased width and they seemed positive he had grown taller.

"Your shoulders are wider. You just look so much stronger," his mother mentioned several times and then shook her head. "You've changed so much in the two years since we've seen you. Have we changed that much?"

CJ looked at his mother and noticed a few more lines on her face, more gray hair, but all in all, still his own dear and sweet mother.

"You look wonderful," he assured her.

Arrangements had been made with the Smiths to stay the night at the manse and to travel to the homestead early the next morning. CJ and his parents enjoyed the gracious southern hospitality and robust conversation at the supper table with their hosts.

Deborah Lynn, CJ was relieved to note, looked far healthier than the last time he saw her, and her little daughter also seemed to have a livelier manner.

During an infrequent lull in the conversation, Deborah Lynn gave him a studied look before remarking about his beard and mustache.

"I declare, CJ, those whiskers just make you look worlds different. I don't know if I even like them. What does Joanna say?"

"Joanna has decided a fist full of whiskers is a good way to keep my attention." There was an outbreak of amused chuckles at his remark.

"We haven't heard the latest about John David," Drew said. "What's the little man up to these days?"

CJ pushed back his chair slightly so he could stretch his legs out. "John is growing, getting fatter, no teeth yet, crawls, says 'mum' and 'da' and 'eye,' which means either his own eye or Isaac."

He thought he had covered the subject well. Mrs. Smith, however, wanted more details.

"Has he taken any steps yet?"

"Not yet. Joanna discovered him crawling up our porch steps with Burr, our dog, following him, and Ruby, the other dog, leading him on. Between the dogs and Isaac, they keep John well entertained."

"Ruby? What kind of name is Ruby for a dog?" Deborah Lynn asked and her dimples flashed merrily in her cheeks.

"Ruby is Burr's puppy. Isaac thought we should call her Rub, which he explained was Burr spelled backwards, but Joanna said it would have to be Ruby because she didn't want anyone to hear her hollering Rub."

Drew had just taken a drink of tea and almost choked on it when he heard CJ's explanation. When he finally recovered, he laughed until tears flowed from his eyes.

Deborah looked at him in astonishment. "Why Drew, I don't believe I've ever heard you laugh this hard at anything!" She was a lovely picture, with her eyes dancing and her slender hand on her husband's arm.

"I just have this mental picture of someone riding up and Joann shouting 'Rub! Rub!'" Drew started laughing again, which seemed to create a ripple effect around the table with everyone joining in, whether they were laughing at Drew or his mental picture was hard to tell.

The two weeks CJ's parents stayed at the homestead seemed to end before they even began. They adored their grandson and their daughter-in-law and made no bones about it. CJ's mother also enjoyed Isaac and became Isaac's best friend when she fussed over and petted both Burr and Ruby.

It became a common sight to see Isaac pulling the wagon Simon made, with CJ's mother walking beside him, John David contentedly riding in the wagon box, and two dogs racing around them. There seemed to be no end to the walks they made on prairie trails and sometimes were gone for over an hour. When they returned, John would be sound asleep in the wagon.

CJ's father made the round of chores with Simon and CJ, admired the sheds and barn, and especially the houses. On several occasions, he and CJ, along with Joanna, saddled up the horses and took rambling rides.

"This is God's country," Reverend John Crezner said one evening as they sat on the porch. "I understand now why you wanted to stay here, Carl."

It was a perfect late summer evening, with a touch of autumn in the air. Cicadas were making their whirring sound in the trees and the prairie was bathed in golden twilight.

"It isn't always as nice as it's been these past days," CJ said, "but when South Dakota wants to impress someone, she does quite a number."

CJ's mother was rocking John David, and CJ thought he had never seen a more contended look on her face.

"I know you have blizzards and bugs and hardships, but this is surely wonderful. There's a certain peace here."

"There's peace because there are so few people around, which will change when all the homesteaders charge in," Joanna said and gave an exasperated sigh. "Just like those Tinners who came from out of the blue. He drinks like a fish, and is just a horrible, mean man. I worry about Isaac running into him while he's herding the cattle. I don't believe Zed's wife ever smiles."

"Usually homesteaders bring towns, schools, and churches into an area," CJ's dad said. "Maybe it won't be as bad as you think, Joanna. Of course, I can understand why you wouldn't want too many close neighbors if they're all like the Tinners."

"Well, the closest neighbor she had, she married just to get rid of the clutter on his homestead." CJ winked at his wife.

"Hah!" Joanna snorted. "And instead I got all his clutter in my own house."

"But just think," CJ countered, "you also got his super dandy rocking chair."

CJ's mother was rocking in said chair and commented, "This *is* a super dandy rocking chair. Where did you get it?"

"Ah, well. Well, actually, my employer at the lumberyard gave it to me." CJ floundered and then glared at Joanna who was hiding her smirks behind her hand. He changed the subject.

"Dad, everyone enjoyed the message you gave here Sunday. They were wondering if you could come to the Anderson's next Sunday."

"Yes, of course. I'd like that," his father replied. "CJ, you may not want to preach to your neighbors, but have you ever thought of having Bible study meetings?"

The Smiths and the Wilsons had suggested the same idea to CJ. It was a good thought. CJ didn't know why he had no enthusiasm for it.

"I never thought of that," Joanna said. "CJ, we could have it here with the dining room table all spread out. It could handle at least a dozen people. What do you think?"

"Well, it's certainly something to think about." It was lame on his part, and he knew it.

"Our church has some older Bibles we could send up, just in case someone didn't have one," CJ's mother offered.

"That's a good idea," Joanna said, and the two women immediately began to make plans on everything from coffee being served to a potluck supper along with the meeting.

CJ knew his father was watching him with questions on his mind. He managed as hearty a smile as he could muster and said, "Well, I guess that's all taken care of. Our ladies are working out the details." He also knew his father wasn't the least bit deceived by his remark.

The church in Pierre seemed bigger than CJ remembered it. It was packed on the Sunday morning his father preached there. For being a man on vacation, Reverend John Crezner had managed three Sunday sermons; one at CJ's home, one at the Anderson's home, and the final one at Pierre.

It was also a début of sorts for Deborah Lynn's first singing appearance since her baby was born. Both Drew and CJ were singing with her, although CJ's presence was under strong protest from CJ himself. He argued that he was too rusty, too rough-looking, too out-of-practice. Deborah Lynn would not be dissuaded. She wanted both men with her lest she "swayed or fainted or both".

Joanna listened to the arguments with uncharacteristic silence. When CJ appealed to her, she merely said he had to make up his own mind.

He would not, he said adamantly, sit up front on the podium. He wanted to sit with his wife, his mother, and his son. That could be arranged, Mrs. Smith said soothingly.

He would not, he said adamantly, sing the new fangled song Deborah Lynn wanted. He wasn't about to learn new lyrics, new harmony. That was understandable, Mrs. Smith said soothingly. She suggested one of their old favorites that they all knew, and Deborah Lynn concurred.

He managed to grumble a great deal about the whole affair to Joanna in private. Finally, she placed both hands on each side of his face and grabbed a handful of whiskers. "My love," she said softly, "do this for me. I want to hear you sing. In fact, I wish you would sing one verse by yourself. CJ, you have such a good voice. Your parents would enjoy hearing you. Just do it. Sing for us."

He was ashamed of himself then. He put his arms around her and kissed her. He never thought about his music being pleasing to his wife or his parents. "Since you put it that way," he muttered, still holding her, "I don't see how I can refuse."

They agreed upon the "Old Rugged Cross." Whether it was planned by some of them or just incidental, CJ took the solo part in the chorus and Deborah Lynn and Drew harmonized the echoing part. Mrs. Smith beamed and applauded when they finished rehearsing. "It's beautiful," she declared, and with the one practice, they deemed they were ready to sing at church.

Their music was, indeed, beautiful. The church had perfect acoustics, which enhanced their blended voices. The congregation loved the song and the message. The fact that Deborah Lynn had finally recovered enough to sing again made more than one of them misty eyed.

Afterward the church service, people clustered around Deborah Lynn and Drew to offer their praises and their thankfulness she was on the road to recover. They also clustered around Reverend John Crezner and told him his preaching was dynamic.

However, Mrs. Ordin sought out CJ and Joanna and John David as they stood beneath the golden beauty of the church's cottonwood tree. "Honey," she said as she tried to hug all of them, "you just plan to sing at my funeral. What a way to go to Glory Land! Make him promise, Joanna."

"You promise me I'll be an old man before you head out to Glory Land." CJ laughed while he patted her broad shoulders.

"Well, now, the whole service was good, but I loved a-hearing my boy sing. Does he sing much at home, Joanna?"

"Not enough to suit me." Joanna smiled and shifted a squirming John David to her other side.

CJ watched idly as a young man with a decided limp started walking towards them. He used a cane and his progress was measured in slow and careful steps. Recognition came swiftly to CJ as he studied the determined face.

"Mickey!" He hurried towards the slender youth. "Mickey O'Reilly! Drew told me you were back after your surgery!"

"Hey, CJ!"

"You rascal! Here you are walking after all those years of crutches!" CJ threw his arm around the thin shoulders. "Your dad told me this summer you had gone back east. How is it going?"

"Well, slow. Painful. But I'm getting there, I think." Mickey's smiling grimace probably told a truer story than his words.

CJ gave him a searching look and lowered his voice. "Was it pretty rough?"

Mickey's face flushed and he looked down. "Yeah."

"I heard it was. Feet are tender critters. I hope in the long run you'll be glad you went through all that pain and agony."

Mickey nodded. "Limping with a cane beats the heck out of hobbling on two crutches. The doctors done what they could with my club feet. They're not perfect, but the doctors told me they wouldn't be before they ever started the operation." Mickey reached out to shake CJ's hand.

"I want to thank you for all you've done for me. I heard you might sing and I told Ma this good Catholic boy was gonna go Baptist for one Sunday."

CJ clasped Mickey's hand with both of his. "I'm proud of you. You're one tough guy."

Joanna and Mrs. Ordin joined them, and Joanna handed their son to CJ. "He's ready to see his dad," she said, shaking her head and smoothing her rumpled outfit. "Good to see you're up and going,

Mickey," she added, and both her and Mrs. Ordin inquired about Mickey's surgery.

Soon Mrs. Smith and CJ's mom joined them, and more questions flowed to Mickey until CJ felt he needed to rescue the bashful lad from all the attention. He started to say something and Joanna shook her head at him.

"Let him have his moment, CJ. He's had one of the hardest summers of his life back east, and I think he can use some caring fellowship," she murmured.

CJ's parents boarded the train early the next morning. CJ wondered if saying goodbye ever became easier. He was thinking the older he got, the harder it was to see people leave.

His team trotted the better part of the first miles heading west. Now they were clipping along at a fast walk, as eager to be home as the ones in the buggy. Isaac and John David were both snoozing, and Joanna had been unusually silent all morning.

"What are you thinking about?" CJ gave her knee a gentle squeeze.

"Three things."

"Three things. Let's hear them."

She took a deep breath. "First thing. I think you married the wrong woman. Now don't get mad when I say that, CJ," she said in response to his negative muttering. "You belong in a church and with people."

"I don't want to hear this again," he said shortly.

"You said you wanted to hear what's on my mind, so now darn it, listen." She answered him just as shortly. "You looked as relaxed singing in front of that crowd as you do when you milk cows. How can you not be scared to death at singing, but even the thought of preaching seems to scare the daylights out of you?"

CJ thought for several seconds. "First of all, wife, I married the right woman," he said gruffly. "Let's get that clear right now." He looked at her with raised eyebrows. She gave him a slight smile.

"Singing is like praising God. I can praise God with all sincerity and humility, and it's natural for me." He flicked a fly off one of his horse's rump with his whip. "But preaching is like, shall we say, teaching. It's not natural for me to teach anyone. I don't think I'm qualified to try and explain the mysteries of God." He looked at her. "Does that make sense?"

"No. You've had access to hearing and reading and studying the word of God all your life. That should qualify as something."

CJ was silent. No matter what Joanna or anyone else seemed to think, he knew he was not meant to stand in the pulpit and deliver a message at this point in his life.

"You know, Joanna, after my grandparents died, I was in turmoil about what I should do about my life. All Crezners are preachers. I was ashamed I was running away from my family and faith." He had never shared these thoughts with anyone, but maybe his wife deserved to know. "When you and I came back to the homestead, I was more physically and mentally exhausted than I've ever been in my life." He looked across the prairie at the first tinges of the autumn colors. It was hard to bare his soul.

"I finally broke down one evening and begged God to tell me what He wanted me to do. There's nothing more restless than a mind going back and forth on what it *thinks* it should do and never coming to a conclusion." He cleared his throat before he continued.

"That night, for the first time in my life, I felt close to God, and I knew eventually He would guide me into what He wanted me to do. I just needed to be patient and wait. And the thought occurred to me that while I was waiting for His will I would enjoy being a homesteader."

A whirlwind rose up before them. They watched in silence as it scurried across the brown grass.

Joanna touched his arm. When he looked down at her, there were tears in her eyes.

"I—I guess we've taken care of my first thought," she said.

He sighed and asked her what the second thing on her mind pertained to.

Joanna stared straight ahead as the feather on her hat bobbed in the breeze. "Yes." Her tone was brisk. "Second matter. I love your parents. I love your mother more than my own mother, and it bothers me to be so fickle to my own flesh and blood."

CJ chuckled softly. "Everyone has always loved my mother. She's sweet, gentle, and caring. It's easy to be very fond of someone who supports you, and she is your champion supporter. I think you've never had acceptance from your own mother. I don't know why. Simon has said she was especially difficult towards you."

"Someday, CJ, when I don't have this third matter on my mind, I will tell you about living with my mother."

"Third thing. Third thing. Do you know how hard it is to say 'third thing' without lisping?"

Joanna's laughter peeled over the prairie until John David and Isaac stirred from their sleep. She waited until the boys were back in dreamland before she told him about the third thing. "We're going to have another baby. In April."

Twenty-two

May 25, 1902
Stearns, South Dakota

Dear Mom and Dad,

I'm sorry I haven't written since I sent you the brief letter announcing Theodore Simon's birth in April. I neglected to tell you then that he was born about 7:30 p.m. on April 18. I dashed off a quick note to send with our neighbor Otis Addison and seems like the days haven't quite been long enough since then to get another letter with more details written.

You wondered if Theodore was named after President Theodore Roosevelt. Yes, for several reasons. President Roosevelt seems to be a man of action and courage and one who actually had a ranch in the Dakotas, and also (and probably the main reason) the name Theodore goes well with Simon. We wanted our son named after his uncle, and his modest uncle said only if we used Simon as a middle name. Isaac calls our little man Teddy. That works for us.

There were some complications with this birth. Mrs. Anderson had almost decided we needed to get a doctor. However, she was finally able to turn Teddy into position, and after that he came quickly. Joanna has chaffed at taking longer to get back on her feet. However, both she and Teddy are gaining in strength every day, and I had instructions this morning I should get the garden plowed.

Spring roundup is gearing up, but I will only be helping on the days the crew is on Brave Bull Creek. Our cattle don't seem to stray too far away. We have fenced most of our property, but our cattle also graze the public domain. Lots of grass in this country, but we see more and more people filing for land.

Lots of talk about the fall roundup. Sounds like the government might impound illegal cattle on the Pine Ridge and Rosebud Indian Reservations. Believe the big outfits are going to gather and ship their cattle and then bid for leases the following year. I understand that one of the biggest, the Minnesota and Dakota Cattle Co. (better known as the 73 Outfit) has around thirty thousand head of cattle. They say there are about sixteen big outfits like that, so you have an idea of how many cowboys will be needed to gather so many herds in such a big area.

Thanks for the gifts for the baby and John and also for Joanna. She says she will get a letter written soon to thank you for everything.

Our love,
CJ, Joanna, John and Teddy

"Want to read this?" CJ asked Joanna. She had poured each of them a cup of coffee and was sitting across the table from him. The unsettled spring weather had turned into a light drizzle that fluctuated from rain to snow during the afternoon.

She nodded at him sleepily. She and her boys had snoozed part of the afternoon on the big feather bed in their downstairs guest room. The boys were still sleeping, but Joanna had decided she would try to perk up with caffeine.

He handed her his letter and took a sip of coffee while he watched her read. She looked up from reading and gave him a small semblance of her usual perky smile.

"I don't want you to look at me that way," she commented.

"What way was I looking at you?"

"Worried-like, like you looked when we talked about Deborah Lynn last year."

"I am worried-like."

"I'll be fine, CJ. Really. I'm getting my pep back—more every day." She nodded reassuringly at him and resumed her reading.

CJ pushed back his chair. The stoves needed wood again, and he thought as he stoked the parlor stove that keeping busy was a good alternative to worrying. When Mrs. Anderson told him they might need to get started for Pierre to fetch a doctor, his heart fell clear to the bottom of his feet. Simon took one look at him and hurried out to get the fastest horse they owned saddled and bridled. The persistent neighbor kept trying, however, and "by der grace of ord goot Lord" Teddy was turned. Joanna fainted, which Mrs. Anderson said was a blessing.

CJ's heart pounded just thinking about Joanna's suffering. He decided two boys was all the bigger their family was going to be, and Joanna agreed, which scared him even more. Joanna seldom agreed to anything that easily.

He poured them both another cup of coffee and gave her shoulder a slight squeeze. "Did you leave Teddy in bed with John when you got up?" He set the coffee pot back on the stove.

"No, silly. I put our little man in his own bed. He grunted a few times and put out a fist before he went back to sleep." She frowned slightly before she lifted her coffee cup. "If I was smart rather than lazy, I'd get him up so he would sleep tonight."

"Didn't you say once it was foolish to wake a sleeping baby?"

She looked at him with the first hint of humor in her eyes since Teddy was born. "That's right! Thanks for reminding me. Now I know I'm both smart and—and—"

"And definitely not lazy." CJ gave her a thumbs up as he sat down.

Joanna sighed. "I feel like I haven't done one blasted thing for over a month. It's aggravating as all get out."

"You can work all the rest of your life, Mrs. Crezner. For right now, you can recover and enjoy our two little boys."

"Mm. It would help if I had a maid. Deborah Lynn had her mother to help with the work."

"Do you want your mother to come and live with us for a while?"

"Good heavens! No!" Joanna sputtered and set her cup down with force. "And if you ever met her you would know better than to even suggest such a thing!"

CJ chuckled softly. The fire was back in his wife's eyes.

She glared at him a while before her look softened. "Think you're funny, don't you? You better hope and pray your wife won't become like her when she gets old."

"Joanna, when Teddy was trying to be born, I prayed a whole lot that God would allow my wife to grow old with me. I was worried I might lose both of you." CJ gave her a tender look. "You scared me, woman."

CJ thought she looked at him like a sleepy old cat looks at a dish of cream. "I know. You're a pretty great guy, Mr. Crezner. I think I'm in love with you."

"Well. I'm speechless."

A wind gust blew rain and sleet against the windows. The sound of running footsteps on the porch caused them to glance toward the entry in anticipation of Isaac bounding through the door. Instead of Isaac, however, a hesitant knock was followed by the door slowly opening. A shivering young girl stood on the threshold in threadbare and wet clothing. Her very being radiated fear, and she seemed poised to dash back out the door as if she was even more scared of them then of what she was running from.

"Hello?" CJ stood slowly, hoping he wouldn't frighten her away.

Her trembling increased and she took several deep gulps of air.

"Don't be afraid." CJ spoke softly. "We'll help you. Come on in and stand by the stove to warm up."

"No!" Her voice was shrill. "Pa's going to kill 'em with his pitchfork! We have to hurry!"

"Is your pa Zed Tinner?" Joanna asked sharply.

The girl nodded and CJ and Joanna exchanged alarmed glances.

"I'll get my horse." CJ hurriedly put on his coat and cap.

"Get Simon too, and tell Isaac to come over here." Joanna's voice sounded strained.

The bedraggled little form started to follow CJ out the door. "Wait here with Joanna," CJ spoke kindly. "She probably has a cookie or two she'll share with you. I'll pick you up when I get the horses saddled."

"Her name is Lizzie," Joanna informed him when he returned to the house to fetch their visitor. "She says Zed is drinking and got mad at the older girl for letting a horse out of the corral. Something about not feeding the horse because it kicked at him." Joanna's voice lowered to a whisper. "CJ, do you have your pistols?"

He nodded. "Promise me, Joanna, that you won't try to do outside chores while we're gone. I don't want you to get any sicker. Promise me?"

She promised. When he left with Simon and Lizzie Tinner, he could see her watching them from the kitchen window.

It was two miles over to the Tinner's place. The girl spoke only a few words to him as she clung to the back of the saddle. Joanna had persuaded her to wear an old coat of Isaac's, but he could feel her shivering in the sharp wind. All he garnered from her terse sentences was that her pa had flown into a rage at 'poor Ben and Sissy'. Apparently they tried to hide in a small stack, and Zed was determined to rout them out with a pitchfork. CJ had no idea how Lizzie was able to find their place. When he asked who sent her to them for help, she shivered even harder and said, "Ain't nobody sent me."

When they were almost to Zed's place, a hideous unhuman scream rolled in the wind and seemed to hover around them. Both horses came to an abrupt halt and CJ caught his breath in alarm. He had never heard a sound that held such terror. It came again and as they urged their nervous horses into a trot, the sound of rifle fire echoed across the prairie.

As they rode into Zed's yard, Simon pointed to a small stack. Zed Tinner sat on the ground beside it, holding his head with bloody hands. A short distance from him a young girl was sobbing hysterically beside a roan colored horse. They could see a pitchfork protruding from the animal's chest, and as they rode closer on their snorting and stiff legged horses, they could also see the animal had been shot. CJ noted the single bullet hole that pierced the white star on the horse's forehead. Whoever had killed the horse knew exactly where to aim. CJ could feel the hair on the back of his neck stand up.

Lizzie let out an ear tingling screech. "Pa killed Sissy's horse!" CJ's horse bolted and it took several seconds to settle the frightened animal down.

"Whoa boy." The authoritative voice boded no disobedience. Mrs. Tinner seemed to emerge from nowhere, and as she stood beside CJ's jittery horse, she raised her long powerful arms to take Lizzie off the saddle.

"Get into the house," she said as she set Lizzie on the ground. Lizzie flew into the tar paper shack as if demons were chasing her.

Mrs. Tinner's grey-black hair was pulled away from her face and wadded in a tight bun on top of her head. Her dirty skirt had hay and blood mixed together on it, and her work boots were muddy. He remembered well the lined face and bitter expression from their garden episode.

As he dismounted she turned to the girl beside the dead horse. She didn't yell, but her voice carried loud and clear. "Sissy, quit your bawling. Get in the house and help me with Ben."

Simon had gotten off his horse and when he heard Mrs. Tinner's command, he walked over to the sobbing girl and gently helped her up. Sissy Tinner's crying was almost a hysterical laughter. She kept making the same sound over and over again, and as Simon led her towards the house, she stumbled several times but that never interrupted her frenzied crying.

"Stop it Sissy." Mrs. Tinner's voice was cold. "It's done with. Pull yourself together."

The words acted as if icy water had been thrown on Sissy Tinner. She stopped crying and she stopped walking. Her face became contorted with anger. "I'll kill him some day! I'll take a pitchfork and slam it into his gut and watch him scream! And I'll enjoy it Ma! I'll enjoy watching him die!"

"Get in the house." Mrs. Tinner's voice never rose, in contrast to the screaming tirade of her daughter.

"Sissy!" Zed Tinner's whining voice lashed out from where he was still sitting by the stack. "It's your own fault girl! You shoulda listened to your pa, and not let your horse out. I was learning him not to kick at me!"

211

If CJ hadn't reached out to help Simon hold her, the girl would have attacked her father. She screamed at him into the increasing wind and rain and sleet. "You was starving him! He was gonna die! I hate you!" She gave CJ a wild, glazed look, and then broke away from their grasp and ran into the house repeating her hatred for her pa all the way.

"Is your boy—do you want some help with him?" CJ asked.

Mrs. Tinner's face was like a chiseled mask. "No."

Simon cleared his throat and said, "Will you be alright Mrs. Tinner? I mean, will Zed---"

Mrs. Tinner interrupted brusquely. "The day I can't handle Zed Tinner will be the day I'm six foot under the ground." She turned to go back into the house and her dismissal of them was obvious.

Simon and CJ looked at each other in astonishment. There seemed to be nothing more for them to do but remount and leave.

The skittish horses broke into a trot as they rode past Zed. He raised his fist at them and yelled, "You keep those cattle away from us, do you hear me?"

Sweat trickled down CJ's back as he pitched hay from windrows onto the hayrack. Mid-June had brought sweltering days of humid air and swarms of mosquitoes. Their constant whine was followed by muttered cursing and swats from Simon and him as they continued across the creek bottom on each side of the lowered rack. Isaac was on the broad back of one of the work horses to guide them with gentle urgings. He had given up trying to kill mosquitoes on himself and concentrated on keeping the pesky insects off the horses' necks.

Neither man spoke as they trudged along. It was a hot, demanding work, and they'd been going since sunrise. Added to the misery of the whole affair was the constant concern of rattlesnakes coiled under the hay. Twice already they had heard the buzz of the snake's rattle above the droning of the mosquitoes. Pitchforks weren't the best weapon to kill snakes with, so they each carried a rope with a piece of metal ensconced in the knotted end. It was effective, but slightly cumbersome to carry.

There was no breeze. Where, CJ fumed, was the South Dakota wind when you needed it? Only one row left and they would be finished with this hay meadow.

"Boy howdy!" Simon erupted, and the hay he meant to pitch into the wagon was hurled in all different directions. There were two rattlesnakes coiled only feet away from Simon and their rattles quivered with indignation.

Simon had taken several backward steps and was frantically reaching for his rope. CJ raced over and tried to stab the largest one with his pitchfork. Instantly, the repulsive reptile struck, its tongue darting in and out with rage. Even though the handle on the pitchfork was long, the distance between CJ and the snake seemed much too close. The tines of the fork had gone through part of the snake. CJ dropped the handle and found his own rope. With a few savage whacks on the ugly head, the snake was stunned, and several more hits killed the thing.

Simon was tangled in his rope. The faster he backed away, the more entangled he became. CJ was as vicious with the second snake as he was with the first one; and when both reptiles were slithering in death, he looked up to discover Simon lying on the ground.

"Well." It was all CJ had energy to say.

"Isaac! Stay on the horse!" Simon yelled from his prone position.

CJ turned to see the undecided boy ready to bail off his perch to come and help.

"Just stay there," Simon ordered and slowly got off the ground. "I'll tell you what, CJ, anyone that would give up preaching to get in on all this misery must have a loose screw," he muttered as he hunted for his fork. "Snakes, bugs, heat, and the likes of Zed Tinner—worst country in the world. Only thing that's left is a hail storm. That would be the last straw."

CJ looked uneasily at the western sky. He thought the weather seemed ripe for any kind of major storm.

"Let's finish this last row. It'll be time to quit then, anyway," CJ suggested and stood on the biggest snake's head while he pulled the tines of his fork away from the still quivering body. While he was doing that, he decided to cut off the rattlers. There were thirteen buttons on the rattle. CJ walked over to the team and handed the rattles to Isaac. "May as well add this to your collection."

"It's the biggest one ever!" Isaac grinned and put the rattles in his shirt pocket.

"I ain't cutting the rattles off this one," Simon said as he gathered up the loose hay he had scattered. "I can't stand to get that close to the blasted things."

CJ looked at his brother-in-law for several seconds. "And when did 'boy howdy' come into your conversation?" he finally asked. "Come to think about it, what happened to 'by jingles'? I haven't heard that for a long time."

Simon leaned against his pitchfork and grimaced in CJ's direction. "I read in the Good Book that our 'yes' and our 'no' should be said without an oath. I decided maybe 'by jingles' might be thought of as swearing. What do you say about that?"

CJ started laughing as he gathered up hay in the windrow to toss into the wagon. "I say I'm hot and tired and dirty and bit up, and I'll think about it later!"

Simon grinned and suddenly it seemed as if the work was easier. They finished up the last row and headed towards the stack. In no time, they had pulled the hay off the hayrack, and with Isaac still guiding the gentle team, they rode home on the wagon.

It was late by the time they milked the cows and shut up the chickens. All the while they swatted mosquitoes and wiped sweat off their faces. The air wasn't cooling down for evening. CJ surmised it would be miserably hot in the house and hoped Joanna hadn't started the kitchen range to cook anything.

Isaac's face was puffy from the bites he endured all day. CJ was sure his and Simon's were the same. They started wearily towards the house when Simon gave a low whistle.

"Look at that!" he said, pointing to the west. A low bank of swirling dark clouds was moving towards them at a furious pace. Lightning bolts were sharp, and the low rumble of thunder could be heard.

"I'm gonna shut windows," Simon said, hurrying towards his house. Isaac and CJ watched the storm come closer and CJ was amazed at the high rate of speed it traveled. Suddenly, a crack of lightning slashed through the sky and almost instantly thunder boomed around them. CJ and Isaac forgot their exhaustion and sprinted into the house. Joanna looked at them in amusement as they came bursting into the kitchen.

"You must have thought you gazed at the sky long enough," she said. "I wondered if you were going to stand there and let it rain on you."

"Funny. What windows are open?" CJ started towards the living room to close the front door.

"All of them. Isaac, run upstairs and—" Lightning cracked and thunder rumbled before she could finish.

Isaac raced upstairs while Joanna hurried to shut the windows in the guest bedroom where Teddy was lying in his crib.

An eerie darkness suddenly descended, and the wind CJ had wished for earlier in the day came howling across the prairie like a banshee witch.

"Joanna," he hollered, "where's John?"

"Playing in the living room," she said as she hurriedly left the bedroom and headed towards the laundry room to shut those windows.

"No, he's not," CJ said sharply.

Joanna's face paled as she turned to look at him. "He has to be! He was there minutes before you came in!"

Without a word, they each searched the nooks and crannies John played in. Joanna repeated several times "he has to be here, he couldn't be outside." Pelting hail stones were hitting the windows and bouncing onto the grass.

The noise was so loud they didn't hear Isaac coming down the stairs. "Guess where I found this guy?" he said, holding a frightened John David in his arms.

Joanna gave a smothered cry and reached for her toddler. She hugged him tightly and John started to cry.

Isaac looked questioningly at CJ.

"We couldn't find him," CJ said, putting one arm around Isaac to give him a quick hug. "I was about ready to look for him outside. And where would I start?"

Joanna suddenly remembered the open windows in the laundry room. CJ made haste to attend to that matter and spent considerable time getting rags to mop water from the rain that had poured in before he closed the windows. It was too dark outside to see what damage the hail was doing to the crops and the garden. A faint light from Simon's house glimmered through the downpour of rain and hail. He thought Simon was probably grumbling about this horrid ending to an equally horrid day.

By the time he returned to the kitchen, Joanna had lighted the lamp, and their supper was on the table. Isaac was looking hungrily at the sandwiches, and John was firmly tied in his high chair.

"Where did you find him, Isaac?" CJ pulled out Joanna's chair for her. Isaac grinned. "Under your bed. I was shutting windows in your bedroom and heard something. I thought maybe Burr had sneaked in and Joanna didn't know it."

Joanna shook her head at her little boy as she sat down. "And how, I'd like to know, did this kid crawl up all those stairs and me not know it? I need eyes in the back of my head to keep track of him. Scared me half to death, and it scares me even more to think of him falling down those steps."

CJ sat down beside his son and ruffled his downy hair. He was rewarded with a toothy grin from John. "I was scared to death he got outside. That would have been terrible. I wonder if you won't have to start locking doors, Joanna."

"Let's say grace," she said, and as usual, CJ prayed.

"I did have the front door locked. I knew he didn't get outside that way," she continued after the prayer. "And if he had gone out the back door and on the porch, you would have seen him." She sighed. "But those steps, CJ. You'll have to build some kind of gate there. And I hate to mention this, but you two guys really smell bad."

Isaac's mouth was full but he nodded his head in agreement. CJ scowled slightly. He had a feeling Joanna would want him to start the stove in the laundry room to heat water, which meant she intended him to use the big cast iron tub to take a bath, which meant dipping out water and cleaning it up afterwards. The fact of the matter was he had forgotten to even wash his hands.

"I'm wondering how the roundup crew is faring," he said, hoping to divert what he surmised was on her mind. "It'll be hard to hold the cattle in this wind, and with the hail, even the horses might get away."

Joanna raised her eyebrow at him and smiled. "Do you wish you were there?"

"Well, truthfully, no."

"Good. After supper, you can start the stove in the laundry room."

Isaac reached for another meat sandwich. "I should have run home with Dad, but I don't think we have much for supper there."

The rain continued to beat against the house, but at least it had stopped hailing. Before they finished eating their supper, the storm left as suddenly as it came. When they reopened the windows, the world smelled fresh and the temperature had pleasantly cooled.

Isaac and CJ dawdled as long as they could eating supper, helping Joanna clear the table and even offering to put John David to bed.

"Go!" She laughed at their dismayed faces. "Get the fire started to heat the water! You smell so bad I can't endure either one of you any longer!"

CJ and Isaac grumbled as they poured water into the tub. "You first, Isaac," CJ muttered as he added the boiling water.

"Wished I'd run home with Dad," Isaac said again.

The garden definitely suffered from the hail. However, the rain would probably perk it up in a few days CJ mused as he pulled broken vines away the next morning.

It had rained a good solid inch, and mosquitoes were hungrier than ever. The upside, Simon said, was the moisture would sure make grass and crops grow.

Several riders came through later in the day looking for cattle and horses. They told about hail the size of hen's eggs and wind and rain that scattered cattle and horses for miles. They said their wagon boss, Tom Jones, tried to hold the herd, but when the other roundup crews had cattle scattering in all directions, Tom had to let his go too.

It blew their cooking supplies and tents everywhere, and the cook ended up sitting in the rain with a cast iron kettle over his head for protection from the hail. They laughed a little at that, but CJ could see it had been a grueling night for all the roundup crews.

Joanna brought coffee and sandwiches onto the porch, and the riders quickly dismounted. In a very short time, she had an empty platter and profuse and sincere thanks from the cowboys as they finished drinking her coffee.

"This is a little different from what we got at the Tinner place," one of the riders said. "Old Zed is always whining about our cattle on his land. The old coot had those two older kids file claims right beside his, and I know they ain't legally old enough to do that."

Another rider joined in the conversation. "Yeah, now he's got a section of land, 'cause him and his wife both filed. He won't fence it out, and he seems to think it's our duty to keep cattle off from it. I hear his boy almost lost his arm because of something old Zed did to him. You folks know anything about that?"

CJ and Simon briefly told them what they had seen, but neither of them knew the extent of the Tinner boy's wounds.

"They're trouble. Nothing but trouble. I ain't so sure Zed's wife is any better than he is. I hear she's a wicked shot with her rifle. I sure hope more of the likes of them don't settle here." The rider started towards his horse to remount. "Good neighbors are great, but ones like the Tinners we can do without."

"Oh, by the way," one of them said after they were mounted and ready to continue their hunt, "someone said Smokey Stearns had a fire at his place on Bad River. Burned his house, no one seems to know what caused it. It's a strange deal." CJ started to ask questions but the cowboy shrugged and said that's all he knew.

"I wonder if he meant lightning started it or what," CJ mused as he watched the riders trot towards the creek.

"Well, who would know," Joanna said, balancing cups and platter as she opened the door. "CJ, maybe you could get the little gate built for the stairway since you can't work in the fields today."

"Were you ever at Smokey's house?" CJ wondered as he followed her into the kitchen.

Joanna set the dishes down with a bang and gave him a disgusted look. "Of course not." She shook her head. "Why do you even ask me that?"

"Because it was a nice log house. I thought maybe he would have shown it to you since he claims he wanted to marry you."

"Oh horsefeathers, CJ!" Joanna picked up a dish towel and swatted him with it. "Go measure the stairway so you can get the gate built."

CJ grinned at her. "Just asking, just asking. Where's a measure at?"

While he was writing down measurements and figuring out how to go about building a gate, he thought about Smokey and his ranch on Bad River. It was a picturesque place, no doubt someone would come along and take it off his hands if he wanted to sell it. He also thought of the Tinners. If Zed Tinner would stab his own son, and kill his daughter's horse, what might he do to the rest of them?

Twenty-three

October 8, 1904
Stearns, South Dakota

Dear Mom and Dad,

As usual, after you leave, we all feel a bit bereft. I can't begin to tell you how much we enjoy your visits here. We see the changes in the countryside on a daily basis, but when you come and see the changes from year to year it makes us realize how fast the homesteaders are moving in. And they tell us it will get even more hectic when the trains go through.

I wouldn't be surprised if next year when you come, the train will be quite a bit closer than Pierre. I guess that has good and bad consequences. We will be more connected to the world, but there will be a great deal more of the world at our doorstep.

Wanted to tell you what Joanna overheard while John and Teddy were playing one day. John has decided he will be a preacher like "Grandbob." He practices all the time, and Teddy is supposed to be his congregation. Teddy must have decided John's sermon was overlong and begin to sputter and play with his wooden spools. To add insult to injury, he got off his chair and started to head outside. John put his hands on his hips and ordered him back to his chair, to which Teddy replied, "You talk-talk-talk. I go now." Guess that's playtime for almost-three- and almost-four-year-olds.

As you mentioned several times when you were here, Isaac is growing up fast. Twelve years old this fall, and he works like a man. Sometimes we forget he is still just a young boy, and I want to thank both of you for reminding us of that. He enjoyed going to the softball game at Midland with the two of you. It was a good chance for him to meet and enjoy young kids his age. He always has been dependable, but he needs to be a kid once in a while.

I think we were all surprised to learn that Drew and Deborah Lynn and little Grace were planning on heading to Missouri this winter to be with Deborah's aunt Coramae. You will enjoy having them close to you. Maybe Drew can fill in for you some Sundays and give you a much-needed rest. I feel guilty when you come here and preach several times. Your inspirational messages refresh all our souls, but I'm afraid they drain you somewhat, and hopefully next year when you come, we can keep it down to one message.

Beautiful day here in South Dakota. I better get to work. Joanna has been ironing for an hour already.

Take care, both of you, and God bless.

CJ, Joanna, John, and Teddy

CJ reread his letter on the porch while his two sons tumbled and played at his feet. The fresh October breeze was a breath from heaven. He made up his mind to enjoy the day to the fullest.

"Joanna," he hollered as he went back inside, "do you want to read the letter to the folks?"

"No. I'm busy ironing."

He stuck his head in the laundry room and saw her laboring on a little white shirt. When she was done, it would be ironed to perfection. A waste of time in CJ's mind, as little boys usually played hard and rough and the perfect little shirt would be wrinkled in a matter of minutes.

"I have an idea." He walked into her laundry domain. "Why don't you and I and the boys take the buggy and meander down to Stearns? I want to mail some letters and you said you needed some supplies."

She looked up with exasperation. "Today is Tuesday, Mr. Crezner. Today I iron. And with six of us on this place and some extra besides, I have no time to meander with you."

"It's a rare and beautiful day, Mrs. Crezner. One of South Dakota's finest, and if tomorrow never comes, you will have spent this last day cooped up in your laundry room and not enjoying God's gift."

"Horsefeathers." She renewed her attack on the little shirt and he could see the light of battle gleaming in her eyes.

CJ had learned several battle tactics himself in the first five years of their marriage. The first lesson, he knew, was not to argue with this strong-willed woman.

"Well, I'll take the boys and get the buggy ready." He ran a finger down her flushed cheek. "I really would enjoy having you come, Joanna. If you change your mind, we'll wait for you."

Even though it was early morning, John and Teddy were fed, clothed, and were playing on the porch with Burr and Ruby supervising. They were always excited to go anywhere. CJ found caps and jackets and shoes to put on their wiggly bodies, and soon the three of them headed towards the barn.

The boys sat in the buggy while CJ hitched the team up. When Isaac came from the chicken house, they reminded CJ of magpies crowing for attention. Isaac was invited on the little jaunt, and unlike Joanna, he decided the rest of his chores could wait for another day.

Simon waved aside the invitation. His mind was on a new piece of equipment he wanted to buy and he was on a mission to find out more about it.

CJ took his time, purposely. When he finally pulled the team up to the house, Joanna marched down the steps with her new plumed hat setting grandly on her braided hair. She fussed over the boys' and Isaac's appearance before she handed CJ a wicker basket.

Without a word, CJ took the basket and handed it over to Isaac and the boys in the backseat of the buggy. Then he held out his hand to assist Joanna onto the seat beside him, but she remembered she had meant to bring along some blankets in case the weather was chillier on the ride back.

Finally, after two more trips back to the house to get different articles she thought they needed, she was in the buggy and they were ready to begin, as Joanna grumbled, to "meander."

The team needed no encouragement to trot in the brisk air. As they crested the hill south of the homestead, the panorama of fall spread before them in shades of golds and browns, with the circus of red leaves punctuating the scene in colorful abandonment. Joanna murmured "beautiful" several times.

When they reached the flat where the east fork of Brave Bull Creek started, CJ stopped the team. Joanna looked at him questioningly.

"I'm told this is where the railroad is thinking of putting in a dam so they have water for their steam engines. I suppose if the dam is here, they'll be plotting out a town. There's already some homestead claims here."

Joanna gazed at the open prairie with a slight frown. "Are you saying I better take a good look because in a couple of years it will be wrecked with homesteaders?"

"Well, maybe wrecked isn't the word I'd use, but the promoters for the railroads are building this land up to be a utopia for farmers. I think we'll see lots of shanties here."

He clicked his tongue at the team and they were on their way again.

"It wouldn't be so bad," Joanna groused, 'if the government would let them homestead a section rather than a quarter. They could probably make it on that much land in this country and there wouldn't be shacks everywhere."

"I know. I'm glad I bought the quarter to square up our place to make it a section. At least we won't have people right beside us."

A small ruckus was developing in the backseat of the buggy between the younger boys. Joanna squelched it in no uncertain terms. CJ raised his eyebrow at her in amusement and was rewarded with a light tap on his knee. "It's a good thing I don't spoil them like you do," she said with a slight smile.

"I think you let them get away with quite a bit when I'm not around." He chuckled. "You just don't want me to think you're softhearted."

She surprised him. Instead of saying "horsefeathers" like he thought she would, she slid closer to him and put her hand on his arm. "Don't tell anyone I'm really a nice person underneath all this bark. I don't want to blow my image."

"It will be our secret, Mrs. Crezner."

The cottonwoods along White River were adorned in a breathtaking variety of rich colors. Joanna told the boys to notice all the different shades and impressed upon them a sight like this was rare and wonderful. Stearns came into view, and the American flag waving in front of the post office under the blue sky was almost as breathtaking to CJ as the colorful cottonwoods.

CJ guided his team to a grassy area near the stores. His gentle horses could graze while they shopped and visited.

He helped Joanna step down from the buggy and then lifted his two sons out. Isaac took a flying leap and looked about excitedly. Isaac's main joy in coming to Stearns was the cable crossing that hung over the white water of the river. It had an attached basket to it, and when the river was high, folks sat in the basket and pulled themselves across. More than one person got drenched when the basket hovered too close to the water. Isaac often begged CJ or Simon to let him ride the basket back and forth just for fun.

The post office was first on their list. Joanna marched ahead, holding John's little hand. CJ carried Teddy into the crowded little building, and they were greeted by one of the Thode brothers. After congenial bantering, CJ asked about Smokey and his father.

"I think they decided to start a store in Fort Pierre or Pierre, ain't sure which. The folks who took over Smokey's relinquishment on Bad River was through here in August," Mr. Thode said. "Seem like nice folks. The lady was a little upset about her piano. Guess it fell off the wagon when they were crossing the railroad tracks at Chamberlain."

Joanna's eyes widened. "How bad was it hurt?"

"Wasn't hurt at all. It was all crated up. They've got five kids, looks like from about eighteen years old to a little girl about a year old."

"I hated to hear the log house burned. It was a nice one." CJ set the squirming Teddy on the wood floor. "Did they get another house built?"

"Naw. Someone stole the logs that were there. Don't know what they'll do. I guess there's a dugout along Bad River that they might live in until something else gets built."

Joanna shuddered. "Five kids in a dugout. Doesn't sound like fun to me." She turned to CJ. "I think I'll head over to the store and see if I can find what I need." She glanced at her sons, who were preoccupied with a mother cat and her kittens, and left with instructions for CJ to watch them while she shopped.

By the time Joanna was finished and CJ and the boys had made the rounds of places to visit, it was noon. They took the wicker basket with goodies from Joanna's kitchen and settled under a cottonwood tree to have a light lunch before they headed home. The river was shallow at the crossing, and after they ate, Isaac and the boys puddled in the ripples. They came back with white mud crusted on their feet and wrigglers in their hands.

CJ felt a wave of nostalgia as they headed away from the little settlement. Obviously the train would bypass it, and in a few years, who would ever remember there was such a place as Stearns? In fact, he thought, as the team started trotting up the hill to the flat above, who would ever remember the roundups and the way it was before it became settled?

"What is that noise?" Joanna broke into his thoughts.

"What noise?"

"I'm hearing—something. It sounds like a kitten."

"Can't be."

"Can too be! CJ, stop this buggy. I hear a cat!"

"Well, I can't stop the team while they're going up this hill. We'll stop when I get to the top." CJ flicked his whip lightly over the horses' backs.

There was complete silence in the back of the buggy. Joanna turned to scrutinize three young faces and then shifted her gaze to CJ.

He knew she was gathering information in her mind, and he knew what the verdict would be.

"I think all four of you are guilty."

CJ grinned.

"CJ, you know I hate cats."

"So do mice, and we have scads of them in the barn and granaries."

"They'll be at the door all the time. Wanting in. Wanting fed. Wanting something. A cat is never satisfied. I detest the things!" Joanna glared over her shoulder at the boys. "How many of the blasted things do you have in that box?"

Teddy held up two chubby fingers.

"Two. Great. At least they'll keep each other company." Joanna shook her head and settled more comfortably in the buggy seat. "I should be mad as all get out. But I had such a good time with you and your meanderings I'll save my mad until another time."

CJ put the reins in one hand and reached over to hug her with his free arm. "That's my girl. When you feel grumpy, you can use these kittens to be really mad at us."

She flashed him an impish smile. "Good idea!"

They rode in companionable silence for a while before she said, "I hope you got the little tabby one. It was the cutest."

"One tabby, one black."

Isaac cleared his throat. "I thought we could call them Midnight and Tulip."

Joanna gave him a startled look. "Tulip? That's a crazy name. Why Tulip?"

"Because I remember the tulips Mom used to have. Remember how we all enjoyed 'em?"

Joanna didn't say anything for a while. Finally, she turned again to look at Isaac and said with a wistful smile, "I remember. They were beautiful." Another silence then she added, "The tabby will be Tulip."

Twenty-four

May 30, 1905
Stearns, South Dakota

Dear Mom and Dad,

We enjoyed your letter and news. Sounds like Drew and Deborah and little Grace have settled nicely in Deborah's aunt Coramae's house. It's good that you get to see them often, and I imagine little Grace is enjoying having you folks as substitute grandparents! It's too bad Drew and my cousin Kentworth can't see eye to eye on doctrine, and I hope even if they disagree they can still remain friends.

We are just recovering from a spring blizzard that hit after several days of rain. The snow came after the rain, and it became a terrible mess, as there was mud underneath all the snow. The cattle drifted south quite a ways, hit homesteaders' fences and broke them, and they tell us farther west, the cattle drifted over what they call the badland wall. It's where the prairie drops abruptly to meet badlands. We lost some calves, but we were able to bring the cattle in close to home when it first started snowing. Simon and I worked in the wet and cold until we thought we both were going to freeze to death. However, we did manage to get the cattle fed and in a sheltered part of the creek.

A note about the Tinners here. Their cattle drifted on past our place and most of them ended up drowning in the White River. Ben Tinner tried to keep them contained, but the cattle got away from him. His arm that his dad pierced with a pitchfork three years ago never has healed right, and he basically has no feeling in it. He didn't realize while he was working with the cattle that his arm was slowly freezing. I'm afraid now it will have to be amputated. Sissy, the older sister, left home this spring. No one seems to know where she is. Zed hates all his neighbors, and seems to hold us responsible for his problems. We watch him with a wary eye.

Simon caught a terrible cold. Joanna made him and Isaac come over here and stay so she could take better care of him. During the blizzard, Isaac had numerous school lessons from Joanna, and she even started teaching John letters. He can write his name, which pleases him greatly. He immediately desired Teddy to learn to write his name, but Teddy decided he and Tulip, the cat, should play taxi. Which means Tulip is plopped into Teddy's wagon and taken to different destinations around the house. I don't know what the taxi fare is for Tulip, but Joanna discovered both Teddy and Tulip lapping milk out of the same dish, so maybe that took care of Tulip's debt.

Some of the cattle in this area have scabies, which is an infectious mite that burrows under their skins and causes severe itching. The cattle are thin, and of course, this wet and cold weather has really been hard on them. Several ranchers are going together to build a dipping vat, and guess it will be close to Midland. I'll take our cattle there when it gets going. Hopefully it will help control the disease.

Greet the Wilsons for us. Hope Drew gets the pastorate he wants, and in the meantime, it's a break for you to have him preach at your church.

Love and blessings,
CJ, Joanna, John, and Teddy

CJ watched as Joanna folded his letter and placed it inside the envelope. "You write good letters, CJ," she said. "There's really nothing for me to add, but I jotted down a few things on another piece of paper." She gave a deep sigh. "It makes me sick to think of Ben Tinner getting his arm amputated. I heard someone asked his mom about him, and she basically told them it was none of their business. Strange people." She brushed Tulip off her lap before she stood.

CJ and Simon exchanged smiles across the dining room table as Tulip sashayed to his favorite chair and gracefully leaped onto the cushion.

"He rules the roost," Simon's voice was still husky from the cold he was battling.

CJ nodded and reached for another oatmeal cookie. Outside work was put on hold as the moisture from the rain and melting snow made the entire yard a bottomless mud puddle. He and Isaac had spent the greater part of the morning in the barn oiling harnesses. When that job was finished, he had waded in mud back to the house for hot coffee and some of Joanna's cookies.

"Hey, hey, where are you boys going?" He asked as John and Teddy headed towards the kitchen door.

"Outside to play with Burr," John explained, and Teddy nodded agreement.

Joanna put a quick stop to that notion.

"What is all over outside?" She asked her boys, and they knew it was a trick question. Teddy tilted his head to one side and studied his mother, but neither boy said anything. "Water. Water and mud. You would get stuck in gumbo and probably drown in water." She put her hand on her hip, a sure sign she would not be dissuaded. "You can play inside with Tulip."

John, ever easygoing, shrugged his shoulders and started towards Tulip's chair. Teddy, however, was not going to give up without an argument.

"Isaac's outside. I go too."

"Isaac," Joanna said and reached down to propel her three-year-old in the same direction his five-year-old brother was heading, "is twelve, and knows enough to stay out of the mud."

"I know too," Teddy grumbled and marched over to his dad. CJ picked him up and sat his unhappy son on his lap.

"You can have a cookie with Dad," he said, ruffling Teddy's hair. Teddy leaned against him and gave an exasperated kick to show his displeasure.

Joanna sat down in her chair with frown lines puckering her forehead. "Isaac will be thirteen this fall." She sighed and looked at

Simon, "I wish he could go to a regular school and be with kids his own age."

"I know," Simon said, taking another sip of coffee. "Both Ordins and Smiths have offered to keep him in Pierre if I want to send him to school there." Simon hunched his back and coughed. "I've asked him if he wanted to go, and he said no."

CJ was surprised at this news, and from the look on Joanna's face, he gathered she also was.

"I didn't know anything about that," Joanna murmured as she placed her letter along with CJ's in an envelope.

"Isaac and I have talked about it a great deal. Maybe another fall, but I don't think this year we'll tackle that problem." Simon shook his head. "I know this sounds selfish, but I sure would miss him if he left this soon."

"We all would," CJ said and gave his little man a hug. "Isaac is an import part of our family."

❧

"It either rains continually, or else the wind blows forever, or else it's dry and hot in this country," CJ grumbled to Simon as they scooped mud away from their buried wagon.

Simon grunted and threw another shovelful of heavy gumbo mud. "Don't forget blizzards and rattlesnakes and Zed Tinner," he said, and neither man found any humor about the situation.

The last of June had given the area one cool rainy day after another. The water in Brave Bull Creek was higher than CJ or Simon could ever remember it being, and the rain continued.

"If we ever get this wagon loose, let's put it in the barn and leave it there until the middle of August," CJ said, tackling the mud around the back wheels.

"If it wasn't so close to the creek, I'd say to leave it right now. Boy howdy, I'm afraid if we don't get it out, it'll be going downstream." Simon looked worriedly at the rising water.

They finally had the wheels dug out, and once again the work team struggled to pull the wagon up to a drier ground. CJ put his shoulder against the back of the wagon and pushed with all his might. He could feel the almost imperceptible release from grasping gumbo as it moved slowly out of the mire. Simon kept the team working until the heavy wagon finally pulled loose from the bog. Once it started moving, Simon never looked back until he had the team and wagon in the barn.

CJ waded through mud; every step increased the size of clinging gumbo to his overshoes. Several times he stopped and tried to kick loose the additional layers of mud. When he reached the road to the barn, he rubbed his feet together to slide the worst of the mud away.

It was beginning to rain again, and after the horses were rubbed down and the harnesses cleaned, the men trudged towards the house.

"Simon, do you think your house is in any danger from the water?" CJ asked, noting with alarm the water was considerably higher.

"I don't think so." Simon looked at the rushing water and frowned. "Maybe Isaac and I will move some things up high. Just in case."

"I'll help," CJ said.

It didn't take long for the three of them to stack items on top of the table and counters. Books were pulled out of the lower shelves of the bookcase, bedding was stripped off the beds, and soon the tidy little house looked jumbled and disorderly.

Even though they hurried, the water was closer to the house when they finished. They quickly shut the door and began the slippery journey to CJ's house. The rain had diminished to a light drizzle as they walked and slid in the lengthening twilight.

By morning, Brave Bull Creek was roaring inches from Simon's house. Hay bottoms were flooded, the lower back corrals were flooded, and still the drizzle continued and added more moisture to an already sodden ground.

Joanna paced nervously from one window to another. Her garden was under water, the current pulled and tugged at the young plants. Rabbits huddled on tiny islands made by the flood waters and were in danger of being washed downstream.

CJ worried about their neighbors who lived close to Brave Bull. He began thinking about others he knew that lived along Bad River. If the usual placid Brave Bull was this high, what were other creeks doing? He could picture all sorts of scenarios, and each one became more nerve-wracking.

231

"Daddy," John tapped his leg. "Uncle Simon told me to tell you it was Sunday, and maybe you could read us a Bible story."

CJ looked into the living room and saw Simon in the old rocking chair with Teddy on his lap. In a drenched world, Simon remained an oasis of calm.

"Joanna," CJ said as his wife stared bleakly out the kitchen window, "it's Sunday. The first of July. Let's read from the Bible."

She turned and nodded. "But not about Noah and the flood."

Simon chuckled. "Nor about the foolish man who built on the sand and the rains came down."

Joanna gave CJ the Bible and settled onto the wing chair with John tucked in beside her.

After CJ added another piece of wood to the stove, he sat on the horsehair sofa and opened the Bible. "I think we should pray first," he said and bowed his head.

"Our Heavenly Father, we are worried about our friends and neighbors. We lift them up to You. Protect them from the rising waters, keep them safe. We know while others are cold and hungry and in danger, we sit comfortably in a warm house. We are unable to help anyone, but we pray for all of them. Wrap Your arms of love around all of them and guide and direct them to safety. In Jesus' name we pray, amen."

"Amen," Simon echoed.

Joanna's hand flew to her mouth. "Oh my sakes! I've been so worried about my garden I never thought about people downstream." She shook her head and pursed her lips. "When you get done reading, CJ, I'll get busy baking. If they've had their homes flooded, they'll need food, maybe some blankets, maybe—" She lapsed into silence. CJ knew her mind was intent on what else she could do.

"Well, let's read about a young boy who had a coat of many colors."

Isaac was sprawled on the rag rug and gave CJ a lopsided grin. "I like that one." He reached for one of Joanna's fancy stitched pillows to put under his head while he listened.

As soon as the floodwater started receding, CJ and Isaac loaded baked goods onto their horses and started downstream to see how their neighbors fared. They saw parts of haystacks lodged high in the cottonwood trees, dead carcasses caught in debris, and wire and posts and trees were snagged everywhere.

Water had crept into the new log home of the Andersons, and the whole family was shoveling out mud and debris. Farther down Brave Bull Creek, Clara Jones and her three children had spent part of the time in a small and leaking building. Their log home also had water in it. Plus, she told CJ, the cistern had mud in it, and the cellar with their food supply had caved in.

CJ and Isaac helped where they could, and Joanna's food was appreciated. It was mid afternoon when they reached Bad River. They could hear the roar of water before they saw it, and when CJ and Isaac crested the high bank and looked down at the angry swirling water, he realized everything Joker had told him about Bad River was true. Whirlpools danced in all directions as the water thundered past.

Isaac backed his horse farther away from the bank. "This is scary," he muttered.

CJ nodded, and even though he was well away from the edge, he pulled back also. Never had he seen such tumultuous waters.

The dipping vats and corrals were on a river bottom on the north side. It would be a while before they would be functioning again, and from the looks of the volume of water going through, it would also be a while before it was safe to cross Bad River.

"Good thing White Man put his teepee on high ground."

CJ and Isaac jerked in surprise and swiveled in their saddles to see who was speaking. The noise of the water had prevented them from hearing the lone rider coming from behind them.

"Joker!" CJ put out his hand to shake the other man's and found Joker's grip was as strong as ever. "You said this river was bad. It lives up to its name."

"Mm. It kill more cowboys. One crossing Jack Dailey Creek." Joker pointed to the north. "Maybe three over there." He pointed west and shrugged. "Who knows how much more."

CJ shook his head. "You can't help wondering when you see the power of it." CJ paused reflectively, and then he added, "How did you know about those men?"

Joker looked at him expressionlessly. "Smoke signals."

"Right." CJ gave him a skeptical grin. He dug in his saddlebag and found three smashed sandwiches. Isaac took his gratefully. It had been hours since breakfast. Joker took his and ate in silence.

"Haven't seen you for a while," CJ said in between bites. "Life treating you okay?"

"No."

"Are you married yet?"

Joker nodded his head and held up two fingers.

CJ looked at him in disbelief. "You have two wives?"

"Two kids."

"What's their names?"

"Boy is Ace. Goes good with Joker. Girl is Little Sparrow, I name her that. My woman is from the north. She's Cheyenne. I'm Sioux." Joker sighed. "We wear war bonnet all the time."

"Does she tell you out-out-out?"

Joker's stoic look crumbled and he started grinning. "No, your squaw says that."

They exchanged a few more tidbits of information, and CJ finally decided they should start for home.

As they rode away, CJ turned to look back and saw Joker sitting motionless on his horse watching them. Joker made a sweeping motion with his hand. "Out, out, out!" he yipped and started his horse trotting west. "Out, out, out!"

CJ started laughing and urged his own horse into a slippery trot. Isaac followed with a puzzled look on his face.

☙

An acrid smell hung heavily in the air when CJ and his neighbors brought their cattle to the dipping vat several weeks later. They were the last to go through, and one by one each cow and calf were pushed into the trough of warm water mixed with sulphur, lime, and Black

Leaf 40, a nicotine mixture. The cowboys closest to the vats were about as drenched as the cattle.

"Guess we're out of a job now, Art," one of the cowboys said to his companion as the last critter waded out.

"Where are you from?" CJ asked the one named Art.

"Burt, Iowa. Me and Howard just graduated from high school this spring and thought we'd see the wild west."

"Well. What do you think of the wild west so far?"

"I can tell you this river gets spooky! We hunted all day in the rain for Arthur Austin when he disappeared in Jack Dailey Creek. Poor devil. His horse just couldn't swim against the current. Then we spent that night out in the rain 'cause our cook shack was going underwater from Bad River. That was pretty wild." Art grinned. "But I like it here. Maybe I'll be back someday and homestead."

"Did they ever find Austin's body?" CJ asked.

Art immediately became somber. "Yeah, four days later. Face down in the creek. And then there were the four guys farther upstream. That was bad. They were trying to cross a swale to get to higher ground, but the current took their horses right out from under 'em. One grabbed his horse's tail and finally managed to grab a cottonwood tree branch. He spent thirty-some hours in that tree."

"I heard the other three didn't make it," CJ said, shaking his head.

"No, guess they buried them on a bluff above Bad River. Ed Cook, Fred Trumbo, and Perry Rifenberg. Sure hard on Perry's brother, Albert. He's the only one that made it. Dang wonder he didn't catch pneumonia hangin' out in that tree so long."

"I'd imagine those hours were the longest of his life." CJ put out his hand. "Nice meeting you. Hope you have a good trip back to Iowa."

The young man gave him a hearty handshake and turned his horse back to the corrals. CJ and his neighbors gathered the wet and bawling cattle and headed them in a southerly direction to take them back to home pastures.

Along the way, they commented on the tar paper shacks springing up like mushrooms all over the prairie. The cattlemen grumbled about the range getting choked with fences, the virgin grass getting plowed under, crooked politicians and railroad men, the vigorous mosquito population, and certainly, the weather came in for a fair bit of criticism. When someone mentioned the Tinners, CJ decided it was time to change the subject to happier talk.

"At least this summer, we'll have all the grass we need and the water holes will have water in them. Come on guys, count your blessings!"

Twenty-five

August 15, 1906
Stearns, South Dakota
(Same name, different location)

Dear folks,

When you come this fall, you will be able to ride the train clear to Stearns! Not Stearns by the river, like you have seen before on your visits, but Stearns near the south fork of Brave Bull Creek. The Thodes have built a new store and have also moved the post office to that location. Now there is even a land commissioner located by the post office.

Interestingly enough, there is another post office located close by. It's called Belvidere. A homesteader's wife talked the railroad into naming it after her hometown of Belvidere, Illinois.

We were glad to hear Mom is once again feeling better and will be up to the trip out here. The boys are counting the days until you get here! John is excited to have some new books to read. Teddy is excited whenever John is excited.

Joanna's mother has also had some health problems this summer. She has been doctoring but is getting discouraged with her medical advice.

We received a letter from Deborah Lynn saying they plan to be in Pierre this winter to help Reverend Smith for several months. I can well imagine how delighted the Smiths must be to have them back for awhile. It's too bad cousin Kentworth and Drew have quit speaking to each other. Maybe you can tell me when you're here what the problem is between the two of them.

It will seem like a different country to you when you arrive here. There are homesteaders pouring into the region. Up the little valley to the northwest of us, where there used to be a beautiful view, is a settlement of Bohemians. It feels like a foreign country when I ride in that direction. Most of them have difficulty speaking English. However, they do seem pleasant, unlike the Tinners.

Isaac had the misfortune of meeting Mrs. Tinner and Lizzie while he was getting our cattle out of an area close to them. Mrs. Tinner claimed the cattle were on their land, but Isaac is positive they were on free range. Mrs. Tinner is known for being a deadly shot with her rifle, and no one, much less a fourteen year old boy, argues with her!

We will meet you at the train only six or seven miles from the ranch. Have a safe trip!

Love,
CJ, Joanna, John and Teddy

CJ took his letter and headed towards the porch to let Joanna read it. He expected her to be darning socks, like she usually was during the summer evenings. Instead, she was sitting motionless on the homemade wooden bench with a faraway look on her face.

"Joanna?"

"Do you hear that?" she asked.

CJ listened. From the upper end of the little valley, the sound of an accordion could be faintly heard.

"I can't quite make out the song, can you?" CJ asked as he listened intently.

Joanna shook her head. "No, but it's a sad song. Makes me feel sad to hear it. I suppose those foreigners feel lonesome for their family and their old country."

"I suppose so. Do you want to read this before I seal it up?"

She held out her hand to take the letter and scanned it quickly. "Mmm."

CJ raised his eyebrow while he sat down on the bench next to her. "What does 'mmm' mean?"

"I'm wondering how comfortable your mother will be on this train that comes out here. It's not a passenger train, CJ. It has some hard old seats for a few people. Maybe you should tell them to come to Pierre after all."

"I think she's up for a little adventure. They can see country they haven't seen before." He stretched out his legs and reached over to pat her skirted knee.

"Maybe so. Speaking of seeing new country and having a little adventure—"

"Joanna. No."

They'd had this argument for the past couple days. CJ had purchased a team and a buggy from Waldron's horse ranch near Bad River, and CJ was going to take John and bring the team and buggy home. He planned to make it a two-day journey so John wouldn't get so tired.

Joanna had decided Simon could take the lumber wagon to Midland and get some supplies, and she and Teddy would ride with him. The problem was, Joanna wanted to take the stagecoach from Midland to Olney's road house, which was a stage stop near the Waldron ranch, and meet CJ and John to join them on the buggy ride back home.

"Why not, CJ?" Joanna's tone was mild, but CJ was not deceived. He knew her arguing tactics.

"I think I've told you several times why not. Those stagecoaches are rough riding, and they go fast and furious. You and Teddy will have the ride of your life, and you, my dear sweet Joanna, will not like it. Trust me."

"Is that the only reason?"

"You'll be thrown all over the coach, and there'll be all sorts of fellows on there you won't want to be bouncing around with."

"Horsefeathers. I won't be bouncing all around with undesirable characters. CJ, really!"

CJ was exasperated. He stood up and paced a few steps on the porch. "Tell me again why you want to do this?"

"I've told you several times. The days of stagecoaches are almost gone, and I want to say I've ridden one. And I want to see some of the country over there. I've never been there. You go riding all over the country. I stay home and work. Simple."

"If you want to go with me, I can saddle up extra horses for you and Teddy and we can all ride over. You'll see the country a lot better that way than on the stage."

"But haven't we gone over this before? I said I didn't want to ride that far and take that long. Riding the stage just works better."

CJ and John left for the Waldron ranch early the following morning. He was still irritated at his wife and gave her a curt farewell. She was, he decided, just as stubborn as the day he first met her. He had promised through gritted teeth he would wait for her at Olney's road house the next day.

The countryside held traces of green even in August. He and John rode slowly northwest, dodging homesteaders' fences as they went, and making sure they missed the Tinner place altogether. They stopped at noon along Indian Creek and enjoyed the lunch Joanna fixed for them. By mid afternoon, they reached their destination close to Nowlin and along Bad River.

The ranch had been one of the bigger horse ranches. The blizzard and the flood of 1905 had destroyed many horses and cattle for both Olneys and Waldrons. On the heels of that disaster came another in the form of a pretty purple flower called locoweed. The critters who ate the weed became "loco," a disease which affected the nervous system.

Both Olney and Waldron had decided to invest in sheep to get back on their feet financially, and the fine team which CJ bought was one of the last of Charlie Waldron's well bred horses.

"You know," Mr. Waldron said conversationally after their business had been settled, "I lost a darn good little roan horse about five years ago. I had put him out to pasture because he was limping. Never saw him again." Charlie paused reflectively. "One of my riders was purty sure the Tinners had him in their corral. I rode over there once to see about it but no one was home. At least, no one answered me when I hollered. I never saw my horse either."

CJ frowned. "Did he have a star on his forehead?"

Charlie leaned forward and nodded his head.

"I saw a roan horse with a star on his forehead at the Tinners about four years ago." He hesitated, wondering if he should say more.

Charlie waited and never said a word, but he gave CJ a scrutinized look that seemed to suggest it would be best if he knew the whole story. When CJ finished telling him about the April storm and what he and Simon had seen, Charlie leaned back and rocked on the heels of his boots. He cussed softly, and shook his head. "I about figured something like that. So the question is did Zed or his daughter Sissy steal the horse?"

"There are a lot of questions when it comes to that episode. I wish I knew the answers. But don't rule out Mrs. Tinner. Sometimes I get the feeling Belle Tinner is a force to be reckoned with."

The following noon, CJ kept his promise to Joanna. He and John arrived at Olney's roadhouse where the stagecoach would change teams. They tied their two horses behind the four-passenger buggy and ate a light lunch from the roadhouse while they sat outside underneath the cottonwood trees.

"Stage should be here about two," Ed Olney informed them. "Not any later unless Art has trouble. The bronc he used this morning was darn wringy."

CJ sat up a little straighter. "You use broncs on your stageline?"

"Sure. Put a broke horse with 'em, they do okay. But the rascal this morning took three guys to hitch 'em up."

After Ed left, John put his sandwich down and looked at CJ with worried eyes. "Will Mama be okay?"

"I'm sure both she and Teddy will be just fine." CJ patted John's little shoulder. Silently, he prayed for their safety.

Close to two o'clock, CJ heard the crack of a whip and the rumble of the stage. It came careening around the river bend with the four horses' thundering hooves beating a sharp staccato on the road.

"Whoaaa-whoaaa," the stage driver yelled and pulled the reins back until the team came to a gradual stop. Even so, they pawed the ground while Ed opened the stagecoach door.

Teddy came flying out first and a young girl was close behind him. When he saw his dad, he let out a whoop and came running. Satisfaction was oozing out of every pore. "Daddy! Daddy, that was fun!"

The girl patted Teddy's shoulder and said, "Next time your mother will know about the steep hill and won't scream."

CJ frowned and looked at Teddy. "Your mother screamed?"

Teddy kicked at an invisible rock. "Only once."

A slight man was descending from the stage. His glasses were perched crookedly on his nose. "My word. My word." He looked pale and hurried into the roadhouse.

Two burly foreigners stepped off next. One spit out a stream of tobacco and said something to his companion in his own language. They both looked grim.

Following them was a slender man, and it soon became evident he was the girl's father. He nodded at CJ before asking his daughter if she wanted one of Mrs. Olney's sandwiches before they headed to Philip.

While Teddy gave John all the details of the ride, CJ walked to the stage door and peered into the gloomy interior. "Well, Mrs. Crezner, are you going to come out?"

Joanna sat ramrod straight in the corner. Her plumed hat angled in a peculiar manner and wisps of hair straggled in forlorn abandonment down her neck. She seemed to be collecting her thoughts and paid scant attention to the fact she was now the only passenger on the stage.

When CJ spoke, she gave a startled jump. "Yes!" she snapped the answer to his question and gathered her skirts and reticule as she prepared to descend the steps. "And I want a word with that driver!"

"Well, ma'am, I reckon that'd be me," a cheerful voice said from behind them. "I sure hope you enjoyed your ride!"

Joanna marched over to the speaker and placed a forceful finger on the young man's chest. "You, sir, should be ashamed of yourself!" Two little red spots appeared on Joanna's cheeks.

The driver quickly doffed his hat and looked decidedly unashamed.

"Whipping those horses to make them plunge down hills at breakneck speed! I certainly did *not* enjoy that ride!" Joanna dusted her hands together and gathered up force for her next words. "The children bounced all over the stage. It's a wonder they didn't break bones!"

"That would be terrible, ma'am." The young driver put his hat back on his head and grinned. "I know Mary is okay, she's ridden with us before and knows the bumps." He granted Joanna another engaging grin and asked, "Is your little boy up and running?"

It was quite obvious Teddy was ready to begin his career as a stagecoach driver that very minute.

CJ put his arm around his wife's stiff shoulders and gently moved her aside. "Art—didn't I meet you someplace before?"

The young man reached out his hand to shake CJ's offered one and said, "I think last summer when you were at the dipping corrals."

"Ah yes, now I remember. You must have decided to come back to South Dakota and take a homestead."

"My parents came and filed about a mile west of where they think the town of Philip will be." His words were almost drowned out by horses whinnying and stomping.

Another mixture of broke horses and a bronc were being led towards the stage to get harnessed. CJ understood the stage would be ready to leave in less than thirty minutes, and from the hustle of the men hooking up harnesses, he well believed the passengers would soon be herded back into the stage. Minus, of course, his wife and son.

CJ gave a farewell nod to the driver and guided Joanna towards their own team. Neither said a word as he helped her into the buggy. John and Teddy scrabbled into the backseat, with Teddy still giving vivid illustrations of the stagecoach ride. After CJ checked the harnesses, he climbed onto the seat. With a soft click of his tongue, the team pulled ahead, and in no time, they found a stride that ate up miles without seeming to hurry.

Joanna turned towards him after they had traveled a while in strained silence. "Just say it and get it over with."

He noticed for the first time the plume that decorated her hat was definitely bent in an unfixable manner.

"Your feather is broke."

"Oh, CJ! I'm not talking about the feather." She looked at him in exasperation and seemed to be waiting for him to say something totally different.

"Do you want me to tell you 'I told you so'? Because I'm not going to say it." His tone was sharp, he knew, but he decided he would be as obstinate as she was.

"I know that's what you're thinking." She turned away from him.

"We probably better have this conversation when we're alone," he told her quietly. The two little red spots were back on her cheeks, a sure sign of impending war. CJ frowned. Or maybe it was a sign she was almost ready to cry. That bothered him. Joanna never cried, but she seemed to be having trouble swallowing and her eyes were suspiciously moist.

They rode in silence for a couple of miles, and even Teddy's enthusiasm was beginning to wane.

"What about those cookies, Dad?" John asked suddenly.

"I'd forgotten about them. I'll pull up here by the creek and we'll have some. Are you hungry, Teddy?"

"Are they Mom's cookies?" Teddy wanted to know.

"Of course, their Mom's," John reassured him, and when CJ halted the team, both boys were ready to bail out.

After checking to make sure there were no snakes or other varmints by the sluggish little creek, CJ handed the boys each a couple of cookies. When they finished eating, they rolled up their pant legs and began wading and splashing in the shallow water.

CJ watched them for a while and then lowered himself down beside a silent Joanna.

"Now. Tell me about your stage ride." He gave her knee a gentle squeeze.

She took a deep breath and soon the words were tumbling out. It was suppose to have been fun, an adventure for her and Teddy. She was the first one in the coach, and she and Teddy sat by the window. The man and his daughter got in next. They seemed nice, and he said his name was Nels something, and his daughter was Mary. They lived on the north fork of Bad River. Then the two foreigners got in. One muttered continuously, and the other smelled like he hadn't had a bath for a long time. They sat next to her. The little wimpy guy got in last.

The Nels guy told her they might be traveling fast, and there was a particular place where the driver liked to crack his whip as they started downhill. It was quite a thrill, the girl said, and sometimes people screamed.

Joanna smirked at that. She would not condescend to such a low practice. But they raced up a hill at breakneck speed and then broke over the top and plummeted downward with the coach swaying back and forth so severely she was sure the whole thing was going to tip over. She screamed, and Teddy bounced out of her lap right across to the Nels guy's lap, where he stayed the rest of the ride.

To make matters worse, the foreigner was trying to grab onto something to steady himself, and her fine-feathered hat caught the brunt of his flailing hands.

"It was just terrible, CJ, and all I could think of was how you said it would be just like this, with me bouncing all over the place." Joanna ended with a wail and a sniff.

CJ handed her his hankie before he spoke. "Well, I guess it was an adventure of sorts. You can still say you rode on one of the last stagecoaches in the country. And Teddy had a great time."

Joanna looked skeptical. She gave a wan smile and slumped against him. A tiny tear trickled down her cheek. "I don't feel so good, CJ. I have a headache and my insides are tied in knots."

He put his arm around her and kissed her flushed cheek. "We'll just sit here for a while. Maybe when it starts cooling down you'll feel better."

"Maybe when we get home I'll feel better. I wasn't made for traveling."

Twenty-six

March 28, 1907
Belvidere, South Dakota

Dear Mom and Dad,

We were glad to hear about the new associate pastor at your church. Hopefully he will work well with you and your congregation. It will take some of the workload off your shoulders, Dad, and that is definitely good news. I understand Drew and Deborah Lynn are settled in Pierre again, and Drew is back with his father-in-law.

We are concerned about Joanna's mother. She's in failing health, and we don't know what the problem is. Joanna's siblings are urging her to come to Minnesota to see her mother. Simon wants to buy train tickets for them, but Joanna hasn't decided yet if she is going. I've volunteered to keep Isaac and John and Teddy. Teddy is sure he can't live without his mother, which further discourages her from going.

You probably noticed that our new address is Belvidere. Several of us wanted to retain Stearns as our post office, but majority rules, and when the votes were counted, Belvidere had more votes than Stearns. Belvidere has become a booming little town. We have a grocery store, lumberyard, drug store, plus several more businesses, and of course, all the homesteaders. The foreigners have even started what they call a Bohemian Band. Culture has come to the prairie.

I've been doing a great deal of research on the two opposing views of Drew and Kentworth. I believe each of them has a point, but am concerned that neither are altogether correct in their argument. I guess the church has always argued over certain matters. As you said, the message should always be Christ and our faith and trust in Him. I feel blessed to have grown up listening to you and Granddad preach directly from the Bible.

A note about the Tinners. We were surprised to learn young Ben died and was buried on the Tinner place before anyone even knew he had passed away. Some say Ben hadn't been feeling well for quite some time. Now only Lizzie is on the place with her folks. She's just a little younger than Isaac.

Teddy is waiting for me to finish so we can saddle up "his" horse. He and Isaac have plans to check our cattle and make sure they're not bothering a homesteader who has filed west of us. He's a young bachelor and an easygoing fellow. He's building a log house on the higher bank of the creek. I think his name is Nels Christenson, so sounds like we gain another Norwegian on Brave Bull!

Always enjoy hearing your news. Take care and God bless.

Love,
CJ, Joanna, John, and Teddy

CJ left his letter on the table for Joanna to read. Teddy needed warmer clothes to go riding; the March breeze had coolness that slowly seeped through jackets. After Teddy was bundled and his horse saddled, CJ lifted him onto the saddle with admonitions to ride carefully and mind Isaac.

The boys had only been gone a short while before CJ heard their horses whinny and the sound of hooves beating a quick tempo back home. He was alarmed and dismayed that Isaac would ride so fast with Teddy. He became even more concerned when he realized Lizzie Tinner was racing ahead of them on her spotted horse. He was prepared to give them all a lecture when Lizzie's screeching voice informed him that her Pa was hurt and they needed help fast.

"It's all the government's fault," Lizzie informed him and Simon as they hurriedly saddled their horses. "They told Pa if his family had four claims, he had to have four cellars, and so Pa is digging a hole and putting boards up for the roof. And those darn cattle runned right through there!"

CJ and Simon exchanged puzzled looks as they mounted their horses. Lizzie's account of the accident raised more questions than answers. Isaac came with them, but much to Teddy's chagrin, his mother insisted he would have school lessons with John.

By the time they arrived at the Tinner place, a small group of homesteaders had already gathered there. One of them, a small man named Frank, had tried to crawl through the busted boards to see if he could reach Zed. He was just crawling out of the collapsed cellar as CJ and Simon dismounted to join the group

He spoke in rapid Bohemian to several of the other men and they shook their heads. With halting English he tried to explain to Mrs. Tinner that her husband was very badly hurt.

"I know that," she snapped. "We'll have to dig him out."

It took a couple hours to do that. By the time they were able to reach Zed, he was barely alive. CJ wanted to lift him out on a board but Mrs. Tinner would have none of that. She said it would take too long and she wanted CJ to pick him up bodily and carry him to the house. From the set of her jaw and the determined expression on her face, CJ knew it was useless to argue with her.

He thought Zed would be heavy and was surprised at how light the man was. Helping hands steadied CJ as he carried Zed out of the demolished cellar and into the tar paper shack. He laid him carefully on the small cot Mrs. Tinner pointed to. Zed made a gurgling noise, and opened his eyes for one brief moment. "Sissy," he whispered hoarsely.

CJ quickly stepped aside assuming Mrs. Tinner would want to be at her husband's side as he died. He was mistaken. Mrs. Tinner had other matters on her mind.

"Since you're here, you can dig his grave. Put it by Ben's."

CJ looked at her coldly. "Generally we wait until someone has died before we dig the grave."

"Mr. Crezner. Does he look to you like he's gonna live?" She turned to Simon and some of the other men who had crowded into the little house. "Dig the grave."

The other men silently filed out of the house, but Simon and CJ stayed behind. Mrs. Tinner looked at them defiantly. Her hair was still pulled in the same tight bun on top of her head as it was the last time they were there. The lines on her face had deepened and once again her skirt was dirty but this time there was no blood or hay on it. "If you're too good to dig, you could build a box to hold him. There's some lumber in the barn."

They found the lumber. They also found Zed Tinner's liquor cache. Bottles and bottles of homemade whiskey. "No wonder he was so light," CJ muttered to Simon as they framed the casket. "He was pickled in whiskey."

"This is strange business." Simon hammered some nails into the wood. "Did you look at the tracks around the cellar? Those cattle were being chased. Do you see the saddle blanket over there? It's been used today, I'm sure of it. And where's the horses? I think the old girl drove those cattle over the cellar when she knew he was in there, and then unsaddled her horse and turned him out so no one could see he'd been rode." A worried frown creased Simon's forehead.

CJ felt the hair on the back of his neck raise. "I think we better check and double check to make sure Zed is dead before we bury him."

"Dad, are you in there?" Isaac's voice sounded shaky.

"Come in here Isaac! I was wondering where you were."

"Dad," Isaac hurried toward them. "Lizzie came out of the house just now and said her pa was dead."

"At least," CJ told Joanna several mornings later while they were drinking coffee, "I was able to say a prayer when we buried him. I thought for awhile Mrs. Tinner wasn't going to let me do that."

"What kind of prayer could you even say?" Joanna looked mystified.

"I—well, it was difficult. I asked God to help us understand His children, and said we were all children of God, and we needed His guidance."

"Do you think we'll ever know what really happened there, or where Sissy Tinner is, or why Ben died and was buried so mysteriously?" Joanna was wide eyed as she asked all her questions.

"Who knows? Only God knows," CJ shrugged as he answered his own question. He was ready to put the Tinners out of his mind. They were a strange family. He was more concerned about Joanna's family, or more specifically, Joanna and her mother and their non-existent relationship.

Simon knocked lightly before he came in, and announced it froze again during the night. He took off his jacket while Joanna poured him a cup of coffee and the three of them made the usual small talk about the weather as they sat around the table drinking their morning coffee. During a lull in the conversation, he produced two train tickets from his pocket. Joanna eyed them with misgivings written on her face.

"Little sister," Simon said quietly, "I know you don't want to do this, but you really need to come with me to Minnesota. Not so much for Ma's sake as for your own."

Joanna looked pleadingly at CJ. "I—do you think I should? I mean, what about you and the boys?"

CJ put his coffee cup down and looked at her intently before he spoke. "We'll be all right, Joanna. I think you do need to go. You haven't seen her for years, you've both changed. You've become a wife and mother, she's become an old woman, and she needs you right now. And maybe you don't think so, but in a strange way, I think you need her too."

Joanna folded and refolded a piece of paper that was lying on the table. Finally she looked up and said, "I've been thinking about the Tinners, and all the hate in their family. I don't hate Ma, but I'm not sure I love her, either. I suppose——I mean I know— the Christian thing to do is go and not expect anything from her because, well, because Ma is Ma, and she won't change. If I can't love her, at least I could care for her like a good daughter should." Joanna tapped the table with her forefinger. "However, for the record, she really did treat me terrible."

"I know she did," Simon said. "She was in her mid forties when you were born. She couldn't handle you, and it made her mad that Pa could always make you mind with just a word or two."

Joanna gave CJ a sheepish smile. "I really was a handful. Sometimes even Pa told me that."

"For being a handful, you grew up to be quite a woman." CJ winked at her and was delighted when she blushed.

"Before I say yes, I want to make sure those tickets are for a round trip. I don't intend to spend the rest of my life in Minnesota with my mother!"

Simon nodded. "They're definitely round trip tickets. We leave on April seventh. We'll be on one of the first passenger trains leaving Belvidere."

Joanna gave a huge sigh. "All these years I've dreaded those darn trains coming. Now I'm going to hop on one and the only good thing about it is I'll be able to come back here a whole lot faster than I ever thought was possible." She shook her head. "I hope it isn't another stage coach experience."

✀

When the train came to a thunderous stop beside Belvidere's depot, CJ realized with a sinking feeling that he might have been wrong to assure Joanna a hundred times he and the boys would be fine. Nothing could possibly be fine without his wife by his side. He gave himself a mental shake for being so selfish and plastered a reassuring smile on his face.

He noticed Joanna had the same kind of smile on her face as she told Isaac and the boys goodbye. For that matter, Simon's smile looked extremely forced also.

"What's wrong with us?" He whispered as he held her close before she got on the train. "We act like we'll never see each other again. Good grief, you're just going to Minnesota."

"I love you CJ. Even if you are sending me away to my mother." Her voice was low and husky.

He kissed her quickly. "When you get back, I'll never send you away again."

"Promise God?" She asked with a tremulous smile.

"Promise God. And I love you too, Mrs. Crezner."

"Well then, since my husband loves me, I guess I better board." She determinedly squared her shoulders before she gathered her traveling skirt in one hand and the metal railing on the train with her other hand. When she reached the top of the narrow metal steps she turned and waved goodbye to the boys and blew a kiss to CJ. And for good measure she waved at the curious onlookers who enjoyed the novelty of the passenger trains. The hissing steam was growing louder. Joanna raised her voice and shouted "Goodbye Belvidere!" and gave CJ a last lingering glance. He watched with a lump in his throat as she entered the car and followed Simon to her seat.

He picked up Teddy, and held John's hand tightly as he moved a safer distance away. As the steam built up and the train whistle blew, Teddy buried his face in CJ's shoulder and cried, "I want Mama back!"

The four of them watched silently as the train moved down the tracks. They watched until the crowd had thinned out, and the train was just a tiny speck on the horizon. Finally CJ released John's hand, and set Teddy on the ground.

"Well. Well boys, maybe we should have a look around town and see if we can find a good place to eat before we head home." He knew his voice sounded flat but the thought of weeks without Joanna was overwhelming. The boys showed little enthusiasm for his suggestion.

They slowly moseyed up the hill to where some of the business places were. When Isaac saw the sign that read 'Home Restaurant. Get a good square meal for twenty-five cents' his eyes brightened. "I'll bet this is a good place!"

Isaac and the sign were correct. They were served a good square meal by a friendly waitress, and by the time the pudding desert arrived they were in better spirits.

CJ glanced up as another person entered the small restaurant. He grinned as the waitress fluttered over to the newcomer and asked where he'd like to sit.

"With his old friend," CJ said loudly. "Come and join us, Smokey. I'll even buy your dinner."

"Hey, what is this? How come you aren't home eating your wife's good cooking? And who are all these gentlemen with you?" Smokey hadn't lost his smooth talk or his ability to enjoy a free meal.

When the boys began to get restless listening to their conversation, Isaac volunteered to take them for a walk around town. After they left, Smokey moved a little closer to CJ and said in a lowered voice, "Do you know a Sissy Tinner?"

CJ gave a startled nod and looked at Smokey questioningly.

"She asked about you. Said she used to live nearby. She told me quite a story CJ, and I'm wondering how much of it is true. I can't say she's a gal I'd trust very much."

"She asked about me?" CJ was incredulous. "I only seen her once. Simon and I were there when Zed was on his pitchfork frenzy."

"You're a babe in the woods, CJ. The girl practically thinks you walk on water."

"Ridiculous!" CJ snorted.

"What do you know about Sissy's roan horse with a star on his forehead?"

CJ briefly went over the episode and his own speculations that the horse was stolen from Charlie Waldron's herd.

"That's what I think. When she told me the brand on it, I thought it had to be Charlie's. Ma Tinner is the one who brought the horse home and gave it to Sissy. Now there's a woman I wouldn't want to meet." Smokey reflected on that thought for several seconds while he drank some coffee.

"In a nutshell, CJ, this Sissy said her old man got kicked by the horse and was starving it in the corral for spite. The kids let the horse out to graze, the old man was drunk and Ma Tinner was out riding. When he discovered the horse was gone he went into a tirade with his pitchfork The kids hid in the stack, and when Ma Tinner came riding in leading the roan horse, things really got bad. Ma was mad, charged into the old man with her horse, he plunged the fork into the roan, hurt the horse so bad Ma had to shoot it. Then she got the boy into the house because the old man managed to hit him with the fork while he was in the stack."

"And that's about the time Simon and I rode in with Lizzie," CJ interrupted. "But what I want to know is where has Sissy been all these years?"

"Ma was worried Sissy was going to lose her mind over the horse, so she saved some money and sent her back east to a relative. I ain't so sure she isn't a little touched. She has a terrible hatred for the old man. I met her on a train and started visiting with her and she told me all of this."

CJ grinned. He wasn't surprised Smokey started a conversation with a young woman.

"Wipe that grin off your face, Crezner. I was purely bored and needed a diversion." Smokey tackled the pudding desert.

"The rest of the story, Smokey, is that Zed Tinner was killed about two weeks ago."

Smokey choked on the pudding and looked at CJ in disbelief. In few words, CJ described what had happened, and Simon's speculation that Mrs. Tinner might have been responsible for the cattle running over the cellar. There was silence at the table as Smokey digested that information. Finally he took a drink of coffee and set his cup down with a thud.

"It's this country, CJ. It's hard. It affects people's minds and they do crazy things. It's too lonely and it's too harsh. It makes people mean. You should take Joanna and the kids and get out of it before something weird happens to you."

CJ drummed his fingers on the table and gazed out the window of the restaurant. Finally he tipped his hat so it rested a little higher on his forehead, "I've heard that augment before, Smokey. "But I think this country doesn't change people. I think it brings out what was always there. The weaknesses, the strengths. It makes us honest with ourselves. When all you see is sky and prairie, it puts it in perspective that man is a small entity in God's overall design. Man is important to God, but man is puny, and this country proves it."

Smokey looked at him steadily for several seconds before he broke into a slow grin. "CJ, my friend," he said softly, "it occurs to me that maybe you should have been a preacher."

THE END

This is the first book of the Goodbye, Belvidere trilogy and it is entitled, *Goodbye, Belvidere, A Hundred and Sixty Acres.* It's an accurate account of homestead days in western South Dakota.

The second book, *Goodbye, Belvidere, His Eye Is on the Sparrow,* continues with more Tinner problems along with the growing war clouds of WWI.

The third book is called *Goodbye, Belvidere, I much love you.* CJ and Joanna waltz again along the shores of White River, blissfully unaware that a young cowboy is stealing their daughter's heart.

If you have enjoyed Joyce's style of writing, you'll want to read her western romance novels.

My Lady is the intriguing story of young Jolene O'Neil and the men she loved. With its setting in the Nebraska and the Dakota prairie, *My Lady* is a contemporary novel that carries mystery and romance to an unusual ending.

Laughter in the Wind brings British nanny, Abbie Miller, to South Dakota's capitol city and the Jackson ranch. Redneck Wade Jackson, and red-haired Abbie cuss and discuss the strange decorating habits of Mrs. Jackson. Will the old ranch house give up its secrets?

The juvenile book, *The Countries of Whine and Roses* is an allegory that beautifully describes God the Father, God the Son, and God the Holy Spirit, in an easy-to-understand story set in the Kingdom of Roses. Ages 8-12, but enjoyable reading for anyone.

Joyce can be contacted on her facebook page
www.com/joycewheelerbooks

For twitter users, you can find her at
www.twitter.com/grasslandrose

For more information about Joyce and her books, check out her website www.prairieflowerbooks.com

If you want to contact her by e-mail, send your inquiries to joycewheelerbooks@gmail.com

CPSIA information can be obtained
at www.ICGtesting.com
Printed in the USA
BVHW04s0921091018
529539BV00013B/52/P

9 781634 925754